GET ALL THIS FREE
WITH JUST ONE PROOF OF PURCHASE:

$50 VALUE

◆ **Hotel Discounts** up to 60% at home and abroad ◆ **Travel Service -** Guaranteed lowest published airfares plus 5% cash back on tickets ◆ **$25 Travel Voucher** ◆ **Sensuous Petite Parfumerie** collection ◆ **Insider Tips Letter** with sneak previews of upcoming books

You'll get a FREE personal card, too. It's your passport to all these benefits— and to even more great gifts & benefits to come!

There's no club to join. No purchase commitment. No obligation.

SSE-PP5A

W9-BWB-290

Enrollment Form

☐ *Yes!* I WANT TO BE A *PRIVILEGED WOMAN*.
Enclosed is one *PAGES & PRIVILEGES™* Proof of
Purchase from any Harlequin or Silhouette book currently for
sale in stores (Proofs of Purchase are found on the back pages
of books) and the store cash register receipt. Please enroll me
in *PAGES & PRIVILEGES™*. Send my Welcome Kit and FREE
Gifts -- and activate my FREE benefits -- immediately.

More great gifts and benefits to come.

NAME (please print)

ADDRESS   APT. NO

CITY   STATE   ZIP/POSTAL CODE

PROOF OF PURCHASE
ONLY

**NO CLUB!
NO COMMITMENT!**
*Just one purchase brings
you great Free Gifts and
Benefits!*

▼ DETACH HERE AND MAIL TODAY! ▼

Please allow 6-8 weeks for delivery. Quantities are limited. We reserve the right to
substitute items. Enroll before October 31, 1995 and receive one full year of benefits.

Name of store where this book was purchased_____

Date of purchase_____

Type of store:

☐ Bookstore   ☐ Supermarket   ☐ Drugstore
☐ Dept. or discount store (e.g. K-Mart or Walmart)
☐ Other (specify)_____

Which Harlequin or Silhouette series do you usually read?
_____

Complete and mail with one Proof of Purchase and store receipt to:
U.S.: *PAGES & PRIVILEGES™*, P.O. Box 1960, Danbury, CT 06813-1960
Canada: *PAGES & PRIVILEGES™*, 49-6A The Donway West, P.O. 813,
North York, ON M3C 2E8

SSE-PP5B

"You're quite the hero, Mr. Stuart,"

said Trisha Stewart, the pretty social worker running the Boys and Girls Club. "Thanks for letting us share your new van."

Pat felt more like a trapped rabbit as the media closed in on him and the vehicle in question.

"How about a group shot?" a photographer shouted. "Hey, Pat, stand between that cute little girl and Miss Stewart."

"We should all be so lucky!" a reporter said, laughing.

Pat forced a smile for the cameras. He should have stayed in L.A. He should have become a hermit. He should have moved to the Gobi Desert.

"Hey, butthead," the "cute little girl" muttered to him. "You know how to drive?"

"Angie," Trisha murmured, "be nice to Mr. Stuart."

"Ya can't never trust no Pretty Boy, Miss Stewart," Angie advised sagely. "They'll break your heart every time!"

And Pat sighed....

Dear Reader,

September is an extra-special month for Special Edition! This month brings you some of your favorite veteran authors, three dynamite series and a celebration of special events! So don't miss a minute of the fall festivities under way.

Reader favorite Christine Rimmer returns to North Magdalene for the latest JONES GANG tale! THAT SPECIAL WOMAN! Heather Conway meets her match—and the future father of her baby—in *Sunshine and the Shadowmaster*. Gina Ferris Wilkins's new series, THE FAMILY WAY, continues in September with *A Home for Adam*, a touching and poignant story from this award-winning author. Diana Whitney's THE BLACKTHORN BROTHERHOOD continues with a story of the redeeming power of love in *The Avenger*.

And this month, Special Edition features special occasions in three books in our CONGRATULATIONS! promotion. In each story, a character experiences something that will change his or her life forever. Don't miss a moment of any of these wonderful titles: *Kisses and Kids* by Andrea Edwards, *Joyride* by Patricia Coughlin, and from a new author to Silhouette, *A Date With Dr. Frankenstein* by Leanne Banks.

But that's not all—there's lots in store for the rest of 1995 and Silhouette Special Edition! Not to give away our secrets yet, but safe to say that the rest of the year promises to bring your favorite authors in very special books! I hope you enjoy each and every story to come!

Sincerely,

Tara Gavin
Senior Editor

Please address questions and book requests to:
Silhouette Reader Service
U.S.: 3010 Walden Ave., P.O. Box 1325, Buffalo, NY 14269
Canadian: P.O. Box 609, Fort Erie, Ont. L2A 5X3

KISSES AND KIDS

Silhouette ®

SPECIAL EDITION ®

Published by Silhouette Books
America's Publisher of Contemporary Romance

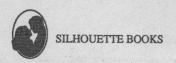

SILHOUETTE BOOKS

ISBN 0-373-09981-9

KISSES AND KIDS

Printed in U.S.A.

ANDREA EDWARDS

is the pseudonym of Anne and Ed Kolaczyk, a husband-and-wife writing team who have been telling their stories for more than fifteen years. Though Anne is a former elementary school teacher and Ed a refugee from corporate America, they love small towns, are fascinated with family and local history, and are intrigued by ethnic legends and myths. Their four kids are pretty much grown, but they still have two dogs and five kids to wreak havoc in their books.

Dear Readers,

Congratulations. Due to your persistence, dedication and pure optimism, the torch of love is burning brightly in a world that sometimes seems to be unraveling.

You have kept alive the belief that love does conquer all, for you know that it alone gentles anger, bridges chasms of misunderstanding and allows us to reach the full potential of our humanity. Love costs us nothing to give, yet it is so precious to receive.

This book bridges a range of congratulatory themes, but the real congratulations should be at the end, when love is found and hearts are healed. A reason for us all to celebrate.

Andrea Edwards

Prologue

August 22
Fifteen years ago

"**I**'m going now, Gran," Patrick called as he went on into the kitchen.

Even over the old refrigerator's hum, he could hear the rain coming down—the constant rustle as drops hit the leaves, mixed with the splatter on the back steps from the water pouring through the crack in the gutter. It was going to be a miserable night at the station. Nobody would want to use the self-service pumps and he'd be outside all night, pumping gas.

But it didn't make any difference. Working nights paid good, and the more money he earned now, the farther he'd be from working crummy jobs like this the rest of his life.

"Patrick?" His grandmother had followed him into the kitchen, then stopped with a frown. She looked at him from top to bottom and back again. "You're going to work."

He opened the refrigerator and took out a can of soda. The August night was so hot that he could see the cold air tumble off the shelves. It billowed out around him and fell to the floor in tiny swirls. "I told you I was going out." He closed the refrigerator with reluctance. "And work is *going out.*"

"I thought you were going out with some friends. Land sakes, boy, it's your birthday."

"It's the night shift and I get a bonus."

"There's more to life than money," she said. "You're eighteen. You should go out and have fun once in a while. Maybe take some nice girl to a movie."

He took out the bread and peanut butter. "Fun's not going to pay my tuition next year."

"Neither is one night of work, even with a bonus." She snatched the peanut butter jar from him. "And that's no kind of dinner for a growing boy. We've got ham left from Sunday. I'll make you a real sandwich."

"It doesn't matter, Gran," he said. "It all tastes the same anyway. I don't care what I eat."

"What do you care about?" She took a covered platter from the refrigerator and put it on the counter with a force that added emphasis to her words. "Nothing, that's what. Nothing but running farther and farther from yourself."

She pulled the foil off the platter and began stacking thick slabs of ham onto his bread. "You did the right thing leaving your father and brother. You've got to accept that. You didn't start your pa drinking and you weren't going to stop him. And Angel's got to want to leave because it's good for him and only him. So stop feeling you could've changed things."

Pat sure wished she'd stop looking for hidden reasons in everything he did. He'd put that part of his life behind him and refused to look back. "I don't feel that way." He wrapped the two sandwiches she had made and slipped them into a bag.

"You're not wanting to feel any way at all, that's the trouble." She put a bunch of grapes and an orange into the bag also, then wrapped a double handful of cherry-topped cookies and put them in, too. "You think by working and studying all the time, you can keep from feeling, but you can't. You're too much like your mother, God rest her soul. She had a heart stuffed chock-full of love, needing to be shared, just like you do."

"No way." He got his nylon rain jacket from the hook by the door and slipped it on. He'd had his fill of sharing and caring. It had done nothing but suck him dry. "Living with Dad was a good education. It taught me that love is just a weight around your ankles, pulling you down."

"Lordy, if your mother could hear you talking such nonsense, she'd be spinning in her grave. Love is what makes life worthwhile."

He picked up the soda and the bag of food. "That's about as much of a crock as your story about a treasure hidden in this old house. Money's what makes everything worthwhile, not love," he said. "In a few years, I'm gonna be checking the time on my Rolex while the Romeos around here will still be using the bank clock."

"Patrick, Patrick, Patrick," she muttered as she followed him to the door. "You mark my words. There'll come a birthday when folks will be singing your praises and pretty girls will be wanting to have their picture taken with you. But it won't mean a thing because you'll have nobody to share it with."

"I'll share it with you," he said as he leaned over to give her a quick kiss on the cheek.

"Ha! You think I'm going to live forever?" She pushed him away. "You need someone. A special someone. Your soul's twin. But to win her heart, you're going to have to throw away all your pride."

He pulled the door open. "Don't wait up for me. I'm working a double shift."

"Double shift." She snorted in derision. "Fancy gold watches won't warm your bed."

Patrick just put his head down and hurried through the downpour. Her words echoed around him but he didn't look back.

Chapter One

The stale air in the taxicab smelled like the remains of a bad party—cheap wine, greasy french fries and cigarette smoke—but Patrick Stuart was too beat to even roll down a window. Besides, after a week of Los Angeles smog followed by six hours in an airplane, he wasn't sure his system would accept clean air.

The caffeine from endless cups of coffee had drained away, leaving him feeling disconnected. All he wanted was to jump into bed and sleep until the cows came home. Or until tomorrow morning, whichever came the latest. Unfortunately, he had a big appointment this afternoon.

"Hey, you hear about that new plant coming to South Bend?" the cabbie said, tossing a newspaper over the seatback along with his words.

"Uh-huh." Pat blinked to clear his bleariness before picking up the paper. The article about the new plant shared the front page with a photo of a young blonde surrounded by kids from the West Side Boys and Girls Club. Typical small-town newspaper stuff—hard news mixed in with neighborhood filler.

"Four hundred new jobs," the cabbie went on.

Pat just grunted a reply.

"They ought to take this Stuart guy and make him emperor. Or at least mayor."

Oh, yeah, he'd be perfect for the job. He'd love being in the limelight twenty-four hours a day. "Maybe he doesn't want to be mayor."

"Hey, the guy's doing a great job," the cabbie said, ignoring Pat. "Town should show its appreciation. A parade would be nice."

Closing his eyes, Pat slumped back in the seat. A parade? That would be great. He couldn't remember the last time he'd thrown up.

Sure, he wanted to be appreciated as well as the next guy, but a quick handshake was enough. Stopping to pat yourself on the back would lose you the game; playing high school football had taught him that.

"Here we are, 20 East Colfax." The cab slowed down. "Hey, you somebody famous?"

Pat opened his eyes to find trucks from the local TV stations parked in front of his office. Guys with cameras balanced on their shoulders were crowded around the entrance to his office.

"I was a rock star in another life," Pat said as cameramen converged on the cab. "But I'm just an ordinary kind of guy now." What the hell was going on?

He barely noticed that someone was paying the cabdriver as his door was opened and hands reached in to yank him out.

"Yea, Pat." The crowd cheered and clapped their hands as they parted, leaving him a path to his door.

For a moment, he was back in high school, an eighteen-year-old jock, running the gauntlet of fans onto the football field. Filled with dreams and certain that success was his for the taking.

Then he shook his head sharply. He wasn't eighteen anymore; he was thirty-two. And he wasn't a Friday-night hero; he was the executive director of the county's committee for industrial development, responsible for bringing new industry into the community.

Pat went into his office. And stopped. It was filled with banners and bouquets of balloons as if he really were a rock star. Pat shook his head. What was going on? This wasn't his first contract, or even his largest.

"Folks," he said. "I appreciate your intentions but—"

"Congratulations, Pat," a tall, shapely brunette said just before she wrapped her arms around him and kissed him hard on the lips.

Flashes exploded all around him, filling the bleary shadows in his eyes with multicolored pinwheels. As he struggled to disentangle himself, Pat recognized the woman as the current Miss Indiana, who did promotional work around the state.

For some odd reason, his grandmother's words from years ago came floating out of the mists of his past. Something about folks singing his praises and pretty girls wanting him. And how it would mean nothing.

But Gran had been wrong. Even though he hated the attention, this meant a whole lot. It meant he was a success.

"What's the matter, Pat? Does she bite?" someone called out.

"She can bite me anytime she wants," someone else answered.

A roar of laughter filled the packed reception area of his office. His office staff was there, along with a lot of other people. Business owners from down the street, the mayor and his entourage and bigwigs from the chamber of commerce.

Everyone was filled with good cheer, except for Pat. He needed to cut this hoopla short and get back to work. In a few hours, he had a meeting with a group looking to locate a warehouse in the Midwest.

"Don't you folks have business of your own to do?" Pat asked.

That remark brought on more laughter.

"He's a grumpy sort, ain't he?" the mayor said.

"Yeah," Ben Mackley, the president of the chamber of commerce, replied. "But he sure knows how to get the job done."

* * *

Patricia Stewart stepped out of the old brick building that housed the West Side Boys and Girls Club of South Bend. It was going to be a standard August day in Indiana—hot, sticky and mellow.

Too bad she wasn't equally mellow. She could feel the acid starting to eat at her stomach lining as she walked over toward the broken-down van parked at the back of the lot.

"How is it going, Rusty?" The mechanic was leaning against the sick vehicle, parts strewn about his feet. It was obvious how things were going, but she was the director of the club and had to stay on top of things whether she liked it or not. "Gonna be able to put Old Bertha back together again?"

"Yeah, I can." He spat out the matchstick he was chewing on and shifted his position slightly. "But she still won't run."

"But she has to." Trisha heard the pleading tone in her voice and hated it. Management didn't plead, they issued orders. Unfortunately, when you worked in a not-for-profit agency devoted to children, pleading was sometimes your only weapon. "I have eight kids to take to camp this weekend."

"Old Bertha ain't gonna be no Lazarus raised from the dead," Rusty said, shaking his head.

"Maybe we can have someone else look at it." Trisha swallowed hard. Rusty was a proud man and she hated intruding on his turf, but she really needed the van for this weekend. "I know you're a good mechanic, but there are times when everyone could use a little help."

"Way ahead of you, ma'am." He tapped the side of the van with his middle knuckle. "Already got me an expert."

A man rolled out from under the van and stood up. The emblem on his shirt said that he worked for an automobile dealership in the area and that his name was Wayne. Rusty introduced her anyway. The man nodded as he wiped his greasy hands.

"I don't know how you kept it running this long, Rusty," the man said.

"Spit, bailing wire and prayer."

"Can you guys patch it together for one more trip?" Trisha asked.

"No way, Miss Stewart." The young mechanic shook his head. "This old heap should've been buried years ago."

"But the children have worked hard all summer." The camping trip was a reward for the kids who had read the most books over the summer and helped out with the club's community activities. "They've earned this outing."

"Gonna have to find some other way to get them to the camp." Wayne scratched his chin for a moment. "Maybe you can rent a van."

Trisha just shook her head. After a new furnace this winter and a new roof in the spring, her budget was stone dry. Things were so bad that she was paying for this month's arts-and-crafts supplies out of her own pocket.

"Well, I gotta be going," Wayne said, shaking hands with Rusty. "Give my boss a call. Maybe he can give you a deal on renting a van."

"Do we owe you—"

"Nah." The mechanic waved his hand dismissively. "I was just trying to see if I could beat the old master here."

"I wish you could have," Trisha said.

"Yeah, me, too." Wayne laughed and then the two men walked off toward Wayne's car, leaving Trisha alone with the old van.

She felt like crying. She was so tired of trying to squeeze nickels and dimes from empty purses. At times, it seemed as though all her energy went toward that instead of the kids.

"The old girl's dead, huh?"

Trisha didn't even have to turn around. It was Clarissa, Trisha's secretary, assistant, confidante and the club's chief disciplinarian. Trisha nodded, not daring to speak yet.

"Well, ain't no reason for you to look so down in the mouth, honey. Anything that's got a beginning, got an end. Just like you and me."

"It's my job to provide for the club."

"Oh, don't you worry now." Clarissa put an arm around Trisha's shoulders. "My mama always said every cloud has a silver lining."

"Where's the silver lining in a dead van?"

"You gotta have faith, honey. Faith and patience."

Faith and patience. An ability to just relax and handle things as they came up. Trisha wished she had those traits tucked away in her attic, but she was about as patient as a six-year-old at Christmas and had faith only in the fact that another crisis was waiting around the corner.

"Stuart? P. Stuart?" a young man called over to them. He had headphones over his ears and his head was bobbing to the beat of music only he could hear.

"Hey," the man said louder. "Like, where is the dude?"

Trisha stepped forward. "I'm Patricia Stewart."

"Cool." He pushed a clipboard at her. "Sign at the X mark."

Trisha stared at the form on the clipboard. It bore the letterhead of the dealership that employed Wayne. Were they giving her a bill for his time? They couldn't be—the mechanic had dropped by on his own. "What is this for?" she asked sharply.

"For your new vehicle, dudette." He nodded over her shoulder at a shiny new van parked near the club door.

Trisha turned to stare at it, at the wide red ribbon stretched around it as if it were a Christmas present. "New van?"

She had no idea where the van had come from or where it was supposed to be, but her hand scribbled her name without hesitation. Was someone donating this vehicle? How would they know one was needed so desperately? It had to be a mistake.

But it couldn't be. The club's address was scrawled across the top of the form—2020 West Colfax. And her name was on it, though it was spelled wrong—Stuart, not Stewart.

"Thank you, ladies." He tore off a copy of the form and gave it to Trisha. "Now y'all have yourselves a bodacious day."

He unhooked a small motorbike attached to the van. After kick-starting the cycle, he gave them a last wave and hummed off down the street like an angry bumblebee.

"I can't believe it." Trisha just stood there staring at the van. "How many people even knew that we needed this?"

"Maybe we got a guardian angel, after all," Clarissa replied.

Trisha moved toward the new vehicle. A huge banner was strung along with the ribbon. It read Congratulations, Pat.

No one called her Pat, but she certainly wasn't going to quibble over that. She opened the front door. A bottle of champagne sat on the passenger seat, a note attached to it.

Congratulations, Pat. You're doing one hell of a job. Hope you like the van. Now you can haul your "cargo" in the comfort and style that they deserve. Good luck for the rest of the year.

The Chamber of Commerce of St. Joseph County

Signatures of numerous local dignitaries were scrawled all over the card. Trisha let her arms drop and stared again at the van. "This is just so weird."

"Wowee," a childish voice called from behind them. "That's one cool vehicle."

Trisha had been concentrating on the new van so hard that she hadn't noticed that a number of children had come outside. "Be careful, kids," she warned. "Don't go out into the street."

"Miss Stewart, are we gonna get to ride in this?" The children were scrambling into the vehicle, opening and closing the sliding door. "Lookit these seats."

As the children oohed and aahed over the seats, Trisha quit staring at the exterior of the van and switched to staring at the interior.

It was indeed furnished sumptuously, with captain's chairs and little tables for refreshments. A vehicle with bench seats would carry more kids, but she quickly rejected the thought. *Just thank your lucky stars,* she told herself, *and be grateful for any favors that come your way.*

"Come on, kids." She herded the screaming kids out of the vehicle. "Let's not wreck our new van the first day out."

Clarissa leaned closer to Trisha. "I'm gonna make me a few calls," she said. "The world needs to know when someone gives us a gift like this."

* * *

"I don't understand," Pat said. Riding halfway across town wasn't what he needed to be doing. "Why didn't someone from the office pick up the van in the first place?"

Ben paused for the stop sign and looked both ways before he proceeded through the intersection. "Because the media people were going to be at your office and the delivery would have made good press. You know, showing how the whole city is behind you in your efforts to bring new jobs to the area."

Pat just shook his head. The air-conditioning in Ben's car was turned on high, sealing them in a world apart from the sweltering heat outside. But it wasn't enough. He could feel a trickle of sweat amble down his back.

"So then why couldn't our summer intern go get it now?" he asked. "Why do we both need to troop out here?"

"Hey, just relax," Ben said. "We're almost there. You can drive the van back. The media guys'll take your picture and then you can get back to work."

Pat dropped back against his seat. Ben was right. He should relax. It just was hard, coming back out here to the westside after he'd vowed never to return.

His old west-side neighborhood slid past the car window— dilapidated buildings looking much the worse for wear. About the same as it had looked fifteen or twenty years ago, back when he was a kid roaming these streets.

He'd gone through a lot since then—a lot of anger and bitterness and disappointment. But no matter what his grandmother said, he'd found true happiness: he'd achieved his financial objectives and had no one and nothing tugging on his coattails to pull him down.

"I don't know what's with people these days." Ben paused to pull around an old station wagon, filled with house-painting gear, lumbering down the street. "They had the address totally wrong."

"They didn't check the name?"

"That's the funny part," Ben said. "We had it set up to be delivered to you, P. Stuart. And there's a P. Stewart at the other address."

"It's not an uncommon name," Pat said.

"Yeah." Ben laughed. "Or maybe you got a twin."

"No." Pat popped up in his seat, his stomach twisting into a knot, as yet another echo of his grandmother's words danced around the back of his mind.

Pat forced himself to relax and lean back. He casually glanced down at his watch. August 22. His stomach took a sideways dip but now he knew what was going on. It was his birthday. His subconscious had been working overtime and dredging up birthdays past to haunt him. He just needed a good night's sleep. "I don't have a twin."

"Relax," Ben said. "This one's a woman and she spells her name S-T-E-W-A-R-T. She's the director of the West Side Boys and Girls Club."

Pat just grunted. That was where the kids in that photo in the paper had been from. And the good-looking blonde. Her image came back; something in her eyes seemed to speak to him. Jeez, he was tired. This was not his sort of daydream. He closed his eyes, pushing the image away.

"You grew up around here," Ben said. "Didn't you?"

"I lived in a lot of places," Pat replied, keeping his eyes closed.

It wasn't that he was ashamed of where he came from; the west side had its share of good people, and some not so good, just like any neighborhood. But he didn't want to talk about it. Something that Ben wouldn't understand.

No amount of explaining could make Ben understand the dark side of this kind of neighborhood—the lure of the streets, of a life where polite society's *do's and don'ts* had little meaning. Mackley had grown up on a farm about fifty miles east of the city. To him, streets were just something to drive your car on. No, Ben wouldn't understand at all.

"Uh-oh."

Pat's eyes flickered open. "What's the matter?" They were approaching the Boys and Girls Club and the van was standing out like a Christmas tree in a snowswept field.

Ben slowed his car to a crawl. "Look at all those kids around the vehicle."

"So what?" Pat said. "Kids like cars, especially new cars."

"We could have a problem here."

Pat sighed. "What kind of problem?"

"The kids might get upset."

"Why?" Pat's voice was sharp, but he was getting tired of everything. "The damn thing belongs to us, doesn't it? We're not stealing it."

"Of course we're not." Ben stopped down the block from the club and turned off the ignition. The August heat started oozing into the car with a vengeance. "But when it first got delivered, the kids thought it was for them. You know, for the club."

"These kids aren't dumb," Pat said. "They know mistakes happen."

Ben rubbed his chin. "Unfortunately, they need a new van of their own."

"Fine," Pat said. "Give the damn thing to them and let's go back to the office. I have work to do."

"The chamber bought the van for your outfit."

"All right, then." Pat opened his door and stepped out. "Let's take it and get out of here. Make up your mind—which is it going to be?"

Ben got out of the car, so Pat strode ahead. But he hadn't taken more than three steps when he stopped. That wasn't just a crowd around the van. That was a—

"Oh, great," he muttered. The damn kids had gone and formed a human chain around the van, with arms interlocked and fierce looks on their little faces.

He didn't have much experience dealing with kids, but he suddenly found himself agreeing with Ben. This smelled like trouble with a capital *T*. A dull ache grew in his head as he watched a high school girl step away from the crowd around the van and walk toward them.

She looked cute in her summer blouse and culottes and, dressed properly, she might even be beautiful. But first she'd have to get rid of that wide-eyed innocence that dominated her face. Probably some suburban kid spending a summer saving the world, looking for something that would look good on a college application.

"Hi," she said, thrusting her hand toward Pat. He was surprised to see how firm both her hand and voice were. "I'm Trisha Stewart."

"Hello," Pat replied. "I'm Pat Stuart."

"Ah," she said. "The lucky P. Stuart."

"Lucky?"

"You get to keep the van."

Suddenly Pat recognized her as the blonde from the newspaper picture. Or he thought he did. But the person in the picture had been the director of the club. And this woman looked awfully young.

"Hello, Mr. Mackley." She turned her attention to Ben, shaking his hand. "I'd like to thank the chamber again for our new roof. It was very generous of them."

Pat grimaced. This certainly wasn't a high school kid. That wide-eyed innocence was just a facade. She knew what side her bread was buttered on, and the unobtrusive, inoffensive way she handled Ben said she was probably very good at milking dollars from the fat cats.

"We're always glad to help." Ben had cleared his throat and was fingering his tie. "Now, do we have some kind of a problem here?"

The woman shrugged, a pixielike grin on her face. "The children really love the van."

"It is a very nice vehicle," Ben agreed.

Pat took a deep breath and sighed. He had things that needed doing. He didn't have time to play all these games. "I'm sorry about their feelings," he said. "But we really need to get going. Will you tell them to step back?"

"I've already discussed that with them."

Left unsaid was that since they were still clinging to the van, her talk had been ineffective.

Pat tried another tactic. "How about I load them all into the van and drive over to the Ice Cream Shoppe? I'll spring for cones all around."

She stared at him for a moment. "Your generosity is just too much."

"You can come along." Pat was uncertain what her tone meant, but knew it wasn't positive.

Her lips twisted into a frown. "You plan on spending ten, maybe fifteen dollars max," she said. "And then you'll drive away with a van worth around twenty-five thousand dollars."

"But it's not your van," Pat protested. "It's ours."

The little blond twerp just glared at him.

"You know," Pat said, "I could just call the cops."

"And you expect the police to march in here with clubs and start throwing ten-year-old kids off your vehicle?" She glanced at something behind him, then a broad smile filled her face. "I don't think so."

Pat slowly turned around to see two TV Minicam trucks parking and other media people pulling in behind them. He turned to glare at Ben.

"I guess they got tired of waiting," Ben said with a shrug.

Well, it looked as if someone had to take charge here and, since no one else was stepping forward, Pat figured he'd better. He walked over to his van, turning on his charm-the-visiting-executives smile as he went.

"Okay, kids," he said, making sure his voice was deep and authoritative. "Let's break it up. You guys go back and play inside, while I take this van to where it belongs."

"Stuff it, Pretty Boy."

Pat looked down at the kid who'd spoken. It was a little girl, around ten or eleven, dressed in a T-shirt and shorts. A wild mass of dark hair framed a face so full of innocence that Pat barely realized she was glaring at him.

He tried again. "I know you don't want to keep something that isn't yours, so—"

"I said stuff it, butthead."

"Angie." Trisha had moved up alongside him. "Remember our chat about manners? You're supposed to treat others as you'd like to be treated."

"But Bozo here is a jerk, Miss Stewart. I can tell. He just wants to take our van."

"It isn't your van," Pat pointed out, fighting to keep his voice reasonable as the cameramen and reporters moved in on them.

"It got delivered here," Angie said.

"Yeah," the other kids shouted. "Finders keepers, losers weepers."

The TV cameras were rolling. Pat glared over at Ben, who appeared to be discussing the fortunes of South Bend's baseball team with the reporters. Swell. Pat hadn't made the mess, but he had to fix it.

He turned to Trisha. "I understand you need another vehicle."

"Pretty Boy's a real genius, ain't he, Miss Stewart?"

"Angie, be nice, please."

The girl was now smiling sweetly at him, but Pat wasn't fooled. She probably figured "nice" would be hitting him with a broomstick instead of a baseball bat.

"What we really need is money," Trisha said.

"So, you get this van when we get a new one," Angie said.

Pat took a deep breath. He wished the media people were someplace else at the moment.

"Angie's right," Trisha said. Her smile was soft and kind, but her eyes looked like a banker's foreclosing on a widow's farm. "If you want to give us the money for a new vehicle, I'm sure the children would release this one."

"Get cash, Miss Stewart," Angie said.

Pat kept his smile in place. "I'd be happy to help with fund-raising," he said. "And in the meantime, if you need transportation, I'm sure we could work—"

"You mean that whenever we need a ride, you'll drive us?" Angie said.

"Well, essentially, but that's not exactly—"

"Yahoo," Angie shouted. "Pretty Boy's gonna take us to camp, Miss Stewart."

The other kids started cheering and Pat felt his stomach falling. "What?" He looked quickly to Trisha for help, but she had adopted an angelic smile.

"Great idea, Pat," Ben said. "Just fabulous."

Pat was about to protest that he wasn't taking anyone any-place, but Ben had pushed past him and started talking to the reporters. Something about how hard these children had worked to earn their way to camp. How the club's van broke down and how Mr. Patrick Stuart, the executive director of the Committee for Industrial Development of St. Joseph County, was stepping in and helping out.

Ben went on about the new plant that Pat had brought into the community and the club's new roof that the chamber of commerce helped pay for. There were a lot of words about community and people working together, but Pat just looked at Trisha, his eyes pleading for help.

All she did was smile at him. "Thank you, kind sir," she said. Then, after a quick glance at the media, added, "You're quite the hero."

Everybody was smiling, but Pat felt like a rabbit who'd been caught in a cage. And everyone was closing in on him.

"How about a group photo?" someone shouted.

"Wonderful," Ben said, stepping back now that the damage was done. "Wonderful."

"Hey, Pat, get between that little dark-haired girl and Miss Stewart, will you?" one photographer asked.

Pat moved where he was told, forcing a smile for the cameras. He should have stayed in L.A. He should have gone straight home. He should have become a hermit and moved out to the Gobi Desert.

"What a life our old Pat has." Ben laughed, inviting the reporters to share the humor. "Look at him, there between two beautiful women, without a care in the world. We should all be so lucky."

"So, butthead," Angie hissed at him from the side of her mouth. "You know how to drive, don't ya?"

"Now, Angie," Trisha murmured. "Be nice."

"I'm telling ya, Miss Stewart. Ya can't never trust no pretty boy. They'll break your heart every time."

Chapter Two

Trisha stepped into the office of the Committee for Industrial Development and looked around. She ought to feel at home in the place—its plain utilitarian furniture was similar to the club's decor—but she didn't. It was too quiet; the air was too cool. And instead of crayon drawings covering every inch of wall space, there were modernistic prints hung at wide intervals. It all increased the sense that she didn't belong.

Maybe she should just leave well enough alone and go back to the club. After all, she had transportation for the weekend. She should just concentrate on that and not worry that Mr. Stuart had been roped into it against his will. It wasn't the first time she'd made use of an offer that had come from somewhere other than the goodness of someone's heart.

"May I help you?" The woman behind the receptionist's desk looked efficiently brisk, but then suddenly her face split with a smile. "Oh, I know you. You were on TV."

Trisha stared. "I was?"

"The noontime news on channel sixteen," the woman said. "You're Trisha Stewart, aren't you? The woman who runs the West Side Boys and Girls Club."

"Yes." The word came out soft, almost hesitant, and that made Trisha mad. She'd negotiated peace treaties between street gangs, broken up fights in alleys and shaken the money men in this town until they gave big. There was no need for her to act like some confused little freshman who'd been sent to the principal's office.

"Yes, I am." The words came out stronger, more satisfying. "I was hoping to see Mr. Stuart. Is he in?"

"No," the woman replied. "His afternoon appointment got canceled, so he's working at home this afternoon."

"Oh." Trisha hesitated. She felt stupidly disappointed and it brought disorientation with it. She shook herself mentally. This wasn't like her; she was immune to good-looking tough guys. She forced a measure of briskness into her voice. "I'd like to leave a message for him, please."

"Why don't you just go over and see him?"

"No, that's okay." The idea was tempting, but only for a moment. "It's not urgent."

"He won't mind," the woman said pleasantly. "He's very much into the community. And he grew up on the west side. I'm sure the Boys and Girls Club is at the top of his list."

Trisha felt her mind go blank for a moment. Pat Stuart, *the* Patrick Stuart, grew up on the west side? She couldn't believe that. With his custom-made suit and distant manner, he seemed like a yuppie who was spending a few years in Indiana before he moved on to greener pastures.

"No, no. I don't want to bother him at home," Trisha said slowly. "Besides, I don't have much time."

She had to digest this new information. Not that she doubted what the woman said, but he certainly hadn't shown any fondness for his old stomping ground this morning. The real question, though, was why did any of this matter to Trisha? He was going to drive her and the kids to camp, nothing else.

"He lives just a few blocks from here," the secretary said. "He has a home of his own in the Washington Street historical district."

Trisha swallowed hard. She loved the Washington Street historical district. And she'd always thought that the finest people lived in that area. People who loved the city and all its citizens. People who were sensitive, with a feeling for history.

"He lives in the block just past the Studebaker mansion," the woman said. "At 823 West Washington."

Trisha lifted her chin slightly. No stereotypes were universally true, good ones as well as bad ones. Just because he lived in the historical district didn't mean he cared about the city.

"Thank you for your time," Trisha said, forcing a smile to her lips. "But there's really no need to bother him."

"Pat's a bachelor. You won't bother him." The woman paused and smiled, one of those know-it-all smiles that mothers with grown daughters tended to wear. "At least, not in a bad way. Unless you're married."

Trisha felt her face glow, her cheeks radiating warmth like a pair of hot coals. She hardly thought her single status mattered to Patrick Stuart, any more than his single status mattered to her. Why was it people always reduced things to such an elemental man/woman level? She was a professional first, woman second.

"You said 823 West Washington?" Trisha asked, pausing only long enough for the woman to nod, before turning to the door. "Thank you."

She hurried back into the August heat, anxious to return to the club. She still had so much to do before the camping trip Friday; she had no time to waste trying to check out a grown man's motivations.

So why then, when she got in her car, was she making her way over to Washington Street?

This was crazy, Trisha told herself. He knew what time they were leaving and he certainly knew where the Boys and Girls Club was located. All she had to do was show up at the club, load the kids into the van and let him drive them all up to Camp Weekie-Wookie.

For some unknown reason, though, she didn't want Pat to do something because he had to. She wanted him to do it because he wanted to. Because he would enjoy doing it.

Trisha pulled into Pat's driveway and turned off the ignition. Then she got out, refusing to admire the clean lines of the old frame house or the way the wide wooden porch seemed to reach out and embrace guests with welcome. She just stomped up to the door and rang the bell.

There was no answer, so she tried again. After a third ring, she turned to leave. Either he wasn't home or didn't want company. It was just as well. She didn't know why she was there anyway.

"What do you want?"

Caught before stepping off the porch, Trisha slowly turned around. Her heart just about stopped at the sight of Pat framed in the screen door, wearing nothing but a pair of jeans.

His hair was disheveled, his eyes were red rimmed and his face bore the gosh-awfulest frown she'd ever seen on a person, but she was shaken with the strongest wave of desire she'd ever experienced. She wanted to take him in her arms and kiss that frown away. She wanted to feel his bare chest pressed against hers and let her hands roam over the cords of his back muscles.

"Let me phrase this another way," he said. "What the hell do you want?"

His tone was enough to light a spark of irritation in Trisha. She was not intrigued by his bare, well-muscled chest. She was just surprised at finding him dressed in nothing but his jeans at two in the afternoon.

"Your office told me you were working."

"So sue me."

They exchanged glares. When she first met him, Trisha had thought he was a stuffed shirt. Now she was glad to see there was more to him than that—he was also a jerk.

"The Committee for Industrial Development isn't supported by any public funds," he said. "So you can't go running off to the media with some irate taxpayer act."

"I had no intention of doing that."

"How noble of you."

Trisha paused to put some order in the gaggle of words that were spinning about in her mind. She was not in any way attracted to him. Not in the slightest. All she wanted was to put him in his place. She pushed away a sudden vision of him sitting on her sofa, his eyes alight with invitation.

No, first of all, she'd tell him what she thought of him and his rude attitude. Then she'd tell him she didn't need him to drive—

This was just too suspicious. She had no more than stepped on his porch and he was insulting her, obviously trying to goad her into anger. She might be a bit naive at times, but she wasn't stupid. He was trying to get out of the trip.

"I just dropped by to go over our weekend trip," she said lightly.

"Weekend trip?"

Trisha held his stare. She'd gone eyeball-to-eyeball with some really bad people in her career and she wasn't going to back down now. Not from someone who was a gold-watch, silk-shirt type, in spite of what his secretary said he had once been.

"You mean the one where I have to transport you and a bunch of wet-nosed brats to camp up in Michigan?"

"Uh-huh." She could feel her smile grow even wider. "That's the one."

He opened the door and held it for her. With the door open, Trisha could see that the jeans were indeed the only thing he had on. His feet were bare and the jeans were tight enough to pretty much confirm the absence of underwear. Looked as if Pat slept in the nude. Trisha took a deep breath and marched resolutely into the house. A grump was a grump, no matter how handsome he was. And she was a complete professional. Her kids were all that mattered.

"Go straight back to the kitchen," he said, waving her down the hall. "I'm still a little sparse on furniture in these front rooms."

Although there was no air-conditioning on, the old house was comfortably cool. Trisha glanced into the first room. There was no furniture in it beyond an old sofa pushed up against the windows, but the pale blue on the walls was so clean and the wood trim around the windows gleamed with such newness that it was obvious a lot of work had recently been done in the room. The next room she passed, with its litter of paint cans and drop cloths, confirmed her suspicions. Another surprising side of Patrick Stuart revealed.

"These old homes are a lot of work," she said as she walked into the kitchen. "But they're so beautiful once you've re-done them."

"Yeah, I guess."

Trisha turned to look at Pat. He was rubbing his eyes and didn't look lively at all.

"You certainly sound enthusiastic," she said.

"That's me. Pat the Enthusiastic. Twin brother to Pat the Generous."

He looked so suddenly vulnerable that her heart wanted to give way. She looked away from him and found it easier to be strong.

"The kitchen is very nice," she said, truly admiring the pine cabinets, plank floor and Parsons table. It was so much more homey than her apartment's tiny kitchen. That had all the charm of a can of sardines. "It's modern, yet retains a definite flavor of the past. Did you do it?"

"Mostly." He paused a moment to pinch his eyes across the bridge of his nose. "But I don't hire out."

As if she wanted him working in her kitchen. "If you don't like refurbishing the house, why did you buy it?"

"I didn't buy it. I inherited it." He rubbed his face with both hands. "It was my grandmother's. I lived here during my senior year of high school, so she thought I'd want it."

"Don't you?"

He shrugged. "Want something to drink?"

It was her turn to shrug. "What do you have?"

Pat made a face and looked around the room for a long moment. "Water?"

What a charming host. She tried to be annoyed at him, but found it hard to maintain. She kept slipping off the path and sinking up to her knees in his vulnerability.

"That's okay," she finally said. "I won't be staying long."

He walked over and slumped into a seat at the kitchen table. He was close, too close, and she found her eyes wanting to watch that little pulse point at the base of his neck. She took some more time to admire the refurbished kitchen.

A glass-door hutch stood at the far end. The china on its shelves looked old and sturdy, like something that could weather the storms of time and still be strong. What would it be like to live in a house that held so many family memories, that was such a part of who you were? Her childhood house was a Dutch colonial in the suburbs of Chicago, filled with such bitter memories that she had no desire to even drive down its street. And she had lived there only until she was eleven, and had no idea who had lived there before or since.

"What is it you wanted to tell me?"

Trisha turned back to him, staring for a long moment. What had she want to tell him? Her original intention had been to tell him he didn't have to do anything he didn't want to. But she didn't really want to do that anymore. It was because of his attitude, she told herself. And because she really needed help this weekend. But her eyes kept straying to that pulse point.

"You came here," he reminded her. "I didn't call you."

"I was just wondering if you had any questions."

He looked at her, and his expression was not pleasant. Trisha quickly turned her attention to the kitchen table. The scratches and worn spots bespoke of a lifetime of service, of dependability.

"I'm going to meet you and the kids at the club Friday afternoon," he said. "I drive you guys to some camp for which I presume you have directions and/or a map." He paused and she nodded. "Then I drive all of you back Sunday afternoon. What's there to question?"

"I was just checking," she replied, running her finger along a deep scratch in the table's surface.

He didn't say anything in reply, and when Trisha stole a glance at him, he had his elbows on the table, his chin in his hands and his eyes closed. It took all of her self-discipline to keep from walking over and pulling his head to her chest to plant tiny kisses along his forehead.

"Do you share all this space with anybody?" she asked.

He opened his eyes slowly. For the moment, his eyes showed only weariness, not annoyance. "Just some assorted mice and spiders."

"No pets?" she asked. "No cat or dog?"

He shook his head.

"Gerbil? Fish?"

He managed to glare at her, but it was a halfhearted attempt at best. She felt sorry for picking on him when he was so tired.

"Are you running some kind of survey?"

Poor guy. He probably worked long, exhausting hours. Or was this all a trick to make her weaken and let him off the hook?

"You better get some sleep," she said. "You're going to have an action-packed weekend."

"Whoopee."

"Come on now. It isn't going to be so bad."

"Right." He stood up. There wasn't a trace of a smile on his face.

He might not think so now, but Trisha was sure he'd enjoy the weekend. It might even be good for him. Fresh air. Outdoor activities. And the kids were always a joy. Well, almost always.

"I'll see you Friday," she said, moving into the hall and toward the front door.

"I can hardly wait," he replied, following her.

"Are you doing this, too?" she asked, indicating the half-finished rooms.

"Mostly."

"You must enjoy working with your hands."

"Not especially."

Trisha couldn't help smiling. "So why all this work, then? Is it a form of self-punishment?"

He yawned and looked tiredly around him. "There's supposed to be some hidden treasure in the house," he replied. "If there is, I don't want anyone else to find it."

"What?" It was the last thing she expected pragmatic, practical Pat Stuart to say. "A treasure?"

"Not really," he said as he rubbed the back of his neck. "It's just some silly story my grandmother made up. Supposedly her mother said there was a treasure to be found in the house, but I don't believe it."

Trisha looked at him and felt her heart turning into mush. A man who believed in hidden treasure, even though he denied it, was someone who still had the wonder of a child within him. "But it must be fun looking for it, all the same," she said.

"Oh, yeah, great fun," he said. "Mouse droppings a hundred years old. Cobwebs thick enough to make drapes out of. And plaster dust everywhere. Besides, even if there had been some treasure at one time, I had hundreds of down-on-their-luck ancestors who would have dug it up long ago."

"But just imagine if you found some hidden riches. What would you do with it?"

"Hire someone else to drive you this weekend."

His face had hardened, and his voice was impatient, but Trisha knew it was all just for show. She'd seen enough little boys to know they didn't like anybody to know about the soft spots in their heart.

She just laughed at him. "See you Friday at three," she said.

"Right," Pat replied.

She was out on the porch quicker than she would have liked, but her heart was a lot lighter than when she'd arrived. They were going to have a great time this weekend. Pat would be a good role model for the boys and everything was going to work out fine. She just knew it.

Pat slammed his refrigerator door shut and leaned against the kitchen countertop. He should be feeling great about now—rested and ready for action. Except that he hadn't gotten back to sleep after Trisha had come over. He kept seeing those laughing eyes, hearing her teasing voice. He opened the door to the freezer compartment again.

The same stuff was still there. A couple of packages of those healthy frozen dinners, an unopened gallon of ice cream and three bagels of indeterminate age. Wow. All the makings of a great birthday dinner.

He slammed the door shut, a little harder this time, before walking over to the table and sitting down. Hell, he'd never cared about his birthday any other year. Why was this year different? He leaned forward on his elbows, stared out at the yard and let a little irritability nibble at his feelings.

Any fool could see that he didn't need any pets; his yard was filled with critters. There was a ground squirrel on his windowsill. Two blue jays at the birdbath. And a hummingbird flitting about in the flowers in the south end of the yard.

It must be a woman thing, this need to bring creatures into your house and nurture them. Well, he was a man. He didn't need anything in his house. He could relate to all of nature.

He leaned back in his chair and glared around the kitchen. How could a woman who was so small and didn't wear perfume leave so much of herself behind?

"Oh, hell."

He looked outside again. The ground squirrel had been joined by a companion. Seemed like everyone had a companion. Everyone but him. Well, they had what they needed and he had what he needed.

His stomach took that moment to point out that it didn't have what it needed. He was hungry but unable to decide on anything. Maybe he just didn't want to eat at home.

He went upstairs and added a knit shirt and shoes and socks to his jeans. Then, once outside, he was faced with another decision. Where should he eat?

There were a few places downtown but they sat at the extreme ends of the spectrum. Either expensive and touristy or cheap and greasy. His mood wasn't up to the first and his stomach was never ready for the second.

Maybe he'd just walk. That might even help his mood.

It was nicer outside than he expected, the heat of the day starting to wane. He stepped out onto the sidewalk briskly, going west on Washington Street, past the new town houses that had replaced the previous historical row of cheap bars and dilapidated housing.

The whole street had been pretty run-down when he'd moved in with his grandmother. Downtown hadn't been doing all that well, either. A major employer had committed to putting up a skyscraper, but then had run off to the sunbelt, leaving behind a hole in the ground and a string of broken promises.

But things were improving now. Covelski Baseball Stadium stood where an abandoned factory once was. The College Football Hall of Fame was pulling in business. And new office buildings were filling the vacant lots downtown. Things were on the upswing.

Turning onto Walnut and going south brought him to what his neighborhood used to be like. Run-down housing, idle men standing on the street corners and rusting cars sitting in the yards.

He was surprised to see that neither the glaring men nor the tattered atmosphere bothered him. But then, why should it? For the first time in years, Pat admitted to himself this was where he'd come from.

When his mother had been alive, they'd lived over on the far southwest side, but things had gone downhill after she'd died. His father had had to sell the house and they'd moved to the near west side, where he looked more and more to the bottle to fill the void in his life. And the more time Dad spent with Brother Alcohol, the more Pat and his younger brother, Matt, were left to fend for themselves.

Matthew Thomas Stuart, but everybody had called him Angel because of the angelic look about him. It had gotten him out of a lot of trouble over the years, but hadn't helped at all when the combination of a rain-slicked road and alcohol had put him in touch with a tree about eight years ago. Pat had buried him next to their father and mother.

Something pulled Pat back to the real world and he was surprised to see that his feet had taken him to Pulaski Park, a large expanse of green just across the tracks from the rental duplex he'd lived in with his father and brother. The duplex had burned down long ago, but the park had been kept up. Even had some play equipment over in one corner. Pat stood for a moment, watching a group of kids playing baseball.

Pat shook his head. He'd been in South Bend for three years now and this was his first time back in the old neighborhood. Some writer had said that you couldn't go home again. Hell, who wanted to?

His stomach reminded him that the real purpose of this trip had been food and Pat decided that he was *really* hungry now. He crossed the tracks, walking along several blocks of open land. Land that had been cleared of decrepit old factory buildings. Land where the new plant from California would be built.

A neon sign flashing Johnny's beckoned from a corner tavern and Pat hurried his steps. He wondered if Johnny was still there or if a new owner had chosen to save money and leave the old sign.

Opening the door brought him into a dim, cool interior, along with the same sour-mash smells that had greeted him twenty years ago when he'd come here looking for his father. The bar was still worn and polished. The walls were still covered with dark paneling. It said something about a society when the neighborhood bar was a bastion of stability.

"Hey, Pat. Long time no see."

Johnny's thick mop of black hair had gone with the years, leaving behind a thatch that was thinner and whiter. He didn't look as tall as he used to, but his blue eyes were still bright and his voice was still deep.

"Hi, Johnny," Pat said, taking the bartender's hand. His grip was still as strong. "Good to see you again."

"Beer?"

Pat nodded and slipped onto a bar stool, settling in as if the last time he had been here was a few days ago instead of twenty years. "You have a hell of a memory to recognize me after all these years."

"Ah." The bartender carefully poured a draft, trying to minimize the foam. "It was easy. You're the spittin' image of your father."

For the fleetest of moments, Pat clenched his teeth. Just because he looked like him didn't mean he had to be like him. Besides, he'd always liked Johnny. The bartender would save the change from the drinks his father bought and would slip it to Pat, so that there would be something to buy groceries with.

"So, how are you?" Johnny asked as he slid a foaming glass of beer toward Pat.

"Good." Pat picked up his beer and sipped at it. "Although I'm hungry right now. Your wife still cook those burgers like she used to?"

"Martha died."

"I'm sorry." He felt a stirring of sadness for the gentle woman who'd slipped him and Angel "leftovers" whenever they'd come by. He hadn't thought of her for years, and was suddenly conscious that life had gone on after he'd left. Not just his, but everyone's.

Coming here had been a stupid idea. He should have just gone to a fast-food joint. Pat stared into his glass as the taste soured in his mouth.

"But my daughter Sandi makes them just as good. You want one with the works?"

Pat hesitated. He should get out of here, go back where he belonged. But where was that? "Yeah." The word came out slow. "Sure."

Johnny moved toward the kitchen in back. "We still peel our own spuds," he said over his shoulder. "You want some fries?"

Pat nodded and took another sip of his beer. What the hell. He'd been eating mostly rabbit food for ages now; he could have a burger and fries. He'd just run an extra mile this weekend.

Then it dawned on him. This weekend wasn't his own—he was playing baby-sitter. By the time Johnny brought out the hamburger plate, Pat's hunger had disappeared again.

"I'm sure that that doesn't mean anything, honey."

Trisha stopped to stare openmouthed at her mother, a cat in one arm and a cookbook in the other. "Mother, what in the world are you talking about?"

Her mother was helping Trisha make peanut butter cookies for the kids' trip up to camp. There wasn't much room in Trisha's tiny kitchen, but they were used to working together in cramped quarters. The two of them, along with Trisha's older brother, had lived in a lot of small apartments after Trisha's father had left them. The familiarity hadn't helped Trisha's mind-reading skills, though.

Her mother nodded toward the TV news program that was on. "That little clinch you were just staring at."

The television had just shown the current Miss Indiana giving Pat a long and deep kiss, and now a reporter was explaining how Mr. Stuart had just persuaded a major West Coast company to open a plant in South Bend.

"I'm sure that was just for publicity," her mother went on to explain.

"I don't really care what people do or don't do for the television camera." Trisha concentrated on putting the cookbook away, then replacing Lucy on the ledge where she'd been sleeping. The cat glared at Trisha and jumped down.

''Well, the young man didn't act like it was anything serious.''

''Most men, young or old, don't act like kissing a beautiful young woman is anything serious,'' Trisha replied.

''Trisha, that's not fair.''

Trisha swallowed the retort that was on the tip of her tongue. No, it wasn't fair. Or accurate. After all, her father had taken kissing Lisa seriously. Very seriously. Of course, her money might have had something to do with that. With it, he'd been able to shift his practice to downtown Chicago. Never mind that none of his old patients were able to get there, nor could they have afforded his new rates if they had.

But in all the years since her parents' divorce, Trisha had never heard her mother say a negative word about their father. Probably because he was the father of her children—although her mother never said anything bad about anybody.

''You want to shape the cookies?'' her mother asked. ''Or do you want to smash them?''

Trisha just gave her mother a look. She always flattened the cookies.

''I was just checking, dear.''

Trisha sat on a stool, watching as her mother rolled out little balls of dough and put them on the cookie sheet.

''Must be a slow news day,'' her mother said.

Trisha looked at the TV. The station was replaying the big nonlove scene between Pat and that beauty queen woman. Trisha was suddenly conscious of her own mussed hair, her short, no-nonsense fingernails and her slight, almost girlish figure.

''I don't think they really go together,'' her mother said.

''Oh, right.'' Trisha made a face. ''They're both tall, good-looking and sexy. It's a horrible match.''

''Of course, dear. There's no variety.''

''And that's important.''

''As a matter of fact, it is,'' her mother said smoothly. ''Besides, you'll have him all weekend. I'm certain you can keep his mind off beauty queens.''

''Mom, we're taking kids to camp. That's what we'll be occupied with.''

Her mother passed along the first cookie sheet. "The kids have to sleep sometime."

Trisha stared at her mother. "Just what are you suggesting? That I sneak off with him for a quick romp in a sleeping bag? What kind of motherly advice is this?"

"The kind you're misunderstanding, dear. There's much more to a relationship than sex."

"Who says I want a relationship with him, anyway?" Trisha began flattening the cookies. With a bit too much relish, perhaps, because the first few turned into pancakes. "I'll have you know I don't."

"But you should. He's very eligible."

Trisha didn't ask how her mother knew that. She was sure she didn't want to know and just concentrated on her cookies. "And for your information," Trisha couldn't help adding, "he's not too crazy about me, either."

"Oh, I doubt that."

"He thinks I'm pushy and manipulative."

"I'm sure you're exaggerating."

"He was roped into taking us to camp and I refused to let him get out of it."

"Men need a firm hand sometimes," her mother said. "They're shy about getting involved."

Shy? That was about the last word Trisha would use to describe Pat Stuart, but she knew there was no point in telling her mother that. She'd just make her cookies and listen to her own heart.

And that was telling her to stay clear of Patrick Stuart and his broad shoulders.

Chapter Three

"*Eleven bottles of beer on the wall, eleven bottles of beer.*"

Pat gripped the steering wheel until his knuckles turned white. He was sitting in this van with eight kids between the ages of eight and twelve for one reason, and one reason only. And that was to prove to himself that his weird reaction to Trisha on his birthday had been a fluke. She had caught him in a weak moment, but was nothing more than a beautiful woman he'd had a fleeting attraction to. And being with her this weekend would prove it.

"*If one of those bottles should happen to fall, ten more bottles of beer on the wall.*"

Of course, his reasons for coming had totally overlooked the real dangers involved in this trip. He'd thought he was just going to lose his weekend. Now he realized that more serious things were at stake—such as his hearing and his sanity.

Throughout all this mayhem and commotion, Trisha sat in the front passenger's seat, hands folded in her lap, looking at the passing scenery with a face as serene as Botticelli's Madonna. She must be wearing earplugs.

"Are we there yet?"

Gritting his teeth, Pat ignored the question. He remembered that when touring the state prison at Michigan City last year, a guard had told him the inmates interpreted any friendliness as a sign of weakness. Pat knew if he answered that question, they'd jump on him with a million more.

"Ten bottles of beer on the wall."

"Do they have to do that?" Pat asked, loud enough for Trisha to hear through her earplugs.

"Ten bottles of beer."

"Why are you shouting at me?" she asked.

A beautiful, blessed silence filled the van. Pat could almost feel his ears sigh in relief. All right, so she wasn't wearing earplugs; the noise just didn't bother her. Just went to show that they had nothing in common. If she was his soul's twin, she'd be ready to climb the walls the way he was.

"How about if they put a sock in it?" he said, indicating the kids in back with a slight tip of his head.

"They're not hurting anybody."

"If one of those bottles should happen to fall—"

Not hurting anybody? How about him? How about his ears? How about the fact that his brain was turning into oatmeal?

"Are we there yet?"

Pat ground his teeth. It was Rulli again—a skinny little eight-year-old who looked scared of his shadow. Pat wanted to tell the kid to shut up, but Trisha would probably interpret it as an attack on the little punk's self-esteem. Not that it should matter to Pat. It wasn't like he was trying to win points with her or anything.

"Nine bottles of beer on the wall."

If only they were in Colorado, driving to some camp back in the mountains and snaking the van along narrow switchbacks. Then he could just drive off the edge into some canyon about a hundred miles below. Sure, they'd all die, but hell couldn't be any worse than this.

"Nine bottles of beer on the wall."

"Aren't they a little young for that song?" he asked.

"Nine bottles . . ."

The kids' words trailed off and peace again returned to the van. Pat wondered if that was the key. If he talked, the kids didn't sing. But they had almost another hour to go. What in the world could he talk about for that long? If he were riding with some regular business folks, that would be one thing, but a pack of kids and a social worker? Covering subjects of common interests would take about thirty seconds.

"What are you talking about?" Trisha asked.

"Beer," Pat replied. "I'm sure they're not old enough to drink beer."

Trisha stared at him.

"I know that they might sneak some," he said. "But I don't think that as responsible adults, we should condone that kind of thing."

Her frown deepened and it hit him suddenly just how beautiful she was. It didn't matter that she was anything but pleased with him; there was a glow to her skin that was richer than any makeup could cause. And a light in her eyes that spoke of passion and fervor. He looked back at the road.

"I'm sure you realize that alcoholism begins with an attitude," he said. "A lackadaisical attitude that starts with sneaking a few cans in the alley. Then when they're older, they move to social drinking, which, for some people, is a major step on the way to alcoholism."

"If one of those bottles should happen to fall—"

"This is a silly conversation."

"Eight bottles of beer on the wall."

After the few moments of quiet, the renewed singing was putting Pat closer to the edge than he'd been before. It was like pouring salt into an open wound.

"Eight bottles of beer on—"

"I mean it," he said. "Alcoholism is a serious social problem. In many cases, it leads to more serious substance abuse."

Her sigh was very definite and drawn out. "Kids." Her voice was firm. "Enough of that song, please."

"How come?" Angie asked.

"Mr. Stuart doesn't want us singing songs about beer."

Pat glared at Trisha. Why did he have to be the bad guy? The little bandits would probably do something bad to him now. Like putting spiders in his bed.

"They got beer on TV."

"They have a lot of things on TV that we don't need," Trisha replied. "No more beer songs, please."

No one had a reply to that, not even smart-mouth Angie. Pat could feel the tension draining away from him. The pretty country scenery gently floated by them and he was even starting to enjoy the drive. There was a lot of whispering in the back, but he could take that. He could take almost anything after that damn song.

"A hundred cartons of milk on the wall."

Suddenly Pat found it hard to breathe. His fingers locked themselves so tightly around the steering wheel that they hurt. He glared at Trisha.

"A hundred cartons of milk."

"They're not singing about beer." Her voice was sweet and her eyes were dancing.

"If one of those cartons should happen to fall, then ninety-nine cartons of milk on the wall."

"You know," Trisha said. "They were almost done before you made them stop."

That was it. He'd had it. No more Mister Nice Guy.

He pulled the van over to the shoulder and eased it to a stop. He very deliberately put the vehicle in Park, set the hand brake, released his seat belt and turned around to face the kids. Eight pairs of eyes gazed at him. Now he knew what a zebra felt like when surrounded by lions.

"Are we there?" Rulli asked.

"No, we're not there," Pat snapped. "I'll tell you when we are, so quit bugging me about it."

The kid's face started to crumple and Pat felt a twinge of guilt. This was all Ben's fault. Ben's and Trisha's. They had roped him into this without any thought that some people might not deal well with kids. He looked away from Rulli, settling his attention on Angie. The girl was looking daggers at him, firming Pat's resolve to take charge of the situation before it got totally out of hand.

"And the next one who starts singing about bottles of anything falling down is going to get his tongue ripped out by the roots."

For a split moment there was absolute, total silence. It was beautiful. But like so many beautiful things—a snowflake, a soap bubble, a sunset—it didn't last long.

"That's an awful thing to say," Trisha said.

At least, Pat thought that was what she had said. It was hard to hear her since Rulli had begun wailing like an ambulance siren, spilling crocodile tears on everyone within thirty feet of him.

"Miss Stewart, Rulli's gonna wet his pants," Angie called out.

"And not very bright," Trisha told Pat, before turning back to Rulli. "It's okay, Rulli. He didn't mean to yell."

"He's always got to go when he starts crying," Angie was telling them.

Pat could feel the world crumbling around him. All he'd wanted was some peace and quiet, a little consideration for his feelings. Damn, he should have come down with beri beri and called in sick.

"There's a gas station up ahead," Trisha said. "Get us over there, please."

"We better hurry," Angie said. "Rulli's gonna go real soon."

He turned in his seat, fumbling with the hand brake.

"I already have eight kids I'm responsible for," Trisha said. "I don't need another. So get us to that service station or let me drive."

"I'm going, I'm going," he snapped. He got the hand brake released, put the damn van in gear and was off toward the service station. He threw a little gravel just to show everybody that he could move fast when he wanted to.

"You ain't got your seat belt fastened."

Oh, gag. It was Angie again. "I don't need a seat belt," Pat snapped. "I'm Captain Magic's brother."

"Captain Magic don't have no brother," Angie replied.

"How do you know?" Pat asked. "Are you a friend of the family?"

"Children." Trisha ought to have been addressing the kids in back but she was looking at him. "Let's behave."

"I didn't start anything," Pat said.

"Drive."

He wanted to point out that that was exactly what he was doing but he wasn't sure that Trisha was into such fine technical points. How could he have thought she was beautiful or soft and gentle? How could he have felt attracted to her, even for a moment? She wasn't his type at all.

They were at the station within minutes. Rulli took off running for the men's room before they were barely stopped. Then the other kids climbed out. Pat drifted after the boys to keep an eye on them while Trisha did the same for the girls.

It was hot and muggy outside, with waves of heat rising from the blacktop of the service station. But every so often a gentle breeze would bring a hint of relief along with the scent of rich, wet earth and the sound of birds calling in the distance. Pat took a deep breath, feeling his tensions unwind slowly and fall away.

They really weren't bad kids, he thought as he tried to fight off pangs of guilt. They were just lively. And probably nervous about going to camp. He'd bet none of them had ever been away from their neighborhood before.

His conscience began to really rag at him. He should have been the adult, the mature one. He could have done it without yelling.

"Yo, Pat." The kid was a husky, aggressive boy named Douglas. "How about you buy a few pops for me and the guys?" The boys, all done with their turns in the washroom, had gathered around Pat.

He was about to agree but Trisha was really in charge of the kids. "Let's check with Miss Stewart."

The boys all made faces.

"Hey," Pat said, herding the boys before him, "she's in charge."

Like most little boys, they were probably male chauvinist piglets, but everyone kept their mouth shut as Trisha and the girls approached.

"The guys want something to drink," Pat said. "Do you think that's a good idea?"

Trisha glanced at her watch. "We're about forty-five minutes away from the camp. It should be okay."

"It'll be my treat," Pat said. He pulled his wallet out and then held a ten in his hand, trying to decide whether he should go in with the kids or whether Trisha should.

"I'll take care of that."

Before he could react, Angie had snatched the bill from his hand and was leading the other kids into the little convenience store attached to the service station.

"She's such a shy little thing," he said. "I wonder how she'll ever survive in this hard, cruel world."

"Angie lives in a crowded household. She has to be aggressive or she wouldn't have survived this long."

Pat leaned against the van and stared out over the road at the pastureland beyond. Brown-and-white cattle dotted the hillsides, with a few horses mixed in for good measure. He'd bet most of those kids hadn't even seen a pasture before. And he was the one who'd behaved as if he shouldn't be let out of his room.

"I'm sorry for acting like a jerk," he said to Trisha.

She turned from watching the kids in the store to smile at him. There was no doubt about it; she was a beautiful woman.

"They can get to you sometimes," she said.

"I'm an adult, so I should have known better. Kids have a lot of energy and they have to burn it up."

She nodded and turned back to look into the store. "Want a word of advice?" she asked.

"Sure."

"Never make a threat you can't keep."

"You mean the 'rip out their tongues' thing?"

"That's going to come back and haunt you."

"Think they'll tell their parents?"

Trisha laughed. "I thought you grew up on the west side."

"Yeah." He felt that familiar tightness in his stomach. "So what?"

"So you should know that these kids don't go running to anybody for help."

A chattering sound escaped the store, rolled over the blacktop and filled his ears. He turned to watch the kids come spilling out, sipping at their cans of soda and talking at the same time.

"They know you're not going to rip their tongues out," Trisha said. "And you better believe they're going to call your bluff."

He looked away from the kids and into Trisha's sparkling green eyes.

"So, good luck, fella."

"You see all them trees and bushes and stuff?" Douglas asked, waving his arm in a sweeping motion. "Them's woods. You know, like a forest. The kinda place where Bambi and Robin Hood live."

All the other kids were occupied with hauling their gear and following Trisha up the path to their cabin. Nobody seemed to be listening to the big kid. Pat was bringing up the rear.

He had done some soul-searching on the rest of the drive up here and had decided he could do a lot better than he had. His life had been so structured lately that he'd forgotten that sometimes you just have to go with the flow. It would take a little effort on his part, but he could do it. It was how a man handled things.

"And you know who lives in the woods?" Douglas was going on. "Bears. Man-eating bears."

Rulli's head darted from side to side, but none of the other children seemed to be paying attention.

"Oh, yeah?" Angie said. "I heard they like fat people best."

Angie was walking just behind Rulli. Maybe the bigmouth was a mother hen, someone who hated injustice and didn't like to see the weaker ones picked on. Sighing, he tried to put that thought out of his mind. It would be hard to keep a good irritation going toward the girl if he found that she had a good heart.

"And you got enough blubber on your body to feed a hundred bears for a week," Angie continued. "So we're all safe."

"Angie. Douglas," Trisha said without looking back. "We're going to try and get along this weekend, aren't we?"

The two kids stuck their tongues out at each other, but it looked as if Trisha was using the silence-is-consent rule and didn't bother to turn around to look at anyone.

"Oh, look. There's our cabin."

They'd rounded a corner in the path and stopped at the edge of a clearing where a small cabin stood. It was about forty feet by twenty, with an open breezeway cut through the middle.

"It's all made of logs."

"I bet Abraham Lincoln used to live here."

They moved forward, the kids stopping once they stepped into the breezeway. Pat eased past them and peeked into one of the open doors. There was a bathroom to one side, a small enclosed room that was probably for a counselor on the other side, and beyond that a single large room with bunk beds along the wall and a table in the center.

"Okay, guys," Trisha said. "One side is for the boys and the other is for the girls."

"Give them that one," a girl said, pointing to the door where Pat was standing. "It stinks the worsest."

"Mary," Trisha said. "That's not nice."

"It'll be okay," Angie assured them. "The boys already stink."

"Girls." Trisha's voice had grown firmer. "I want us to be polite to one another all weekend."

There was a great deal of blinking by both boys and girls. Pat thought there was also a little pain flitting through their faces, but he refrained from laughing. Trisha probably had enough of his antics for a while.

"So," Trisha said. "I think we should—"

"We'll take this one," Pat said.

"Are you sure?" Trisha said.

"Absolutely," Pat replied. "This is the one we want. Right, guys?"

The boys all looked at one another and shrugged. Well, no one said he had to run a democracy. He opened the screen door and walked into the cabin, pausing to drop his bag in the tiny counselor's room. The boys filed past him into the big room.

"Pee-ew," a boy named Marty said. "What is that stink?"

"Bear pee," Douglas replied.

"I thought they pee in the woods."

"Not when it rains," Douglas replied.

The three older boys dumped their bags on a single lower bunk and started climbing up to the top bunk of one of the beds. Pat found Rulli sitting by himself on a bunk bed farthest from the other boys. The little guy looked like the odd man out and Pat hadn't helped earlier. He walked over and sat down next to the kid.

"Man," Pat said. "This is really gonna be great."

"Yeah." The kid's eyes darted at his companions climbing and jumping on the beds. "Yeah."

"We got a roof over our heads. Someone to cook. A whole big set of woods and stuff to play in." Pat shook his head. "Can't beat that."

They watched the other boys run into the bathroom and listened to them shouting and laughing.

"Are there really bears out here?" Rulli asked quietly.

Pat shook his head. "Nah. You saw how we got here. We drove through a bunch of towns and past some farms. Bears need lots of open space."

"But there's a lotta woods here."

"Still not big enough for bears. They eat mostly berries. And it takes a whole lot of woods to grow enough berries to fill a bear's stomach. Put a bear in here and he'd starve to death in less than a week. The worst they got here are squirrels and raccoons."

Pat looked up toward a window on the far wall. A blue jay was hopping around on the branches, sending insults their way.

"And birds," Pat added.

"We got all that at home," Rulli said. "Douglas don't know nothing."

The other three boys came running back into the room, ignoring Pat and Rulli, to pile on one of the lower bunks and engage in a three-way wrestling match. Nothing was getting bruised, so Pat didn't say anything. The blue jay took umbrage to the goings-on, though, and left.

"You gonna sleep in that little room by yourself?" Rulli asked.

Something in the kid's eyes stopped Pat, something that wasn't quite pleading but damn close. It had been a long time since somebody had really needed something from him, something that had nothing to do with his pocketbook, and it awoke a touch of fear in him. He had stayed clear of this type of involvement, first by choice, then by habit.

He looked away and blew a lungful of air past his lips. Damn it. He knew this weekend was going to be trouble. All he had to do was read the signs. And there had been more than enough of them.

"Are ya?" Rulli asked.

"Nah." Pat turned back to look at the kid. "I'm gonna bunk on one of these beds over here."

Rulli's eyes lit up. The hope growing there was almost too painful to watch. "How come?" he asked.

"That other room's too small, man." Pat put a big smile on his face. "I like a lot of room when I sleep."

"Yeah." Rulli's head bobbed like one of those toy dogs people put on the back shelf in their cars. "Me, too."

"Got more windows here," Pat said. "Makes for more fresh air."

"Yeah."

"And you can hear the sound of the water running in that little brook outside."

Rulli lifted his head and listened, as if he were hearing the gurgling for the first time. "We hear water like that at our house," he said.

Pat looked at him. The kid didn't look as if he were making something up. "Oh, yeah?"

"Yeah, the toilet's broke. The landlord, you know, keeps saying he's gonna fix it but he never does."

Pat slumped back against the wall and exhaled slowly.

"You guys ready to head back to the main area?" Trisha had popped her head through the door. "There's a welcoming ceremony in a little bit."

Pat was so glad to see her that he sprang up off the bed. Unfortunately, he'd forgotten how low the top bunk was and whacked his head into it. Hard.

"Damn." He rubbed the top of his head, biting back the words that wanted to come. "That smarts."

Rulli stared at him while the other three boys roared with laughter.

Trisha rushed to his side. "Are you okay?"

"Sure." He stood up. "My grandmother always said I had solid bone between my ears."

"Well," she said, putting her arm through his. "I have some aspirin if you need it."

"I'm fine. Really." Although he had no objection to her leaving her arm right where it was. She felt good so close to him, her gentle scent teasing his senses and threatening to make his head swim even more than the whack on the head had.

The boys started streaming out of the cabin, pulling Rulli along with them, so Pat and Trisha followed.

"Hey, Rulli," Douglas said. "Is Mr. Butthead a friend of yours now?"

"He ain't no butthead," Rulli said, bristling.

"Well, he sure ain't too smart."

"So what?" Rulli replied. "He's nice."

He could feel Trisha squeeze his arm. "Looks like you have yourself a friend," she said.

"Great." Pat grinned down at her, unexpectedly touched by the boy's endorsement. "But it's a good thing that I don't need a character reference right now."

"Oh, Great Spirit. Give us your light that our fire may burn."

Trisha smiled and stuck her hands in the pockets of her shorts. They'd been welcomed, fed dinner and then introduced to one another through some silly games. Now, after an evening snack of cookies and juice, they were gathered around a huge pile of wood down by the lake. The kids were up close; she and Pat were sitting on a log a ways behind them.

A gentle breeze blew in from the west, easing the weariness from her mind. The trip up had been a challenge, one she hadn't foreseen, and she'd been ready to admit she'd made a major mistake. She shouldn't have forced Pat to come; her instincts had been all wrong. But then he'd seemed to mellow, reacting to the kids with a gentle understanding that had surprised her.

"I don't think the great spirit is listening," Pat said, interrupting her thoughts.

She looked over through the darkness to the still-unburning pile of wood. "Don't be such a cynic," she said.

"I don't see any fire," he said.

"You gotta have faith."

One of the camp's regular counselors had dressed up as an Indian chief and had given a short talk about the earth and all the creatures that shared it. The kids, a little over fifty from various Boys and Girls Clubs in Indiana and Michigan, had listened and behaved very nicely. Unfortunately, the chief's assistant was now having trouble getting the bonfire to go and the little lads and lassies were getting restless.

The chief looked toward a clump of trees just behind him and apparently received a signal.

"Okay, boys and girls," he said. "We'll try again. But this time everybody has to repeat after me."

"Oh, Great Spirit," the chief said.

"Oh, Great Spirit," the kids repeated.

"Give us your light that our fire may burn," the chief shouted.

The children had no sooner finished repeating the words when flames literally exploded from the woodpile. One large, collective gasp of appreciation floated up to the stars above them.

Though Trisha had expected it, she felt herself jump back slightly, bumping into Pat's arm as she wobbled on the log. He reached over to steady her. A sudden warmth that had nothing to do with the campfire raced through her. This was not the plan for the weekend, she told herself, no matter what her mother had advised. Trisha gingerly moved aside a few inches as if returning to her former spot. He let his hand fall.

"That was pretty neat," she said quickly, hoping to cover up her reaction to him.

"It's just old wood," Pat said. "A little gas, gunpowder for oomph and a battery on a long wire for a spark."

She kept her eyes on the fire, now burning nicely. "I know how they do it, but I still think it's neat."

"And how long have you had this fascination with fire, Miss Stewart?"

His teasing was unexpected, causing her to burst into laughter. He seemed like a friend suddenly, and her heart forgot its caution. The dark starry night and the campfire and light sparkling off the lake just beyond all wove a spell around her.

"There's something so magical here," she said.

"How can it be magic when you see how it's being done?"

Trisha turned toward him. She couldn't really see him in the dark, but could feel his bewilderment. Poor guy. Was his life so predictable and concrete that he had no room for magic?

"I guess I believe you never totally leave your childhood behind you," she said.

"I guess I believe you should always keep your feet planted firmly in the real world."

A lot of hardness lay behind his words. Or was it bitterness? She had a strong urge to soothe away his hurts and bring back the magic. "So you grew up on the west side."

"So what?"

His voice held a challenge, a dare to find fault and, for a moment, she was taken aback. She didn't believe that where a person was born or grew up had anything to do with his value as a human being, but he didn't seem to be inviting a philosophical discussion.

"So nothing," she mumbled, angry at herself for backing down but angrier still that she'd thought he was mellowing. She'd seen him change his colors often enough to know he was as prickly as a cactus when anyone tried to get close.

She turned to watch the fire, now burning very well. The flickering firelight created weird shadows that made things look spookier than they'd looked in the moonlight. Maybe that was the problem. This crazy light was just making things look different and she was having trouble distinguishing their shapes. Maybe she'd offended Pat by her statement.

"I didn't ask anything about you," she said. "Your secretary mentioned it in passing."

Pat just grunted, but she took heart from the fact. If she was trespassing into private territory, he would have said something. She knew that much about him.

"Maybe she thought you'd make a good role model for the kids," Trisha said. "You know, someone who grew up with the same disadvantages they face, yet made something of himself."

"I think role models are vastly overrated."

His voice said he was getting distant, but she refused to let him retreat totally. "I disagree," she said. "At least you could tell them how to succeed. They'd listen to you more than they would to me.''

''The formula's easy,'' Pat said. ''You have to leave the neighborhood and cut all ties to it.''

''All ties?''

''Every single damn one.'' There was something so final, so clipped in his tone that she found no words would come.

Her eyes strayed back to the campfire and the children around it. Some counselors had demonstrated an Indian dance and now the kids were joining in. Angie was one of the first ones up, leaving the others behind. Could she do the same as easily if she was leaving the neighborhood as Pat said?

''What about family and friends?'' Trisha asked, her eyes still on Angie dancing around the circle, getting farther and farther from Rulli and the others.

''They'll just hold you back.''

That sounded so cold and calculating. Trisha didn't know Pat very well—she'd be the first to admit it—but that was not the picture she'd formed of him. Obviously she'd been wrong. She forced herself to concentrate on the activities before them.

''My father was an auto mechanic and my mom was a housewife. The four of us—I had a little brother about four years younger— lived over on the southwest side of the city. It was pretty much country back then.''

A working-class, blue-collar family. Not rich by any means, but the father should have been able to provide adequately for them. More so than a lot of fathers could do in today's economy.

''My mother died when Matt was four.'' Trisha heard him take a deep breath. ''And things sort of went to hell for us after that.''

Trisha had lost her father to divorce but she could see where losing a mother would be even harder. Women tended to hold a family together.

''My father had to sell the house to cover medical expenses and we moved to a duplex over by Pulaski Park, not too far south of the club.''

''Must have been rough.''

Pat didn't answer for a while. And when he did, there was pain in his voice. ''Everybody hits a rough stretch of road now

and again, but we could have made out all right." He fell silent for a moment. "But Mom's death hit my father really
hard. I guess he wanted to hit back at something so he started
hitting the bottle."

"He must have loved your mother a great deal."

Pat was looking beyond her, off toward the lake. "It started
with a few drinks on the weekends. Then he began to lose his
weekends as it took longer and longer to sober up." He took a
deep breath. "Somewhere along the way, the days all merged
into one big weekend."

"How did you and your brother get along?" Trisha asked.
"Did you have any other relatives in the area?"

"Just my mother's mother," Pat replied. "But she and my
father didn't get along all that well when Mom was alive. Once
he started drinking, there was nothing between them but anger."

She felt his pain and hurt and bitterness at life. "It must
have been hard," she said, seeing the inadequacy of her words,
but not knowing what else to say.

The kids had finished with the Indian dance and were now
singing. Their voices all mingled to form such a strong statement of hope and promise that Trisha had to blink back tears.
Surely these kids had a chance to succeed without the pain that
was haunting Pat.

"We did okay." Pat's voice had grown husky. "We did odd
jobs for people. And if things got really bad, we'd sneak over
to my grandmother's. She'd feed us, get us new clothes when
we needed them."

And when did they cut all ties? "I take it you two eventually left your father."

Pat was silent for a long time. The bonfire ceremony was
winding down. The evening was just about over for the kids,
and for her.

"I left," Pat finally said. His voice was almost a whisper. "I
left at the end of my junior year in high school and went to live
with my grandmother."

"And Matt stayed with your father?"

"Matt." He paused and cleared his throat. "Everyone called
him Angel. He had such soft features and the biggest, most

innocent-looking eyes you'd ever seen. He took after my mother."

Trisha thought of the boys at the club. "That kind of nickname could be hard on a boy."

"Yeah." Pat drawled the word, dragging it out. "It worked both ways. With adults he could get away with things. They didn't believe that anyone who looked so innocent could do anything bad. But with boys his own age, he found himself needing to work extra hard to prove himself."

"So his bad habits grew because he was getting away with stuff. At the same time, he was getting into a lot of fights." Trisha paused. A kid didn't keep on fighting unless he survived the last one. "And he got pretty good at it. Practice makes perfect, you know."

Pat laughed. "He always said he was going to be the world boxing champion and make a lot of money." He fell silent again.

The night no longer seemed filled with magic, but with secrets. Painful, awful secrets that lurked in the shadows ready to consume a person. Trisha wanted to touch Pat, hold his hand. But there seemed to be a force field around him, pushing her away, warning her to keep her distance.

"I'm not sure how much he really stayed with my father after I left," Pat said. "By the time he was twelve, his family was on the street, and once the streets get a kid, he's gone. There's nothing anyone can do to get him back. I kept trying, though."

Trisha let the silence ease the raw pain in the air. The fire was burning low, but the kids were still sitting around it and singing soft, slow songs, like "Red River Valley" and "Kum-Ba-Ya."

She took a deep breath and looked up to see the stars dancing high above her head. They always made her own hurts seem so insignificant, but she was unable to let their magic close to her tonight. Pat's anguish was too real and too near.

"Just didn't try hard enough, I guess." His words came slow, like molasses in January. "Certainly not good enough."

"Where is he now?"

"Buried next to our parents." He got to his feet, obviously done talking, and stretched as if he could shed the past like a sweater no longer needed.

Trisha got up also, not knowing what to say. Nothing was probably what the situation called for, but she felt his pain was so raw, his guilt so deep that he needed some sort of soothing. Not that she could give it, though, she thought, knowing her own scars from her father's abandonment were barely healed. She knew no words could make that kind of hurt go away.

"Party's over," Pat said.

Trisha looked below them. The children were milling about, looking for their counselors.

"We'd better get our tribe together before the bears get them," Pat said.

"Right." But there were worse things than bears lurking around these woods tonight.

Chapter Four

"Hey, Pat," Rulli called out.

Pat looked up from the screen door he was patching to see the kid running toward him. They'd had an arts-and-crafts session after breakfast, but Pat had managed to get out of it, saying he wasn't going to sleep another night with the mosquitoes zooming in and out of this hole. Not that he'd slept much, since he'd been mentally kicking himself all night.

He wasn't a person who talked about himself, especially about his past. But last night the damn moonlight and bonfire and Trisha sitting so close had turned his spine to mush. He'd said way, way too much. Stuff he'd never intended to tell anyone.

And stuff he certainly shouldn't have told Trisha—he could see that from the sympathy overflowing from her eyes this morning. She was too used to taking on the troubles of her kids; it was second nature to her. If you let a woman like that peek into your soul, the next thing you knew, she'd be trying to force the doors open. Doors that he'd closed years ago and was going to keep closed.

"Pat." Rulli pulled to a stop in front of him, puffing slightly from running. "How come you didn't answer? I was calling you."

Pat went back to weaving the patch over the hole. "Answer for what?" he asked. "I could see you coming and you could see me."

"Friends always answer each other," Rulli said.

Pat took a deep breath and looked away. That was the trouble with these kids. They had a life full of people hitting on them, so the first person that was polite became their bosom buddy—a role he wasn't qualified for. Angel could testify to that. "I'm sorry," he said.

"That's okay," Rulli replied. "No problem."

Don't be so ready to forgive, Pat wanted to shout, but kept his lips tight. He was mad at the world this morning—no, mad at himself. And he wasn't going to take it out on anyone but himself.

"Look what I made," Rulli said, holding up a small brown square for Pat to see. It was a little wallet, made from two pieces of leather sewn together with a thin strip of plastic.

"Nice. Real nice."

"I made it for you."

Pat looked into the kid's shining eyes, framed by an eager expression, and felt his stomach go sour. Damn it. This wasn't his thing. He didn't know how to be close to kids. Sure as shooting, he'd say the wrong thing or do the wrong thing and end up hurting somebody. There was a reason why he was a loner.

"Thanks, kid," he said lamely.

"I know you already got a wallet," Rulli said. "But Douglas said you got a lota money, so you could always use another one."

Those eager, hopeful eyes ate at him until it hurt. "Douglas is full of it," Pat said. "You shouldn't be listening to him."

"Don't you like your wallet?"

Pat had to look away. "Yeah, I like it fine." What the hell was he doing at this camp, anyway? He didn't know what to say to Rulli. He didn't know what to do that wouldn't hurt everyone more in the long run.

"Angie says it's ugly."

Pat sighed. "Angie's even more full of it than Douglas."

"Full of what?" Rulli asked.

The kid was small but he had the personality of a terrier, worrying at things until they broke. Pat shook his head. "I mean, you shouldn't always be listening to other people."

"Miss Stewart says I'm supposed to listen to my teachers."

"That's okay," Pat said. "Teachers are good. You listen to them."

Rulli blinked at him a few times. "I gotta listen to Angie. She says I do."

"Why? 'Cause she's a bossy know-it-all?"

"'Cause she's my sister."

His sister? Yeah, he guessed he could see the resemblance in those wide innocent eyes, but being related to Angie? The poor kid. No wonder he was a mass of nerves and looking for a buddy. "What does she tell you to do?" Pat asked.

Rulli tilted his head in thought, staring off into the trees. "Not to hang around with Buster Dooley 'cause he sneaks smokes." He paused, his lips twisting into a frown. "To study my spelling list harder." The silence went a little longer this time. "Oh, and to take my snack as soon as I get home from school so nobody else eats it."

Pat's stomach tightened. Maybe he'd been wrong about the little termagant. Though if he was, it was just proof that he shouldn't be here. He was lousy with relationships. Lousy at judging people.

"She sounds like a good sister," Pat said, then glanced at the wallet in his hand. "But she was wrong about this. It's not ugly."

Rulli leaned in close, pointing to the leather pieces. "I tried to line up all the holes real good."

"You did a great job, Super. You should get a medal."

"Angie says we're gonna get a whole buncha medals."

"Yeah, that's—" Pat's brain suddenly connected with Rulli's words. "Medals for what?"

"Oh, gosh." Rulli grabbed his head with both hands. "I almost forgot. Miss Stewart told me I'm supposed to get you. She said you're supposed to come because we're gonna do some 'lympics."

Pat remembered the schedule Trisha had shown him at breakfast. After arts and crafts, the camp Olympics were going to be held—egg-in-the-spoon relay races, three-legged races and a whole bunch of other nonsense. Not exactly his cup of tea, but worse, Trisha would be there, reeking of sympathy and good cheer.

"Go back and tell Miss Stewart that I can't play," Pat said. "Tell her I got another couple of holes to fix."

"Oh, no. You gotta come, Pat. You just gotta. If you don't, Angie's gonna be really mad." Rulli shook his head, his face more than a little concerned. "If we don't go home with some 'lympic medals, Angie says she's gonna kick butt."

"Look, kid." Pat put an arm around the boy's shoulders and pulled Rulli in to him. "You can't let Angie push you around, even if she is your sister."

"Douglas is afraid of her, too."

Pat had a sudden vision of Douglas hiding from Angie; then the figures blurred and became him hiding from Trisha. Was there a difference?

"You have to act tough," Pat said. "Otherwise everybody thinks you're afraid."

That's what he needed to do, Pat realized. He needed to show Trisha that last night's talk was just that—talk. That he wasn't afraid of the past. And he couldn't do that by hiding away here. He had to be around her, but tough and in control.

"Let me just finish this little piece," Pat said and tucked in the end of the wire. "There. Now we can go."

Rulli looked only slightly less worried as they walked down the path. "We gotta win some medals, Pat."

"Hey, we're going to leave everybody in the dust. We're not just going to win some medals, we're going to win them all."

And that's just what he'd do, Pat told himself. He'd forget about Trisha and the fact that she knew so much about him, and just get out there and win some races. He liked winning, whether it was a football game or a new contract for the city. It proved he was worth something, that he could do things better than someone else. It made him forget everything.

He'd show Trisha he was someone to be envied, not pitied. He'd show her he didn't need her sympathy or pity or anything, that he wasn't some old softy who couldn't handle a little bad luck in his past. He saw her up ahead, the kids gathered around her as they stood off to one side in a big open field.

"I was getting worried about you," she said when he and Rulli joined the group.

He felt his chin go up just a fraction. He didn't need her worrying about him. He didn't need anybody. "Hey, we were just getting warmed up," he said, trying for a teasing tone. "You know, ready to take our victory laps."

"You sure you're okay?" she asked.

Her eyes seemed to be trying to look deep inside him, to take another peek at his soul, but he just turned away slightly. "Hey, this is going to be great. I like races. I love competition."

She gave him a strange look, then turned to the kids. "You need to choose up partners for the three-legged race," she told them. "But boys have to go with girls, and girls with boys."

"Are you going with Mr. Stuart?" Mary sang out, a knowing smile on her lips.

Pat's blood turned to ice at the thought of being that close to Trisha, of having his arm around her and hers around him. How long would he be able to stay tough? They'd probably barely start the race and he'd be spilling his guts about some other part of his past. He needed a partner that would concentrate on winning, not on him.

"Nope," he said quickly. "That wouldn't be fair. Our legs are lots longer than yours and we'd win." He glanced around at the kids. "Hey, where's Angie?"

"I let her go get our numbers," Trisha said. "She likes responsibility."

She liked power—total, absolute power. But she also liked to win. "Well, I'll take her for my partner," Pat said.

"Hot dog," Douglas said with a laugh. "That means none of us has got to go with her."

"None of the rest of you guys want to win," Pat said.

There was a lot of snickering, but Trisha seemed to ignore it as she helped the kids pick partners. When they were all paired up, she came back over to him.

"Why don't you give the team a pep talk while we're waiting?" she said to him.

Her smile was warm, too warm actually, and felt as if it could make flowers grow in the coldest regions. He turned away from her with a measure of relief. She was one dangerous lady and he was going to have to be careful the rest of this weekend.

"All right, guys," Pat said. "Listen up."

They gathered in a reluctant semicircle before him; Trisha hovered behind the kids, a confident, knowing smile on her face. She was so sure she knew him. Although, after all the yakking he had done last night, she probably did. Probably knew his Social Security number, what size briefs he wore and the name of the first girl he kissed. He stiffened his resolve and thought back to the speeches his football coaches used to give.

"In a few minutes, the games will start," Pat said. "And I want us to fight hard every minute of the time. If you want to win, you gotta pay the price. You can't quit—losers quit. And I don't want to ride back home with no losers."

"Ah, excuse me." Trisha pushed in front of him, giving him a good glare as she did. "What Mr. Stuart means is that he wants you to do your best, but most of all he wants you to have fun. That's what these games are all about. If you win some medals, that's good. But if you don't, that's good, too. All you have to do is try your best. Do that and everyone will be proud of you. Okay?"

"Okay," the kids mumbled in reply.

"Great speech," Trisha murmured as she turned toward him. "Let's get them all feeling inadequate if they don't win."

Before Pat could reply, Angie stepped in between them. "Here's the numbers, Miss Stewart," she said, handing Trisha a stack of adhesive-backed labels with numbers on them.

Angie took two numbers off the top. "Mr. Stuart will help me with mine," she said.

As Trisha turned to help the other children, Angie indicated with her head that they should step away from the group. Pat followed her, carefully.

"I hear you're my partner," Angie said.

He pulled the backing off her number and stuck it on her shirt. "That okay with you?"

She shrugged. "You know all that stuff Miss Stewart was saying?"

"Yeah." Pat put his own number on his chest. "What about it?"

"It's a bunch of pig barf."

He looked at her. At her soft baby face and long eyelashes, but mostly he saw the girl's eyes—hard as black diamonds.

"I want a whole bunch of medals to take back to school when it starts. And I'm going to wear them every day."

The girl's intensity mirrored his own; he felt a sudden kinship with her. He didn't bother trying to tell her that she was somebody, with or without a medal. He knew what he would have thought about such nonsense twenty years ago.

"Okay, partner." He stuck his hand out. "Let's go out and kick butt."

She took his hand in hers. "Deal."

They hurried back to the others just as someone blew a whistle for the racers to line up.

"Come on, guys," Pat called to the other kids. "Let's show 'em that west siders are winners."

Trisha looked over at them, her face showing concern, but he just turned away. Winning did more for your self-esteem than any schmaltzy pep talk.

Trisha just shook her head as Pat stopped to give her a hand across the short log bridge. A couple of girls ahead of them on the trail looked back and giggled.

"That's okay," Trisha told him as she lightly crossed over the gentle stream. "I have a good sense of balance. And I've always been good at this wilderness stuff, too."

"A woman of many talents," he said.

Trisha looked at him, but he had turned away, staring at something off the forest path. She couldn't tell what he meant. He was in a strange mood this afternoon. A strange mood that morning, too, actually.

First, he'd been avoiding her, staying at the cabin to patch holes in the screen doors even though whole swarms of bugs could get in around the doors themselves. Then, when he'd shown up for the races, he was all charged up and ready for battle, game face on and attitude in place as if he'd been going to some serious competition. The hurting, gentle man she'd caught a glimpse of last night was buried so deep, she wondered whether she had dreamed him up.

She just walked alongside next to him. "My talents as a kid were the balance beam and ballet," she said. "You know, anything that required not falling on my face. My mother said my big feet kept me from tipping over."

He glanced down at her feet. "They don't look very big."

She felt stupid then, as if she'd been fishing for compliments. "And I've always liked hiking and skimming stones across a pond—those kinds of things. But I hated the Girl Scout trips where we'd collect moldy leaves or dead bugs, or something else stinky or slimy."

"At least they were outside where you could avoid them."

Guilt washed over her then. "I'm sorry," she said quickly. "I didn't mean anything."

He turned to frown at her; that was plain even in the dappled shade of the trees. "Didn't mean what?"

She shrugged. "You know. Remind you of your childhood."

His frown deepened but his gaze went to the kids hiking ahead of them. "We had few stinky, slimy or moldy things in my house as a kid unless my brother or I brought them in. I was thinking more about my house now. Every time I start a new project, I find things I'd rather not."

"Oh."

She took a deep breath and let her own gaze wander. It was wonderfully cool here in the woods, with only a few mosquitoes to pester them. Ahead of them snaked a line of kids, with other counselors sprinkled among them and a few naturalists pointing out the different types of trees and bushes.

She should be relaxed, Trisha knew, and enjoying herself. Instead, she was acting like a jerk. Ever since last night, she was having trouble seeing Pat as just another of the club's volunteers. In some ways, he seemed as needy as her kids, and that had awoken a dangerous warmth in her heart. And his distant behavior this morning had only made it worse.

Good thing they would be heading home tomorrow. Otherwise, her great sense of balance would be totally gone. She wasn't looking to take on any more challenges, six-foot ones or otherwise. Her life was just fine the way it was.

The trail widened and Trisha quickened her steps to put herself by Pat's side. "This is a real great experience for the kids," she said. "Look at all these plants and the wildlife. It gives the kids a whole new perspective on the world we live in."

"I don't know," Pat said. "Douglas is still convinced there are bears here someplace. I think he's hoping to see one eat somebody. Angie, probably."

He turned as he spoke, his voice teasing and laugh filled, his smile the type that could lure the mermaids from the sea. Trisha felt a sudden tug at her heartstrings, a sudden yearning to have more in her life than work and her cats. But then just as quickly her heart shied away from the idea. She needed a man she could lean on, someone she could trust, but how did she know who that man was? Without a crystal ball to see into the future, how could she know if this man, or any man, would be there for her through thick and thin?

The path had brought them to a low-lying bog area, and the whole group had paused as a counselor explained how the bog cleaned impurities from the water and about the kinds of animals that found a home there. Angie had pushed her way up to the front, dragging Rulli along with her. Douglas was at the back, looking bored and ready to wander away.

Trisha frowned as she kept one eye on the children and half listened to the lecture. The kids were her priority and what she needed to focus on. What she needed to take care of. And that was just what she'd do. "Angie was certainly wound-up this morning."

"Yeah, the kids did well at the races."

"I wasn't talking about the results—I was talking about Angie's attitude. She acted like it was life or death, not just a few silly races."

"Maybe it wasn't so silly for her."

The counselor up ahead had finished her talk and was leading the kids on. Angie had the cattail that the counselor had passed around, carrying it as if it was a prize. Trisha felt a sudden rush of concern for the girl, wishing there was some way she could shelter her from the world even for a short time.

"And you didn't help things much." Trisha turned to Pat.

"Me? What did I do?"

He looked startled with her sudden attack, but she felt only a slight twinge of guilt. Taking care of the kids, helping them, that was what she was supposed to be doing, not mooning over Pat's voice or smile.

"What did I tell you before the games started? I told you to encourage them, not pressure them." She paused a moment to glare at him. "They're kids, for heaven's sake. Those games were just supposed to be fun."

"Who's to say they weren't?" he asked.

"Angie's just far too competitive," Trisha went on. "You should have toned that down, not encouraged it. She's got to realize that she can't win all the time."

"I'm sure she knows that," Pat said, his tone dry. "She's not stupid."

"No, she's not, but she has to learn which battles are the ones that matter." Trisha stopped walking to face Pat. "Look, I know these kids. I've been with them for four years now. And you may think Angie's a real tough kid, but actually she's very fragile. That determination of hers covers up a lot of fear."

Pat's eyes betrayed his impatience. "I know that a lot better than you. I've been there, remember? You haven't."

His words were spark enough to start her swinging—verbally at least. The kids had moved on, stopping a ways up the path to count the rings in a wide old tree stump. Trisha took advantage of their distance to let off some of her steam.

"Just because you grew up on the west-side and I didn't, it doesn't mean you know these kids better than me," Trisha snapped. "They aren't exactly like you."

"Nobody is exactly like anybody else."

"No, but you're using your own experiences as if they match up with theirs."

"They probably come closer than yours," Pat pointed out. "How many of them are in gymnastics and ballet, or Girl Scouts, for that matter?"

How dare he try to make her feel inadequate because her mother had been able to give her a few extras. A fly buzzed around her face and she brushed at it impatiently. "So my childhood was different. I'm still the one here for them, day in and day out."

His eyes grew distant, as if the shutters had been slammed shut. "Like I wasn't for my brother. Is that what you're saying?"

Her heart faltered for a moment, and her anger vanished in the horror at the way he'd taken her words. But she refused to back down just because she'd accidentally stumbled onto his guilt. Her experience with the kids had taught her that was the worst thing she could do.

"No, that's not what I'm saying," she snapped. "I'm saying that after four years, I know these kids and what they need better than you do after two days. And I know that Angie's self-esteem is very fragile. She needs to know that her worth isn't measured by her medals."

"And how do you propose to convince her of that?"

"Through her schoolwork," Trisha said. "She's an excellent student."

"But doesn't feel accepted by her classmates."

"More because of her tendency to fight all the time than anything else."

"Hey, you guys," Rulli called as he came running back down the path. "Are you lost or something?"

Trisha bit back the rest of her anger, forcing it into a side pocket in her mind. Theirs was a personal battle, not one to be aired in front of Rulli or any of the kids. She smiled at the boy. "We were just talking."

"Douglas said you got eaten by bears."

"Not hardly," Trisha said. She pulled him to her in a gentle hug. "But it was brave of you to come look for us."

"Angie made me," he said. "We're going to play softball and she's captain."

"What a surprise," Pat muttered.

Trisha just gave him a look and turned back to Rulli. "Well, we'd better get going, then. We don't want to be late for the game."

"Or we may wish the bears had gotten us," Pat said.

Rulli gave him an odd look. "That's what Angie said."

"Sounds like we think alike," Pat said.

"That's scary," Rulli said.

"It sure is," Pat agreed under his breath.

They said little else as they followed the path back to the campground, but Trisha carried a frown of confusion that had deep roots in her soul. With each step over the soft, damp ground, her anger and annoyance lessened.

Pat was just like her kids in a lot of ways—presenting a tough, macho image that just barely covered the pain lying below the surface. And if she could help the Angies and Rullis of the west side, maybe she could help the Pats, too. It didn't mean she had to get involved with him, not in a romantic way. She could just help him see there was more to life than being tough.

Trisha held her breath, hoping that the squeaking of the springs wouldn't wake the girls. The even breathing that echoed throughout the little cabin told her all were still in snoozeland. She sighed.

The girls didn't seemed bothered, but it sure seemed hot and stuffy in the cabin to Trisha. No matter how she lay, she just couldn't feel cool. She pressed the light button on her wristwatch; it was 1:20 in the morning. She turned over, settling back down with a sigh.

She certainly was tired enough to sleep. She'd had an active day—arts and crafts, the Olympic games, the long walk in the woods, softball and swimming and then square dancing and a movie after dinner. Maybe she was overtired.

Except every time she closed her eyes, she saw Pat, and that stirred up all her mixed feelings about him. Their softball team hadn't won their game this afternoon and Angie had been very upset, but Pat had pulled the girl aside for what appeared to be a heart-to-heart talk. When Angie had returned to the group, she'd done a passable job of hiding her disappointment while she congratulated everyone on playing a good game. Trisha had been impressed—maybe Pat knew these kids better than Trisha had given him credit for—but she'd never quite had a chance to tell him. Mary had been stung by a bee, then Douglas had an upset stomach, and before Trisha knew it, the kids were going to bed and all her chances to talk to Pat were gone. Her head told her it was just as well, but her heart didn't want to listen.

Trisha turned over in bed again, but knew it wasn't going to help. She needed some fresh air. She eased herself out of bed, glad she was wearing a T-shirt and shorts, and padded across the room. Once out into the breezeway, she paused a moment, letting her lungs fill with the pine-scented lake air. Her head cleared in a matter of moments, but she wasn't ready to go back inside.

She would have liked to walk down by the lake, but she shouldn't go that far from the cabin. The little bench just out in front would do fine.

Trisha stepped out onto the bare dirt, savoring the cool ground on her bare feet, and had gone several yards before she stopped, realizing that there already was somebody sitting on the bench.

"Hi," Pat said.

"Pat? What are you doing out here?"

"Sitting," he replied.

She walked over and stood in front of him. "You must have awful good ears," Trisha said. "I thought I was moving pretty quietly."

"I guess I sensed your presence rather than heard anything." He laughed. "It's a sixth sense that all us west siders develop."

A certain hardness resided in his voice and Trisha wondered what ghosts he'd brought out to sit with him in the dark of the night.

"It's kind of hard to explain," he said.

"You don't have to," she said. "I see it in my kids."

"Yeah," he drawled. "I imagine you would."

A light breeze blew in off the lake and Trisha breathed deeply, burrowing her toes in the dirt. "Couldn't you sleep?"

"Nope. You?"

"No."

They paused a moment, some animal calling out from over on the other side of the lake and another answering. Closer at hand, insects chirped and the breeze rustled the leaves on the trees. It was dark here, darker than night in the city, but it was a soft, protective darkness. One in which a person could actually count the stars.

"Want to sit down?" Pat asked.

"Sure."

She felt him move as she sat down next to him. He put an arm behind her on the back of the bench.

"It's a little tight," he said as he settled his arm near her shoulders.

"Yeah." She'd better go beyond these one-word replies before he decided that she was some pull toy. "I wanted to tell you how impressed I was with the way you handled Angie after the softball game. Whatever you said to her seemed to have worked."

"I just have this way with women," he said with a laugh.

Trisha laughed, too, though her heart was racing with silly abandon as his arm brushed lightly against her back. "Nevertheless," she said with a touch more seriousness, "I'm sorry for blowing up at you earlier. You do understand the kids in a way I never will."

He took his arm from the back of the bench and leaned forward, arms resting on his knees. She felt he'd moved farther away than that and she wanted somehow to call him back.

"I'm the one that should apologize," he said. "That crack about gymnastics and ballet was uncalled-for. You do a wonderful job with the kids and nothing can take away from that."

"Thank you." She was almost surprised her words came out so smoothly, with no hint of the sudden flushing of her cheeks and racing of her heart. This was crazy—she knew she did a good job and even if she didn't know it, she'd received compliments before. Just none out here in the moonlight from a man she was becoming more and more fascinated with.

"How long have you been working with kids?" he asked.

"I've been with the West Side Boys and Girls Club for four years," she replied. "Before that, I was a social worker in Chicago for two."

"Been in social work pretty much since college, huh?"

"Yeah, pretty much. Along with some time-out for grad school."

"Well, the kids are lucky to have you," he said.

"Even with a background in gymnastics and ballet?" she asked with a laugh. "Are you even qualified to make such a statement, seeing as how you said you don't know anything about kids?"

"Hey," he said, "I know people. And kids are just little people."

She looked over at him, but he was staring off toward the lake. The moonlight had softened his features considerably. Was it the light or was he just more relaxed in the darkness of the night?

"Sometimes," he added.

Trisha punched him lightly in the ribs. "They are just little people," she said. "Charming, exasperating, interesting, vulnerable little people."

He turned to face her. "Well, they like you and—probably more important—they respect you," he said. "Anybody can see that."

"Thank you."

"Don't mention it," he replied.

She relaxed and let her body slump down a little onto the bench. He sat back again, his arm going around the back of the bench, but this time it rested more against her than the wood. Not that she should necessarily read anything into that. Her heart wanted to disagree.

"How are you enjoying the kids?" she asked.

"We're getting more tolerant of each other."

"Any of them giving you trouble?"

"Not really."

She looked over at him. She couldn't see him all that well in the moonlight, but he seemed peaceful. More so than she could have imagined. Maybe talking last night had put some of his ghosts at least partially to rest.

"One of the kids hasn't handled sleeping here all that well," he said. "So far, both nights, he's awakened a little after midnight crying."

"Rulli?"

"No. Douglas."

Trisha chuckled softly as she pictured the husky, aggressive boy. "Guess you can't always tell a book by its cover."

"Guess not."

Was that true for Pat, also, that she shouldn't judge what type of man he was by the tough, distant mask he wore? A breeze blew in off the lake and she felt herself move just a touch closer to him. Not that it meant anything, she told herself. It was just a reaction to the moonlight.

Still, she felt the need to fight the silence. "You're doing a great job with the kids, too."

"Yeah, right." His voice betrayed his disbelief.

"Don't argue with me," she said. "I'm an experienced social worker, trained to see these things."

He laughed softly.

"What's so funny?" she asked.

"Nothing."

But they had both turned and were facing each other. His laughter died on the soft breeze and the moonlight seemed to hold a melody. She leaned forward just as he did and their lips met. It was a sweet, gentle touch that stirred some deep part of her soul into song. Then suddenly he was pulling away.

"That's a kind of thank-you," he said.

"I see."

The song in her heart had grown, though, bringing a boldness with it. She leaned forward and kissed him back, her lips brushing his with a teasing touch. A warmth spread slowly through her being, leaving a tingly hunger for more. She slowly pulled back.

"That's a kind of you're welcome," she said, though her voice sounded as shaky as she felt.

Neither of them said a word, but suddenly she was in his arms. No gentle little kisses this time, but hungers raging as their mouths touched, and then crushed, the other. His lips drove the song in her soul into a symphony, and she wanted more. Her hands ran over his back, feeling the muscles tense; her chest was pressed to his so that his heart beat close to hers.

This was insane. She barely knew him. Yet her body seemed to be unbothered by such trivialities. A yearning set her heart to trembling. A whole wild panorama of possibilities of delight raced through her mind, even as his hold on her tightened. His mouth moved on hers; he was speaking straight to her soul with his touch. She had never felt so alive, and then as they moved apart in some unspoken agreement, she had never felt so alone.

There was total silence in the woods surrounding them. No animals crying, no bugs whining, no breeze whispering in the trees. She raised a shaking hand to brush her hair back from her face as if brushing away her response to his touch.

"I'd better look in on the kids," she said, and got to her feet.

He stood up also. "Yeah, me, too."

They walked back into the cabin and into their own sides. Without touching. Without looking back.

"Poor kids," Trisha said softly. "They're all tuckered out."

From the corner of his eye, Pat saw Trisha turn back around so that she was facing out the front window of the van.

"That's good."

His fingers twitched on the steering wheel. His tone had been just as soft as Trisha's. That was ridiculous. He wasn't a kid-caring person like her. These kids were okay, but given the choice, he wouldn't repeat the weekend. Not in a million years. It had been about seventy-two hours too long with the kids and with Trisha. He'd felt as if all sorts of things had been creeping around the whole time, trying to find some chink in his armor to slip in and make him weak.

"I couldn't take another round of that damn bottle song," he added in a normal tone. "Or Rulli asking if we're there yet."

From the corner of his eye, he could see Trisha turn and smile at him. Part of him wanted to turn and smile back, to share for a quick moment all the little things they'd shared all weekend. But the other part of him—the sensible and in-control part—told him getting involved with her and the kids would be like walking through a spiderweb. He would never get totally free of the sticky silk of their neediness. Yet neither would he be able to give them enough to bring happiness. He watched the road pass beneath them.

"Today went very well," she said.

Pat just nodded. After breakfast and a nondenominational Sunday service, they'd had a scavenger hunt, then lunch and a final awards ceremony. Their group had received the Best Athletes Award. Everyone, especially Angie, was happy.

"As far as I can see, the whole camp has done very well," Trisha said. "Don't you agree?"

"I guess." He felt her eyes on him, wanting more. "I don't have any experience in this kind of thing. But it seemed fine."

"You're intelligent," she said. "And you certainly can evaluate what's good and what's bad."

Good was going home and being free of Ben's little schemes. Bad was letting her and the kids get to him and wake up emotions he preferred to let sleep. Pat just grunted, hoping she would drop the subject and catch a little nap herself.

"Do you have any suggestions for improving the camp experience?"

"No."

"Well, just think on it and I'll get back to you. The camp administration appreciates feedback of any kind."

He didn't want her getting back to him. The only thing he wanted was tomorrow morning. Then all this would be gone and his life would be back to normal, back to dealing with adults and hustling new industrial development for the county. That was what he did well.

And that was the only thing he wanted to do.

Chapter Five

Pat settled himself at his kitchen table, a bowl of fresh peaches and ice cream by his right hand and Monday's evening newspaper by his left. He'd had a perfect day—three meetings, a telephone conference call, a ribbon-cutting ceremony in the Airport Industrial District and an argument with the mayor about tax abatement policy. There had been no time at all to think about Trisha.

Although he'd slept lousy last night, he knew that he would sleep well tonight. He'd had himself a full, high-activity day, a good evening run along the river and now a great dessert. His life was just as he wanted it. No kids running around, trying to make him care. No slender blonde making him laugh and hurt and spill his guts out just because she was sitting near him.

He took a spoonful out of the mushy mound before him and raised it toward—

The sudden shrieking of his front door buzzer caused him to jump half out of his seat, dropping the spoonful of ice cream onto the floor. Damn it. His nerves were still on edge from the weekend. He knew he was safe at home but somewhere in the back of his mind lurked an image of a gang of munchkins ready to jump on him and sing about a hundred bottles of beer on the wall.

Pat pushed himself upright as the buzzer sounded again. "Damn it." Whoever was at the door was going to go flying nose over butt down the front stairs. "All right, all right. I'm coming."

He flung the door open wide, ready to do battle with the intruder. "Yeah?"

"Hello," Trisha said. "I'm glad to see you, too."

Hell. He'd been building himself up for a confrontation. And now nothing. He felt as if he'd been making love to the world's most beautiful woman—who looked amazingly like Trisha—when suddenly she slipped out of bed, saying she had to floss her teeth.

"What can I do for you?" He tried to speak freely and easily but his earlier anger seemed to be echoing all around them, coming to rest in the shadows in her eyes.

"Nothing really." She shrugged. "I just brought your van back."

He stepped onto the porch and looked around the corner of the house. The van was there in his driveway. "Oh," he said. He felt like an idiot.

"So," she said. "Thanks a lot."

"No problem." He paused. "I was glad to help."

"Not any more than we were glad to receive, believe me."

Pat just stood there, unable to meet her eyes. Why was he always acting like such a jerk around her? And why was he always half-naked when she came to the house? Last time he had just had jeans on; today it was just a pair of jogging shorts.

"Well," she said, turning to leave. "Thanks again."

Pat's gaze flickered from Trisha to the driveway to the street. The van was there, but it was the only car around.

"How are you getting home?"

"My car is at the club," she replied. "I'm going to walk over there."

"That's a mile and a half," he said.

"I can use the exercise."

He watched her slim, trim figure as she went down the stairs. She needed exercise like Indiana needed corn. Her curves were all just the right degree of curviness, if his sudden shortness of breath was any indication. Trisha was on the sidewalk before his brain connected with his gentleman genes.

"Trisha." He hurried to the edge of the porch. "Trisha, wait. I can give you a ride over."

She stopped and turned halfway back. "That's okay."

"I'd feel better if I did," he said.

"I walk all the time," she said. "Don't worry. It's perfectly safe."

Right. Except that she looked about as able to protect herself as a kitten in with a pack of wolves. "I have fresh peaches and ice cream," he called after her.

She laughed. It was a beautiful sound—so clear and full, like someone tapping on pure crystal. He had this need to hear it dancing through his life forever. But only a momentary one.

"Are you telling me just to make me jealous or are you offering me some?"

Man, was she ornery. "I'm inviting you to come in and have some with me," he replied.

"Why, thank you." She turned the rest of the way and came back up on the porch. "A little dessert would be nice."

Pat opened the door for her, then followed her down the hallway to the kitchen.

"Vanilla ice cream okay?"

"Sure."

As he opened the freezer, he noticed Trisha looking at his own dish on the table. Mostly likely, the ice cream was melted by now and looked awful. He took out another bowl for himself.

He heaped both bowls full of ice cream and peaches. After putting the ingredients away, he put the bowls on the table and his old one in the sink. Then he sat down across from Trisha.

She put a teaspoon in her mouth and murmured her appreciation. "This is wonderful," she said. "Nothing like ice cream and fresh peaches at the end of a long, hot day."

"Yep." Try as he might, he couldn't think of anything else to say. He sounded like the idiot he was acting like. At least he was consistent.

"Getting any closer to the treasure?" she asked.

"No."

"Where've you looked?"

"Everywhere." He ate some more, but the silence nagged at him. "There is no treasure. It was just some old story of my grandmother's."

"Can you really be sure, though? What else did she tell you? A clue maybe."

He sighed, trying not to let his gaze be captured by that look of eagerness in her eyes, or by the note of excitement in her voice. "Just that it was something her mother always told her."

"Which was..."

He bit back his impatience, remembering the first time he'd heard the story. He must have been about nine or so—it was soon after they'd moved to Huron Street, and he'd been so excited. He was going to find the treasure and use it to buy back their lives. He hadn't been foolish enough to think it would bring his mother back, but it could get them their house back and their school and maybe their lives. That was when he'd needed the treasure—when he still had dreams that could be met—not now when he was earning enough to buy what he wanted, and smart enough not to want what he couldn't get. But there'd been no clue. It was all just a stupid game of his grandmother's.

"How sad," Trisha said on a sigh.

He looked up, startled by her tone, and realized he'd told the story aloud. Damn. What was it about her that made words come flying from his mouth?

"My grandmother really loved me," he said stiffly. "If she'd known where it was, and if it had been something that could have made a difference, she would have told me."

"Just because she didn't know, it doesn't mean there isn't one. Maybe you just don't believe hard enough to really look."

He got to his feet and took her empty bowl. "Maybe I'm smart enough not to chase rainbows that aren't really there."

"How can you chase a rainbow? It doesn't move."

"You know what I mean," he snapped. "I don't need a treasure anyway. I have everything I want."

"Everything?" Her eyes questioned him as much as her words did, but she didn't push. "What exactly did your grandmother say about the treasure?"

He left the bowls in the sink and came back to the table. "Just that her mother had always said there was a treasure here in the house."

"Hidden in the house, or just in the house?"

He didn't bother hiding his impatience. "What does it matter? Face facts. There is no treasure."

"Facts are fine but not if you allow them to destroy your dreams."

"What if the dreams are unrealistic?"

"Dreams aren't supposed to be realistic," she said.

This conversation wasn't going anywhere. Pat just held his tongue.

"I take it you don't agree," she said.

Pat let a quiet sigh escape. Unfortunately, Trisha wasn't going to let this go. "I'm a facts kind of a person," he said.

"You can't be."

He made a face and shrugged. "Hey, I am what I am."

"Didn't you grow up poor on the west side? Well, something had to drive you to persevere in the face of all the odds that were against you."

"Yeah." He laughed. "Fear."

She just looked at him, a gentle but inscrutable mask covering her face.

"I was afraid that if I didn't do well in school and go to college, I'd be stuck on the streets the rest of my life. Afraid that I'd wind up like—" Angel's name was on the tip of his tongue, but he didn't want to get into that whole mess again "—like a lot of other people."

"Well, you certainly had to be determined."

That gentle smile remained fixed on her lips, making her even more beautiful. But it was also annoying. It was the kind of smile women wore when they thought they knew more than you did.

"But you needed a dream to pull you through the rough spots," she added.

It was obvious that Trisha was a typical upper-middle-class, suburban-raised woman who'd had everything handed to her on a clean platter. It was amazing how people like her figured that they knew how and why guys like him did anything. Pat suddenly found himself growing tired. Not at all up to an argument.

"Care for seconds?" he asked.

She shook her head, her smile growing ever gentler while he found himself growing ever more irritated. It was time to turn off the streetlights and send everyone home before he put his foot in his mouth again.

"Why don't you take the van?" he said. "I assume your old one didn't have a miraculous recovery over the weekend."

"Are you sure?" she asked, her mood changing. "We really could use it, but I don't want to inconvenience your operation in any way."

"Don't worry about it," Pat replied. "I don't have any visitors coming in this week and after that we can play things by ear."

"That's very generous of you."

"Not really." Pat looked away, out toward his backyard. There were no squirrels there now, no birds, no butterflies, no nothing. Just emptiness—like his life, a little voice noted. "It's good PR and Ben Mackley likes that kind of thing."

"In either case, thank you."

"Like I said, don't mention it." He stood up. "I've got some reports to go over tonight."

Trisha followed suit and also stood up.

"Thank you again for the use of the van," she said, holding out her hand. "But most of all, thank you for helping with the kids this weekend."

He took her hand. It was so soft, so gentle, yet he had a feeling there was steel inside it. He wished he had the time or courage to look for it.

"It was no big deal."

"It was a big deal to the kids," she said. "They really enjoyed having you along. You made quite an impression on them."

"I was just somebody new."

"Well, we could always use new blood, that's for sure."

Pat held his breath. Something in the tone of her voice set off an alarm inside his head.

"Maybe you could become more active with the club."

"Yeah, I guess." His mind raced, searching for ways he could be of help. "I could do fund-raising and stuff like that."

"Stuff like that?" she said.

He didn't like the look in her eyes. "Yeah, stuff like that."

"Safe stuff," she said.

Her words stung like a whip. And he was surprised to see suddenly how old her eyes looked. But then, everyone aged faster on the west side. Even sweet, little suburban types like Trisha Stewart.

"A lot of people can do fund-raising," she said. "I was thinking that someone like yourself, someone who came from the neighborhood, could give something much more valuable. Something the kids could really use. Like yourself."

Her eyes had grown so intense that Pat had to look away.

He knew exactly what she was talking about. Reach out and touch some kids. Get personally involved. Try to wean them away from the streets. But why would she ask him to do that? Hadn't he told her about Angel? Didn't she see that he'd tried once and failed? If he couldn't help his own brother, how the hell was he going to help anyone else?

"School is starting later this week," she said. "A lot of the kids could use someone to guide them. You know, make sure they stay on top of things."

"I thought you usually got college kids for tutors."

"We have plenty of tutors from the high schools and colleges," Trisha said. "I was thinking more of a big-brother figure."

Oh, yeah. That was something he'd be great at, especially with all his experience. He knew how to make a first-class mess out of that kind of a relationship.

"We're having a meeting for the tutors tomorrow night, a get-acquainted, coffee-and-cookies thing," she said. "Why don't you drop by?"

Her manner was so easy, her tone so friendly. Yet she wouldn't quit. He knew that. The odds were high that she wouldn't leave until he said yes.

Which, given his mood and mental condition, was the best thing to do right now. Say yes and get her out of the house. Get those lovely green eyes out of his sight. Then, after a good night's sleep, he could call from the office tomorrow. Leave a message saying that something had come up. Back out gracefully.

Back out like a coward, a little voice told him, but he turned a deaf ear to those words, telling himself that sometimes a body had to fight fire with fire.

Trisha looked out over the small crowd in the game room, making a conscious effort not to let her eyes linger on Pat. "Any more questions?" No hands waved. "Great. Then those people who tutored last year leave your schedule on the back table. New people should see Clarissa for their assignment. Thank you all for coming."

There was a general shuffling of papers and feet as people began to file out. Pat was sitting at the back, but Trisha took her time greeting people, trying to make all feel welcome. She was glad to see Pat here, but she was not going to let her heart make more of it than it was. That kiss Saturday night had been a gigantic mistake; it threw their whole relationship off and she wanted to get it back on the right footing.

"Thanks for coming," she told a pair of college students.

"Good to see you again," she said to a retiree who'd been helping out at the club longer than she'd been there.

Gradually she worked her way to the back of the room, stopping at the table where Clarissa sat. "Need any help?" Trisha asked.

"Honey, if I can't manage this itty-bitty crowd, we're in trouble." She nodded over toward Pat. "Ain't that the van man? And if it is, why are you talking to me when you ought to be rolling out the red carpet for him?"

"I'll get over there," Trisha said. "I think all our volunteers should be made to feel welcome."

Clarissa made a big show of looking around Trisha toward where Pat was getting to his feet. "Funny," she said. "He don't look like he bites."

Trisha frowned at the woman. "Who said he did?"

Clarissa just shrugged. "Must be some reason you're scared to go near him."

"I am not," Trisha snapped under her breath, then smiled brightly at a volunteer who stopped at the table. "Clarissa here can help you."

Trisha kept her smile in place as she nodded at the people filing out and made her way slowly back to Pat. She was not afraid of him in any way, but neither was she going to fuss over him. For all she knew, that would scare him away faster than anything. Still, her heart was beating a little bit faster the closer she got to him.

"Hi," she said and stopped in front of him. "Glad you could make it."

He nodded. "I was a bit late. Guess I misunderstood what time my secretary told me the meeting was."

"No problem." She didn't tell him that she'd purposely told Danielle the wrong time, just so he couldn't drop by early with some excuse why he couldn't get involved. "I don't think you missed anything vital."

"That's good."

They started walking slowly toward the door, following the last few people still in the room. The aisle was narrow, though, and they had to walk closer than Trisha would have preferred. She was all too conscious of his height and how he made her feel small and fragile. She was too aware of his arm brushing against her as they walked and the fact that his nearness seemed to drive all sensible conversation from her brain.

"You ever think of going into sales?" he asked.

She turned to frown up at him. "No. Why do you ask?"

"You really had the troops stirred up," Pat replied. "They were ready to follow you through fire."

"You're exaggerating, but I appreciate the compliment." Suddenly she wondered if he had been praising her or had been sarcastic. "That was a compliment, wasn't it? Not another ballet remark."

"Am I ever going to live that down?"

He grinned at her and she felt as if she'd been sipping champagne—light-headed and giddy. She was sorry she'd made the joke. It had been stupid, an opening for the intimacy that seemed to rise so quickly between them. But that she didn't want.

She went over to the refreshment table and unplugged the coffeepot. Then she began gathering empty cups, tossing them into the trash can near the door. "You have to fire the volunteers up," she told him, her eyes on her work. "You have to get them filled with a positive energy that will carry them through the low points.''

He took the lid off the coffeepot and pulled out the basket of grounds, emptying it in the trash. "And does it work?"

"Most of the time."

Clarissa reached in to grab a cookie. "I got all the schedules here," she said. "We should have most of the kids covered."

"That's great. I'll look at them in the morning."

Clarissa eyed them both, then turned back to Trisha. "Want me to stay and help clean up?"

"I'll help her," Pat said before Trisha could think up a reason to keep Clarissa there.

"Great." The woman picked up the coffeepot. "I'll empty this on my way out. See you in the morning."

Trisha watched Clarissa leave, sighing silently as she heard her footsteps die away down the hall. She was not worried about being here alone with Pat. He was a volunteer, that was all.

She wrapped a plate of cookies in aluminum foil and went back to talking about her speech. "If I told these college kids about all the difficulties they would encounter, half of them would walk out before I finished my sentence."

Pat gathered up all the clean cups and stuck them in one corner of the table, then rolled up the dirty paper tablecloth. "We can't have that," he said.

"You're damn right we can't," Trisha said, spinning around to face Pat. "Without help, my kids are nowhere. My product is turning disadvantaged kids into good, useful, productive citizens. And I don't care how I do it, but I will do it."

They stared at each other and Trisha could feel her hands quiver slightly. So now Pat knew that she would do anything to help her kids. So what? That certainly didn't make her dishonest.

Pat stuffed the paper tablecloth into the trash, then turned back to Trisha with a sigh. "I was going to back out on you," he admitted.

Now they were getting down to the nitty-gritty. "I thought so," Trisha said.

He pulled a chair over, turned it around and sat down, leaning his arms on the back. "How did you know?"

"Law of averages." Trisha leaned back against the table. "About half the people who volunteer try to back out of the commitment. A lot of times they agreed just to get rid of me."

He looked away. "I was going to call you this morning—"

"And leave a message," she finished for him. "Something unexpected came up. You wouldn't have as much time as you'd first thought."

His gaze came back to her, an uneasy smile on his face. "It didn't seem like a very manly way of handling the situation," he said, clearing his throat before he looked away again. "So I thought I'd come down here early and talk to you one-on-one." He turned back to look at her, shrugging a little. "But like I said earlier, I must have gotten the time wrong."

"Those things happen," she replied.

Suddenly his smile changed. Frown lines filled his forehead and his gentle look turned hard. A warmth moved into her cheeks but Trisha refused to look away.

"That was kind of sneaky," he said. "Wasn't it?"

There was no need to answer, so she didn't.

"I mean, giving my secretary the wrong time so we wouldn't be alone when I got here."

Trisha just shrugged. "I told you I do whatever's necessary to help the kids. And Rulli and Angie need all the help they can get."

He just continued looking at her.

"They both have a lot of potential, but they've just had themselves a string of bad luck. Both their parents are dead— their father years ago, their mother just last year—and they're living in a tiny household with a great-aunt and -uncle, and some older cousins. It was supposed to be a temporary situation, but nothing else has come along."

"That's not uncommon," Pat guessed.

"No, but something's going to have to change. Their great-uncle has emphysema and has been getting much sicker. Their great-aunt can't take care of him and give the kids the attention they need. It's a real unstable situation, but with someone like you working with them, they'll have some stability in their lives."

Pat rubbed the back of his neck. "I guess you wouldn't take my backing out very well, would you?"

"I'd hit you with a big stick and stomp you into dust."

"I'm a big boy, you know. You don't have to beat around the bush with me. Just tell me straight out what you'd do to me."

She smiled at him, a genuine smile straight from her heart. "I'd very much like you to work with Rulli and Angie."

He looked down at the floor.

"I know it'll be hard," she said. "But the rewards are more than worth it."

Pat continued looking at the floor. Without seeing his eyes, she had no idea what his thoughts were.

"I mean, when you see them walk across the stage and get that college sheepskin, you'll burst with pride."

Pat's head snapped up, his eyes wide. Oh, Lord, Trisha thought, she'd gone too far.

"Okay. We'll work on getting them into middle school first," she said quickly. "All you have to do is be a role model, a guide, a friend."

That seemed to relax him. She slid off the table and walked over to where he sat, turning a chair around and straddling it, her arms resting on the back, just as he was sitting. Only a few tiny inches were separating them. She could breathe in the woodsy scent of his after-shave and see the tiny flicker of concern in his eyes.

A strange boldness seemed to take hold of her. Maybe it was because she was tired, or still high from the camping trip. She didn't really care as she reached out and took his hand in hers.

"I know you can do it, Pat. You can do anything you set your mind to. You've proven that all your life."

"Right," he replied. "Like if I want to run away, I can just turn around and go."

"Those kids won't let you down." She tightened her hold on his hand, as if she could pass her urgency along to him. "You'll be paid back tenfold for everything you put into that relationship."

"Yeah, right."

"Hey," she said. "You know what happens when you throw your bread upon the water."

"You get soggy bread?" He sighed and got to his feet. "All right. I'd be a heck of a role model and probably a lousy guide, but maybe I can handle being their friend."

"That's great, Pat," she cried, jumping to her feet. Without another thought, she threw her arms around him. "You're going to make such a difference to those kids."

"Anything to please," he said, his voice sounding slightly ragged.

Trisha suddenly stopped, and looked up into his face. She felt a tiny spark flare up in her heart and saw an answering flame in his eyes. Her pulse was racing, her breath was nonexistent, her soul was aquiver. For several centuries, they seemed to stare into each other's eyes, seeing each other's soul, and words were somehow unnecessary.

Then, ever so slowly, he leaned over to meet her lips with his. It was a sweet, deliberate kiss, a pledge of their friendship, a searching of their hearts, an acknowledgment of this strange attraction that seemed to bind them together. They pulled apart gently, but their eyes stayed locked.

"This isn't part of the 'anything' I'd do for my kids," she said.

"It isn't part of what I figured volunteering here would include." His smile turned infinitely tender and he reached over to tuck a curl behind her ear.

"In fact, I'm not sure it's wise," she went on.

"I'm certain it isn't."

"Something between us would just complicate things."

"Or we can just ignore it."

She let her smile grow wider. "That's always a possibility."

"One we should work on."

"More windows to fix?" Carl asked.

Pat nodded as he placed the window sash rope on the counter of the hardware store. It was Labor Day weekend and he had all three days planned—busy hands would keep his mind busy. Too busy to let a certain blonde wander into his thoughts.

"Yeah," Pat said. "That old house has a lot of windows."

"You ever thought of replacing them all with new ones?"

"Sure," Pat replied. "Just as soon as you start selling them. You know, those kind where the frames are made of plastic."

Carl gave him a frown before ringing up the sale. The Howard Street Hardware Store was the place where you could find a bracket for something installed fifty years ago. Pat knew that hell would freeze over before Carl would carry anything like plastic-framed windows.

"When you going to quit fooling around with that house and hire a professional?" Carl asked.

"That house has been around longer than the two of us together," Pat replied. "There's very little I can do to harm the old place." He gave Carl even change and picked up his package. "Besides, I enjoy that kind of fooling around. Helps me wind down from the aggravation of my job."

"You ought to get married," Carl grumbled, handing Pat his receipt. "You won't know real aggravation until you do."

"Can't do that." Pat made his way to the door where he paused and turned. "I got me a real bad case of bacheloritis."

"I've seen bigger men than you fall," Carl called after him.

Pat smiled and waved as he stepped out the door.

It wasn't a matter of falling or standing. What it was, was knowing who you were. Knowing where you fit and where you didn't. And he fit exactly where he was. Bachelor, manager and amateur refurbisher of an old home. He had everything; there was no reason to change. Yep, ignoring that spark between him and Trisha was the best thing he could do.

"Excuse me."

Pat stopped just before running into a middle-aged woman coming out of the bakery next door. She looked almost like Trisha and his heart practically stopped. Was she so in his subconscious that he was seeing a resemblance in everyone?

"Mr. Stuart, isn't it?"

Pat just stared at the woman. Usually he was pretty good at remembering names, but he was just drawing a blank. "Yes?"

But the woman wasn't looking at him anymore; she was leaning back through the half-open bakery door. "Honey, come out here and say hello."

"Mother." The word was said on a sigh and it was only when the other woman came out of the bakery that Pat realized the second woman was Trisha.

"See," the older woman said. A note of pride was in her voice as if she'd bagged the largest salmon. "I told you it was him."

"I didn't say it wasn't." Trisha's cheeks were bright red as she turned to him. "Hello, Pat."

It was such a shock to see her right on the heels of thinking about her that his mind had trouble shifting gears. He kept thinking he'd conjured her up and wanted to ask if she'd suddenly found herself transported there. Luckily a bit of sanity crept in and he just said, "How are you, Trisha?"

"So you're the nice young man that took Trisha camping," the older woman said. "I saw you on television last week. Such a good job you're doing for the county."

"That's nice of you to say." He paused. "Mrs. Stewart, is it?"

"Yes, but most people call me Connie." The woman stuck her hand out while glaring at Trisha. "I don't know what's with my daughter. Normally she's not as ashamed of me as she is today."

"I'm not ashamed of you," Trisha protested. "I'm just not used to you running men down in the street."

She looked decidedly uncomfortable and that surprised Pat. She was normally so in control. He rather enjoyed seeing her flustered for a change. Especially after the way she'd been manipulating him.

Connie was making a face at her daughter. "Hey, he's a celebrity. My chasing him is the price of fame."

He smiled at them both. "I'd call it a benefit instead of a cost," he said smoothly.

"Why, aren't you nice?" Connie patted him on the arm. "Isn't he nice, Trisha?"

Trisha looked as if she was trying to swallow a bitter pill. "He's a real sweetie pie, Mother."

Connie shook her head at her daughter before smiling at Pat. "She's usually a lot nicer."

"I think she's very nice," Pat said.

The red in Trisha's cheeks deepened, if that was possible. But then a couple coming out of the bakery maneuvered around them and Trisha's eyes took on a look of relief. "We're in the way here, Mother. We'd better be going."

"Okay, okay." Connie turned toward Pat. "We're looking for a dress for Trisha. She's going to that United Way dinner at the Century Center Saturday night and was going to wear the same dress she's worn for the last two years. Everyone would think she's got no clothes. Or no taste."

Trisha looked in pain but Pat managed to hold back a laugh. It was definitely payback time. "Oh, I think most of us would be more charitable than that."

"Oh, you're going to be there, too?" Connie asked. "Are you taking that Miss Indiana woman?"

"Mother."

"Well, they were together on television," Connie pointed out.

"No," Pat replied. "That was just a stunt for the cameras. We're not that close. I'm going alone."

"Oh, for heaven's sake. That's the same thing Trisha's doing," Connie said.

"Mother."

"And it's so inefficient," Connie said, going on as if Trisha hadn't just moaned in pain. "Everybody going in their own car. The pollution, the parking. It just doesn't make sense."

"Now that you mention it," Pat said, "it certainly doesn't."

"People should form car pools."

"We could all ride our bikes," Trisha suggested sharply. "Or maybe rent a school bus to drive around and pick everyone up."

Connie leaned closer to Pat. "She's being sarcastic."

Pat nodded. "I thought so. She doesn't seem to understand that individually we don't make that much of an impact, but together we can change the world."

Trisha looked ready to gag. "You know we really should be going," she said to her mother.

"I guess I failed," Connie said with a touch of sadness in her voice. "I tried to teach her about conservation and saving the environment."

"I'm sure it wasn't your fault," Pat assured her. "I've noticed she's a trifle stubborn about things."

"Thickheaded is more like it."

"You know, I am still here," Trisha pointed out.

Pat pretended that she wasn't. "Maybe I could pick Trisha up on Saturday," Pat said. "It would mean one less car on the road, and we have gotten such a good grade from the EPA on our air quality lately. I'd hate to jeopardize that."

"Even though it means putting up with me?" Trisha mocked.

"That sounds like a good idea to me," Connie said. "She'd love to go with you."

"Mom," Trisha protested. "I can answer for myself."

"Of course you can, dear," Connie said smoothly, as if she were settling down a cranky child. She glanced over at Pat. "I presume you two can work out the details?"

"Sure," he said.

"Good, good." She turned back to Trisha. "We really should be going, you know. We haven't got all day to find that dress."

"I'll call you later in the week," Pat said. "At the club."

"Whatever," Trisha called over her shoulder as she hurried her mother away.

Pat watched them leave with a half smile on his face. The exchange had been rather fun and Saturday would be, too. Not that it was a real date. They were just going to a common business function, someplace where they could network with the various movers and shakers interested in the welfare of the city.

Still, he found that he was suddenly looking forward to it. Maybe he and Trisha could ignore that spark, but still have some fun together. Why not? They were adults. They could handle that kind of thing.

Chapter Six

Trisha looked out her office window, frowning. Pat, Rulli and Angie were sitting at a card table in the corner of the club's main activity room, their heads bent over a book. Actually, since the table and chairs were adult-size, Pat was the only one who was sitting. The kids were kneeling on their chairs.

Pat was not supposed to be tutoring them, but their assigned college student was a no-show, so he was filling in. Since Rulli was a third grader and Angie was in fourth, their lessons weren't all that difficult, but Pat hadn't gotten the tutor's orientation packet. Would he know he was supposed to help the kids rather than do their homework for them?

She really should go check, instead of sitting in here like a scared rabbit. Just because her mother had pushed them into that date for Saturday was no reason for Trisha to be embarrassed. If she was going to act like some junior high kid on her first date, he was going to think she was. She pushed away from her desk and walked out toward Pat and his charges.

"Hi, everybody. How are things going?" Trisha asked.

"Pretty good," Pat said. "We're wrestling with Angie's multiplication tables and Rulli's addition."

"And we're kicking butt," Angie said.

"We're getting there," Pat agreed.

"Yesss." Rulli threw his pencil down on the table and raised one fist in triumph. "I did it."

"Let's see it, sport," Pat said, taking Rulli's paper.

"His name's Rulli," Angie said sharply. "Rulli Ingram. After Grandpa Rulli, our mommy's second daddy."

Pat kept his attention on the paper before him. "Good job, Rulli." He glanced over at the gaming tables on the far side of the room. "Why don't you guys take a little break? Then we'll take a quick look and see what you have coming tomorrow."

"You just want to talk to Miss Stewart," Angie said. "Don't you?"

"Come on, Angie," Rulli said. "Let's play Ping-Pong."

Trisha watched the children rush over to the Ping-Pong table, grabbing at the paddles before anyone else could. She sat down in the chair Angie had vacated, glancing idly at the girl's homework paper before forcing her eyes to meet Pat's.

"I'm sorry to drop in in the middle of things," she said.

"No big deal. We were just about done."

He flashed her a smile and Trisha was happy to see that she was unmoved by it. Well, relatively unmoved.

"They just needed a little help with math and reading."

"I'll give the tutor a call," Trisha said. "If I need to, I'll assign another one."

"That would be a good idea," he agreed. "I've got a couple of trips planned over the next few weeks so I'm going to be a bit undependable."

Trisha nodded, though a gentle softness welled up within her. It hadn't been more than a few days ago when he'd objected to working with the kids, saying he wanted to do fundraising. Yet here he was, concerned that business pressures would keep him away.

"How are you and the kids getting along?"

"Okay, I guess." That grin lit up his face again. "Rulli's always been my buddy. And Angie's getting better. She's only threatened to punch my lights out once today."

"It's obvious you've got a way with the ladies."

"Oh, yeah?"

"I mean, very young ladies," Trisha said. "Like Angie."

"I guess that's better than nothing."

There was a sudden increase in volume in kids' voices and Trisha glanced over toward the Ping-Pong table. Two other children had gone over and wanted to play, but things quieted down quickly as the kids paired off. Rulli, as always, went with Angie.

Trisha sighed. "I hope one of these days that Angie gives her brother a chance to do things on his own."

"She's afraid that if she lets go, even a little, she'll lose him."

The smile had vanished from Pat's face and, for a moment, his eyes were deep wells of pain. She put her hand on his shoulder.

"Trisha," Clarissa called.

Trisha pulled her hand back as if it had been in hot water and turned. Her assistant just stood there grinning at her.

"You have a phone call."

"Thank you." Trisha turned toward Pat. "Thank you for your help, Mr. Stuart. You're really doing well with the children."

"Thanks." He slowly stood up. "I'll go referee the game. Then I'll have a chat with Angie and Rulli, make sure things are shipshape for school tomorrow."

"Thank you again, Mr. Stuart." Trisha turned to hurry toward her office.

"Oh, Trisha," he called out.

She turned. Clarissa's totally unprofessional grin was the first thing she saw. "Yes?" she said, forcing herself to look at Pat.

"I need your address if I'm going to pick you up Saturday night."

Trisha totally avoided looking at Clarissa. "It's 1425 North Riverside," she said. "Apartment 4. That's over by the Indiana University of South Bend campus."

He nodded. "Yeah, I know where it's at. Six-thirty okay?"

"That'll be fine."

She turned on her heel and rushed toward her office. After all, it was rude to keep people waiting on the phone. Trisha strode up to her desk and snatched the phone up, at the same time turning to face out toward the activity area. Clarissa was standing in the doorway.

"It's just business," Trisha said.

That just seemed to feed her assistant's grin. "Honey," Clarissa said, "it's always business when you're dealing with a man. Just so happens that sometimes it's monkey business."

"Don't be silly," Trisha snapped. "We're just going to the United Way dinner."

"Oh, ain't that nice."

Trisha didn't like her assistant's attitude at all. And although she knew that she shouldn't keep the party on the phone waiting, she also didn't like misconceptions to get out of hand.

"We're just sharing a ride."

"That's good," Clarissa said. "You save a lot on gas and parking that way. Especially in a big city like South Bend."

"It was my mother's idea."

"She's a nice lady," Clarissa said. "But she's gonna be real upset if you don't talk to her."

Trisha looked down at the phone in her hand as if it were a piece of equipment from an alien spaceship.

"Tell her hi for me," Clarissa said, stepping out of the doorway.

"Yes, Mother?" Trisha sighed into the phone.

Trisha was sitting in Pat's car at the traffic light just south of the Century Center. He'd picked her up at 6:30 sharp, just as he'd said, but after complimenting her on her dress, that had been it. Except for a few remarks about the weather, they'd ridden in silence pretty much the entire way downtown.

He didn't seem annoyed at having been maneuvered into driving her, but neither did he seem too interested in her company. Which was probably just as well. The evening was for politicking, not spending time with Pat. Maybe he was just better than her at keeping his feelings under control.

The light turned green and Pat moved into a line waiting to get into the parking lot. Most of the other cars, after a moment or two in line, were making their way to the parking garage across the street.

"The lot looks full," Trisha said.

"Looks can be deceiving."

Okay, Trisha thought. If it wasn't full, it was almost so. And she was sure that meant they would be parking over near the post office. But that wasn't a problem. Her heels were fairly comfortable. And it was Pat's car, not hers, so he could put it wherever he wanted.

Although, she sniffed appreciatively at the new car smell, she wouldn't mind owning this car. It was a beautiful black sports car.

"Do you get a new car every year?" she asked.

"No." He moved ahead several feet. "Every two years. The Committee for Industrial Development works out a deal with the Oberlin dealership. It's one of the perks that goes with my job."

Trisha wondered if Pat could get a deal on a new van for the club. Or even a new "used" van. And if he wasn't able to, Ben Mackley certainly could. It was something she needed to start working on.

While she'd been lost in her thoughts, the line had moved; they were in the lot now. Pat waved to the attendant at the entrance as they went by.

Another attendant was directing the cars up ahead, sending all the cars to the right except for Pat, whom he sent to the left. That brought them to a parking space close to the south entrance of the Century Center.

"Boy," Trisha said. "If I were driving, I'd have to park at the Wayne Street garage and walk four blocks."

"You want me to drive over there and drop you off?"

Trisha gave him the look, the kind she saved for smart-alecky six-year-olds. Unfortunately, he was concentrating on jockeying his car into the parking space.

"I just thought you were concerned about missing out on your exercise," he said, once he had stopped the car.

She kept the look in place.

"Wow." He shook his head as he put his car in Park and turned off the ignition. "Tough room."

"You better believe it," she said.

Pat put the key in his coat pocket and exited the car, quickly coming around to open her door for her. He held his hand out to help her from the car.

Unfortunately the dress her mother had helped her choose did not have a skirt that was wide and loose, and she really did need some assistance out of the bucket seat. It was something she hadn't thought of when her mother had urged her to be a bit daring and get the red silk sheath.

"You going to be mean to me all night?" he asked.

"Only if you need it," she said, trying for a graceful exit. She thought she made it with only a slight flashing of thigh.

If he saw, he was gentleman enough to pretend not to notice and just shook his head as he took her arm. "And here I told your mother that you were nice."

"She wouldn't have believed you if you'd said I wasn't. She loves me."

The light touch of his hand on Trisha's sent a slow, delicious shiver through her. She'd been dating since high school and had been on her share of first dates, yet she'd never had this strong a reaction to a man's touch. Her heart was climbing on high, wanting to laugh and sing and dance in his arms.

Once they got off the relatively uneven surface of the parking lot and onto the sidewalk, she made a pretense of fixing her earring so she could let go of his arm. *Ignore him,* she told herself sternly. They both knew there were sparks that flew in the air around them, but they were mature enough not to feel something had to be done about it.

They walked into the convention center and down the bricked hallway. Artwork by local artists decorated the walls. It was a good, safe topic for conversation, yet Trisha couldn't think of a thing to say. She was more conscious of how good Pat looked in his dark suit—tall, broad shouldered and strong. He could be here on these walls, her heart pointed out. A local work of art, as it were. Although she preferred art in a more natural state. The suit would have to go as well as the shirt.

What in the world was she thinking of? she scolded herself. She greeted the open convention area with relief. "Good crowd," she said brightly.

"And all came to see you in that dress, no doubt."

The look in his eye matched the hint of fire in his voice. They both were pitiful though when compared to the flame in her cheeks at his remark. She glanced around in panic.

"Oh, look, it's the mayor."

"Hey, hey. Who do we have here?" The mayor was bearing down on them. "Pat. Trisha. It's good to see you folks."

"Hi, Mark," Pat murmured.

"Hello, Mr. Mayor," she said. "So good to see you."

"Are you two together?" the mayor asked.

"Pat gave me a ride," she replied.

"Pat's a great guy," the mayor said with a sly wink. "But be sure to count your fingers when he drops you off at home tonight." He gave Pat a sharp slap on the back. "Nice to see you folks. Maybe we can get together later."

He slowly made his way back through the crowd, dispensing a hearty laugh here, a backslap there, with earnest handshakes all around. The mayor was the consummate politician, but at least he had relieved the tension she'd felt at the moment.

"There's Ben," Pat said.

He took her arm and led her across the room. She wished her dress had long sleeves—long, thick, woolly sleeves. She didn't need to have him touch her again, didn't need to feel the warmth of his hand on her arm and wonder what that hand would feel like in other places.

"Let's see if we can sit with Ben," Pat was saying. "Give you a chance to lobby for more funds for your club."

She jumped at his words. "It's not my club. It belongs to the neighborhood. I just work there."

"What would it be without you, though?"

There was definitely a measure of respect and admiration in his voice and that seemed even more dangerous than his hand. She should have come by herself this evening, the hell with the parking and pollution. She could have taken a cab and made a contribution to the area economy. She could have taken a bus. Walking, even home at midnight, would have been safer than this constant barrage her heart was under. But she was all smiles as they met Ben.

"Pat." Ben shook Pat's hand vigorously. "Trisha. How are you, my dear?"

"Just fine, sir." She paused a moment to get her brain working again. She could swoon all she wanted later; she had the kids to fight for right now. "Although we still need a new van."

"I thought you were using—"

"Oh, Pat's been very generous with us," Trisha said. "But conflicts will arise. Besides, Pat's van isn't really suited to transporting groups of children about."

Ben nodded. "We'll need to look into that. Maybe you should discuss this with Joe Henning. He's in charge of grant requests this year."

"Thank you," Trisha replied. "I'll do that."

Then with a quick nod, Ben was gone, swallowed up by the crowd. Trisha hated to see him go. She was alone—relatively—with Pat again.

"I guess we won't be sitting with him," Pat said.

"Let's go find Joe Henning," Trisha said, moving farther into the hall. She needed to stay busy. "I'd rather sit with him. It'll be a lot more productive."

Pat smiled and shook his head. There was something in his eyes that she couldn't read.

"What?" she asked.

"I don't know how you do it," he said. "The constant pleading would get me down."

She stopped and turned toward him. It was suddenly important that she know exactly how he meant that.

"It's not that you're not good at it," he said. "You aren't too pushy or rude or even impatient when you're pushed aside the way I would be. But don't you get tired of always having to ask for stuff?"

"All the time," she said and let a touch of the weariness seep into her voice. She felt that she could be honest with him and show for a moment some of the frustrations that she felt. "It seems like I spend all my time begging instead of working with the kids. But there are so many good causes, and so many people needing, I know that we won't get much unless I badger."

"I couldn't," he said.

She just shook her head with a slight smile. "Don't you plead with different businesses to locate their facilities here?"

"I don't plead." He looked shocked at the suggestion. "I sell our area. I point out all the advantages to locating a plant, warehouse or whatever here. There isn't any pleading involved."

"Oh, no?" She liked that look of horror on his face. It was almost as if she'd started singing "A Hundred Bottles of Beer."

Little lines of impatience had formed around his lips. "The companies get something when they come here. I'm just pointing out that what we're offering is better than what anyone else is offering."

"And how's that different from me?" she asked. "I try to sell the idea that turning kids into productive citizens is a plus for everybody." She smiled and gently tapped Pat's chest with her finger. "You never can tell how things will turn out. Maybe fifteen or twenty years from now, one of my kids will be the executive director of some civic organization. I've heard that it happened before."

A gentle smile filled his face, one with enough tenderness in it to melt a girl's heart. Trisha quickly put her hands down and behind her back. And kept them there so she wouldn't follow her instincts and throw her arms around him and kiss him until he couldn't breathe. She forced her eyes to focus on the flower centerpiece on a table just beyond Pat, and forced her voice to be matter-of-fact.

"Or my kids may be doctors, or firemen or carpenters. Anything where they can take care of themselves and their families and contribute to society."

"You know—" his voice was soft and low, a whisper into her heart "—someone once said that you were a great salesperson."

She dared a smile into his eyes. "This someone," she whispered back. "Was he wise?"

"Very much so," he said.

They looked into each other's eyes. The hubbub of voices surrounding them faded to a gentle, distant hum. There was a string quartet playing, the music filling the air like a gentle spring rain, bringing life and sweetness to the day. Trisha suddenly found it hard to think.

"Let's find a place to sit," she said, turning and looking quickly around. "All the good places will be taken if we're not careful."

"There's Beth Liederman," Pat said. "Isn't she the corporate fund director for Martin's Supermarkets?"

They made their way around the room, stopping to chat here and there, and found seats at Beth's table just before they started serving dinner. Trisha was glad to sit down, glad to have the chance to talk to Beth and certainly glad to have something else to do besides focusing on Pat.

She was able to pitch the club to Beth over salads and get a promise of some aid from the chairman of a local real-estate firm who was also at the table. Over the main course, Trisha felt brave enough to talk to Pat. And after the introductions and speeches and opening of the local fund-raising campaign, as the evening was winding down, she found the courage to tease him, telling the others about his determination to win all the relay races at camp.

"That's Pat," someone said. "Always has to win. That's why he's so successful."

As everyone laughed, Pat leaned over to her. "Nicely done," he whispered, his breath a teasing tickle on her ear. "I acted like a jerk and you made me look only competitive. Maybe I should bring you along to my meetings so you can interpret all my actions in a positive vein."

"Oh, I doubt that you need me," she said with a laugh.

"Don't be too sure."

The look in his eyes was for her alone and seemed to be a product of the wild dreams plaguing her all evening. The night was suddenly both too young and too old. She wanted it to go on forever, yet her heart shied away in fear.

"Let's go out on the terrace before we leave," she said and cleared her throat, shocked by the hoarseness that had crept into her voice. "I love the view."

He nodded and took her arm, guiding her to the terrace on the riverbank outside. The night had turned pleasantly cool and they walked over to the railing along the river. The water went rushing over the dam below them, the sound drowning out the city noises, but not the beating of her heart. She wanted to slide her hand over just the few inches that separated her and Pat. She wanted to touch his hand, to feel it lying beneath hers and share the night with him.

Instead, she looked out toward the lights on the east bank. They were just shops, restaurants and apartments, but under the cover of the darkness, they added a magical spell to the night. Glittering diamonds of reflected light danced on the water while, far above them, stars danced in the sky.

Pat put his hand over hers. The movement startled her and she turned toward him, finding him closer than she'd thought. But not close enough. She leaned forward, letting her lips touch his.

There was wonder in his touch and a bewitching hunger in his nearness. She moved into his arms, letting the night cast its spell over them. She was tired of fighting her needs, tired of pretending that her heart didn't sing when his eyes found hers. His lips moved against hers, sending a slow yearning through her soul that continued to grow even when he pulled away a moment later.

They stayed at the railing, his arm resting lightly around her waist as they looked out over the river. She could feel her body shaping itself to fit his. It was such a beautiful evening. She wished it wasn't ending.

"Want to go back to my place?" she asked. "I make a mean pot of coffee."

"Sounds great."

Pat flipped through the CDs piled by the stereo, mostly classical music with a few nature recordings mixed in. Sounds of the rain forest? He shook his head and put them back.

"Boy, oh, boy," he murmured. This was a mistake. He shouldn't have come. Just because his hormones went into overdrive around Trisha didn't mean they had anything in common.

"Want to put something on?" she called from the kitchen.

"No, thank you," he replied. "I'm not cold."

Trisha groaned aloud, but didn't say anything more. He walked over to the counter dividing the kitchen from the dining area. Two shorthaired cats were sitting there glaring at him, a small reddish one and a larger, dark brown one. He tried to stare back, but they were better at it than he was, and he finally had to look away. It was obvious they didn't like him.

Trisha put two mugs of coffee on the counter. "These are my roommates," she said. "Lucy and Sniffles. Lucy's an—"

"An Abyssinian," Pat said, indicating the little red. "And that one's a Burmese."

"You like cats?" She seemed eager to find some connection.

"They're okay."

"But you know the different breeds," Trisha said.

"I went to a cat show once. When you're on the road, you can get caught with a lot of time and nothing to do."

"Oh."

They each took a mug and went back into the living room to sit down. He took a chair near the windows. One that was uncomfortable and not quite big enough for him.

He would have preferred to sit on the sofa with Trisha, but her feline companions were already there, cuddling up around her and glaring at him. Defiantly pointing out that he didn't belong. Hell, he didn't need two snooty cats to tell him that. He wasn't a total dummy.

"So how long have you been doing industrial development?" Trisha asked.

Pat shrugged. "Almost ten years. Pretty much since college."

"How'd you happen to go into that?"

Her eyes were on him, but her hand was absently petting the dark brown cat. It was leaning against her leg, purring noisily and radiating contentment. Pat looked away.

"I went to a small college," he said. "Since nobody came recruiting me, I had to go out looking. And that was the first job I found. I became the director of industrial development for a small county in southern Illinois."

"Oh."

"I found that I was good at it and therefore, I guess, enjoyed it."

She sipped at her coffee, so he did the same while he tried to figure out where the conversation could go from there. He already knew Trisha's work history, so he couldn't ask her about that. And he didn't want to talk about the kids at the club; that would just bring back her professional side. The smaller cat walked along the edge of the sofa, as if on a tightrope, until it came to the end. It daintily stretched its neck to sniff at Pat's hand.

"Hello, Lucy," he said softly, but the cat darted away at the sound of his voice. He tried to laugh it off. "So much for my magnetic personality."

Trisha smiled and it lit up the room. "She's a little cautious until she gets to know you."

Something which wouldn't happen in his lifetime. Pat drank some more of his coffee, then leaned forward and put his cup on the end table. "This is a nice place," he said as he glanced around the room. "You been here long?"

"Two years." She also looked around, a puzzled frown in her eyes. "I got it because it was convenient and inexpensive. It always seemed pretty ordinary to me."

His eyes took in the framed wildlife prints, the profusion of plants around the window and the quilted throw over the back of the sofa. "It's what you've done with it that makes it different. It reflects your personality."

"Everyone's home reflects their personality."

That stopped him. He thought of his house and its constant state of disarray, of the walls bare of any prints or paintings or photos revealing secrets about his inner soul. Maybe there were no secrets. Maybe the constant disarray was his way of keeping it all at a distance.

It quickly dawned on him that he ought to go. If he stayed here any longer, he'd be too depressed to move. He got to his feet.

"I should be going."

"Already?"

Pat knew it was just a polite response. She had to have seen how awkward this was. He picked up his mug and carried it to the kitchen counter. The cats jumped up to sniff at the mug.

"I didn't break it," he told them. "I didn't even spit in it."

Trisha just laughed. "They think everything is theirs," she said. "That's how cats are."

"We had one when my mother was alive," he said suddenly. "Buster. But it was very definitely her cat. She had him before she married my father. He sat in her lap, followed her around and couldn't have cared if the rest of us fell off the face of the earth.'' He hadn't thought of Buster in years. And stranger still, why was he suddenly articulating that memory?

"What happened to him when your mother died?"

Pat shrugged. "He was pretty old by that time. Fourteen, I think. My grandmother took him. He lived another couple of years, but never seemed really happy."

What a stupid story to be telling. Why was he always telling these things to Trisha? She must think his life was nothing but one long tragedy. Why didn't he tell her about his successes? Like quarterbacking his high school football team to the city championship in his senior year, or making the dean's list seven out of eight semesters in college, or—

The phone rang and, with a slight smile of apology, she went to answer it. He was tempted to just duck out while she was occupied, but that seemed cowardly. Besides, no one got good phone calls at midnight. She might need him for something. He got her mug from the living room and washed both of them out. He was drying the one he'd used when she hung up the phone. She looked more annoyed than worried.

"The alarm's gone off at the club," she said. "The police think everything's fine, but they want me to come out and let them in the building."

He put the mug down. "I'll drive you."

"No, don't be silly. It's not your problem." She had gone into the living room and picked up her purse.

"I'll drive you," he repeated, and went to the door to wait for her.

She had started looking for something in her purse, but stopped at his words. Her eyes came up and met his, for a moment holding his gaze as if reading something there. Or giving him some kind of test. He must have passed, for she looked away with a nod and followed him out to his car.

"This happen often?" he asked as he unlocked her door.

She waited to answer until he'd gotten in and was starting the car. "Oh, maybe once or twice a month. It's usually some kids fooling around. They trip the alarm and run off before the police get there."

"Ever anything worse?"

"Once a broken window." She paused as he pulled out into the street. "I sure hope it's just a false alarm. We can't afford to get a broken window boarded up, let alone repaired."

"Don't you have insurance?"

"With a huge deductible. It costs too much to get coverage for all the little stuff."

With nothing else to say he drove through the darkened streets. A group of young men, on a corner just down from the club, caught his eye and he traded glares with them as they drove by.

He was glad he hadn't left earlier, or just dropped Trisha off after the dinner. She'd have had to drive out here by herself and he wouldn't have liked that. It was probably safer than a big city, but no place was really safe these days.

He pulled into the club parking lot right behind a police car, its lights flashing silently, sitting near the back door. A young cop was leaning against the car. His canine partner, head hanging out the door, was trying to catch the night breezes.

"Hi, Trisha," the cop greeted her as she got out of the car. "Sorry to drag you out here."

"No problem."

But the cop was eyeing her in that red silk dress, then turned to look at Pat. His eyes said he must have interrupted something. He just nodded at Pat. Pat nodded back.

"You check all the doors?" Trisha asked. "How about the windows?"

"Everything looks tight from the outside." His glance darted back to Pat for a second. "I thought I should have Oscar sweep the interior for you. Make sure everything's fine and dandy in there."

"Guess we'd better." Trisha looked at Pat. "Do you want to wait out here?"

"Yeah," he said, nodding.

The officer opened the door for his dog. It jumped out onto the ground, where he ordered it to sit, and he then hooked a leash to its chain collar. The dog whined and looked over toward a line of bushes along the far end of the parking lot, but the cop just ordered the dog to heel and the three of them walked to the front door. Trisha unlocked the door, then let the officer and his dog enter first.

Pat waited until the door closed behind Trisha, then walked toward the bushes. His years on the streets had given him a kind of sixth sense. And right now that sense was telling him there was someone in those bushes—someone not too dangerous.

"All right, you," he growled. "Come on out of there."

He waited and nothing happened. He was sure someone was in there, but maybe they weren't as cowardly as he'd hoped.

"I said, come out here. Now."

There was a kind of sniffling, sobbing sound; then a little figure stumbled out of the bushes into the light.

"Rulli?" Pat bent down and looked closer. "What the hell are you doing here this time of the night?"

Rulli's reply was to start crying in earnest.

"Are you the one that tripped the alarm?" Pat asked.

The kid, snuffling like an elephant, nodded.

"Come on." Pat took the kid's hand. "Let's go."

The kid started bawling like a calf being branded. "Don't send me to jail, Mr. Stuart. Please. I'm sorry. I'll never do this again. Honest."

"Would you shut up?" Pat hissed. "You keep making all that racket and the neighbors will have a SWAT team out here."

Rulli retreated to snuffling and Pat hurried him to his car. "Get in there," he said, opening the back door. "Lie down on the floor and don't make a sound. Not even a doggone peep."

Then he slammed the door shut and leaned against the car to wait. It wasn't long before Trisha and the canine team came out.

"Nothing," Trisha said. "It was just a false alarm."

"Yeah," the officer agreed. "Me and Oscar swept the place from top to bottom. There's nobody in there."

The dog looked toward Pat's car and whined. Pat took a deep breath and held tension at bay.

"What's the matter, boy?" The dog continued whining and the cop looked at Pat.

"Ah." Pat put a smile on his lips and, after a quick glance at Trisha, looked the officer in the eye. "I helped out a neighbor last night. Drove her and her dog to the emergency veterinarian clinic up on South Bend Avenue."

The officer nodded but his expression was still quizzical.

"Her dog was in heat." Pat cleared his throat. "I haven't had a chance to have the car cleaned yet."

"I see." The cop laughed, a man-to-man kind of thing. "Come on, Oscar. No romance tonight. You're still on duty."

He pulled the dog back to the police car and opened the door to let him in the back seat. After giving them a quick salute, he got into the front seat.

Pat remained leaning against the car until the lights of the cop car disappeared around the corner. Even then he didn't move, barely allowing himself to breathe.

"Are we going to leave?" Trisha asked. "Or are you enjoying the view?"

Instead of replying, Pat just unlocked his door, then reached back to unlock the rear door. "Come on out, kid."

"Rulli?" To say Trisha's voice was full of surprise would be putting it mildly. "What in the world are you doing in Mr. Stuart's car?"

Rulli started sobbing again.

"He's sure got the hang of that," Pat said.

"Rulli, honey." Trisha ignored Pat and put her arms around the kid. "What's the matter? Why are you crying?"

Rulli's answer was to cry louder, which caused Trisha to hug him even harder. Pat could feel his lips turn into a sour expression. He wasn't sure if he was irritated at Trisha's naiveté or whether he was just plain jealous of the kid.

"You can stop that wailing anytime now," Pat said.

Trisha turned so that she was between Rulli and Pat. "Come on now, honey," she said. "Tell me what's wrong."

"It's Angie." The kid paused to intermix his sobs with hiccups. "She's gonna kill me."

"What?" Trisha said.

"So I was trying to get into the club." His sobs were lessening in intensity. "I was gonna sleep on the couch in the study room."

"Why do you think Angie is mad at you?" Trisha asked.

Rulli shuffled his feet and wiped his nose, but couldn't seem to find any words.

"Come on, kid," Pat said. "Out with it."

The kid looked up at Pat, then reached into the back pocket of his pants and pulled out a crumpled paper. He stepped out of Trisha's embrace and gave it to Pat.

Trisha stood up and came to look over his arm as he unfolded the paper. It was a spelling test. Rulli hadn't just flunked it; he'd bombed it. Only three out of twenty words were spelled right. Pat looked down at him.

"Pretty lousy. Doesn't look like you studied."

Rulli just shook his head and wiped his nose again. "I told you Angie's gonna kill me."

Trisha was stooped down in front of the boy again. "Honey, you can't let her—"

"What's Angie got to do with it?" Pat said. There was a bigger lesson to be learned here. One that Trisha was never faced with.

"She's gonna be mad at me," Rulli replied. "She's gonna hit me."

"Is that why you study?" Pat snapped. "Just because your sister hits you?"

"She hits hard."

"So what? In a couple of years, she'll be in middle school with lots more homework. She won't have time to hit you. If the only reason you're doing your work now is because you're scared of her, what are you gonna do then?"

Rulli kicked at the ground with his toe. "I dunno."

"Sure, you do," Pat said. "We both do. You'll stop studying. Why don't you just quit school now? Drop out now and quit wasting everyone's time."

"Pat!" Trisha turned Rulli to face her. "Mr. Stuart doesn't mean that. He—"

"I damn well mean it!" Pat snapped. He spun Rulli to face down the block. The streetlight almost made the corner into a stage for the group of young studs they'd passed on their way in, drinking and mouthing off. "See those kids down there? Is that what you want to be?"

"No," Rulli said with a decided sniff in his voice.

"Why not? They got cars. They got clothes. They got money. And you can bet nobody makes them study their spelling."

"Pat!"

"I ain't like that," Rulli said, some of the sniff being replaced by testiness. "I'm gonna fly jet planes when I grow up. Big jet planes. Those jerks ain't even been in a tiny plane."

Pat found his words had disappeared along with his breath. He swallowed hard, feeling more than a little stunned at the backbone in Rulli's voice and more than a little proud that the kid had dreams. It was more than he expected. He cleared his throat roughly. "Pilots have to know how to spell."

"I know."

"But not because their sisters say so. Because they have to be able to read maps and directions and manuals and all sorts of things."

"I know."

Rulli's voice had grown softer, less belligerent and more tired. Pat put his hand behind the kid's shoulders and gently moved him forward. "Come on, kid. We'll take you home."

Trisha made small talk with Rulli in between giving Pat directions to the house. It was a good thing because Pat could not have talked to save his life. He felt like a balloon with all the air emptied out.

He pulled up to the house Trisha indicated, the only one in the block with all the lights on. The car had barely stopped when Angie came flying out the front door and down the steps, followed by an elderly woman.

"Let me," Trisha said under her breath to Pat. Before he could agree, she was out of the car and leading Rulli up to the others.

Pat just watched the scene as one would watch a silent movie. Some anger, some tears, then some hugs. He was glad Trisha wanted to direct that. It wasn't his scene at all. None of this was. He was glad when she got into the car.

"That was really wonderful, what you did," she told him.

Her voice was brimming over with some emotion. He didn't want to know "what" and just pulled away.

"He needed it." Pat made a show of watching for traffic. He sensed he was heading toward dangerous ground and it had nothing to do with where his car was going. "Now's the time to catch these kids and set them in the right direction. Eight's not too young."

"He's a good kid," she said.

"That doesn't mean he'll make it."

"With you looking out for him, how can he not?"

Pat wanted to give the lady some straight facts, wanted to burst her little rose-colored bubble and introduce her to the real world. He was here for Rulli at this moment. But who knew when Rulli's pivotal moment would come—next week or next year? And would Pat happen to be there at that exact moment when he could make a difference? Pat hadn't known the right moment to save his brother or his father—why should anybody expect he could save some stranger's kid?

But he couldn't tell her that. Hell, she worked with these kids. She should know how the world worked. If she had one last illusion left, he was not going to be the one to destroy it. He pulled into her parking lot in silence and walked her up to the door.

"Thanks for everything," she said. "You really went above and beyond the call of duty."

"Don't mention it."

"Hey, it's not every day I meet a real live Boy Scout," she teased.

But he wasn't in a teasing mood. "I'm about the farthest thing from a Boy Scout that exists," he said. "I'm not loyal, or trustworthy or dependable."

But she just laughed, moving in closer to him. "But you're kind and I am so glad I know you, Patrick Stuart," she said, and reached up to kiss his lips.

He was amazed at the hunger that swept over him, at the way that all his doubts vanished at her slightest touch. He let his arms slide around her, pulling her closer. Her softness was a lure that he could not resist, her lips a temptation that he no longer wanted to fight.

There was no reason to run from this desire. There was no reason to pretend it didn't exist. It didn't matter if they were suited or not. A kiss wasn't forever. It was now, this moment, a flicker in the breadth of their lives. They could touch and kiss and delight in the other; it was as right and natural as basking in the warmth of the sun.

Yet when they finally pulled apart, and he saw the warmth in her eyes and the glow in her cheeks, he was no longer so sure he should ignore the warnings of his heart.

"Thanks again," she said lightly.

Her lips were curved into a smile so tempting, he wanted to crush her mouth once more to his. "No problem," he said gruffly. He was suddenly glad his schedule was taking him out of town soon. He needed time to think.

Chapter Seven

"Sir."

Pat squinted at the waitress, trying desperately to clear the wool—or rather, the thoughts of Trisha—from his mind. Obviously the waitress wanted him to order something.

"Uh, yeah." He picked up the menu. He'd decided on something when they'd first come in, but he was damned if he could remember what it was. Probably steak. That was always a safe bet in these hotel joints. "I'll have a filet mignon, medium—"

"Whoa, Pat."

"Earth to Pat. Anybody home?"

"What?" He looked around the table, bewildered. He was in Cleveland, attending a regional conference of industrial development specialists. After spending the day in workshops, six of them were having dinner in the hotel dining room.

"We were going to order another round first." The speaker was Harry Ales, director of industrial development for Flint, Michigan. "You want a refill?"

Pat stared at his glass of red wine, still almost full. If he said yes, he'd wind up with two glasses of wine that he'd barely touch. "No." He shook his head at the waitress. "I'm fine. Thank you."

The waitress nodded and left to fill the rest of the table's drink order. He didn't want to drink, but he wasn't all that interested in eating, either. In fact, he didn't want to be here at all. He found he was missing Trisha and the brightness of her smile. And even the kids.

"Are you all right, Pat?" Carole Langhorn was gazing at him from across the table, a worried expression on her face.

"Yeah, I'm fine."

"You look like you're someplace else."

"Maybe he'd just rather be someplace else," said one of the men, whose name Pat had forgotten.

"Nah," Pat replied. "I just had a hard couple of weeks."

"Poor baby," Carole cooed.

"Yeah, getting that big plant for your city would tire anyone out."

"I'll say," Harry Ales said. "It must get damned tiresome having people shake your hand, slap your back and tell you how great you are every minute of every day."

"Not to mention the walking on water," Carole said with a laugh. "That gets old in a hurry."

"And the mess it makes of your shoes."

Good-natured laughter filled the air around their table. The industrial development business was a small world and, within a matter of hours after he'd secured the agreement, development people all over the Midwest knew what Pat had accomplished. In fact, he was supposed to give a workshop on it tomorrow morning.

"I was just trying to figure out what to say at my workshop," Pat said.

"Hell's fire, Pat. What's to say?"

"Yeah. Just tell the folks to work hard and get lucky."

"Especially the lucky part."

"That's for sure."

The drinks came and the laughter grew louder. Pat shrank back even further into his cave.

The past several weeks had been hard. Maybe it wasn't Trisha. Maybe he just needed a vacation. He was having trouble keeping track of the days lately. Gran had always said that time flies when you're having fun, but he hadn't been having all that much fun.

Although, to be honest, that wasn't entirely true. Sure, he'd come back from that camping trip a little ragged around the edges, but it hadn't been what one would really call a bad time. And then that dinner with Trisha last Saturday certainly had been enjoyable.

Trisha. He felt—more than saw—her short blond hair, her bright green eyes and her smile. Especially her smile. Happy, full of joy, with a dash of mischief. She filled his dreams nicely but he would much prefer for her to be here in person.

Suddenly he sat straight up as if someone had pinched him. What in the world was the matter with him? He didn't need a vacation; he needed to concentrate on his work. It was a good thing that he was going on to Atlanta from here, then to Pittsburgh.

"So," Pat said, "do you guys think the prime rate will be going up anymore this year?"

The conversation died and they all stared at him, looking like the cattle he'd seen on the way to camp with the kids.

"There is a strong correlation between new plant investment and the cost of money," Pat said. "It's an economic principle."

"What the hell's that got to do with Wisconsin getting to the Rose Bowl this year?"

Now Pat found himself staring.

"We were talking about college football," Carole said.

Pat wasn't the type to blush, but he felt a little warm around the collar. Man, did he sound stupid. He needed to get out of here before he put both feet in his mouth.

"Are we going to eat anytime tonight or what?" he snapped.

"Maybe we better feed him," Harry Ales said. "He's getting more than a little irritable."

Carole signaled for the waitress and their dinner orders were quickly placed; then the conversation returned to the upcoming college football season. Pat sat up and paid attention. No more Mr. Dummy. He was as aware and witty as anyone else at this table.

"So how is Notre Dame going to do this year, Pat?"

His mouth opened and quickly closed. He had this feeling that everything was alive in him except his mind. "Okay, I guess."

"Okay?"

"No national championships?"

As a resident of South Bend, Pat was supposed to have the latest info on the Notre Dame football team. He was supposed to be able to recite who had graduated, who was returning, who was injured, and the name of the priest who said the prayer at the start of the game. He could usually fake this kind of stuff, but not today.

"Filet, medium-well?" the waitress said.

Pat looked up, nodding eagerly. "Yes, that's mine."

The rest of the food was distributed amid small talk that continued halfheartedly as they all dug into their meals. Once they were just about done, Carole waved the waitress over for coffee.

"Say," Harry Ales said. "I hear they have a couple of good nightclubs down in the river district. Anyone want to go?"

Most of the people at the table answered they would.

"Carole?" Harry asked.

"No," she replied, shaking her head. "I want to wash my hair and do a little reading."

Harry nodded. "Pat?"

His mind was still sluggish, but he kick-started the damn thing. "No. No, thanks."

"You two got something going?" Harry asked as he looked from Pat to Carole and back again.

"My husband wouldn't like that." Then Carole looked at Pat and smiled. "Besides, I think Pat's occupied with someone else."

"I am not." They were staring at him again and, for a moment, Pat considered throwing something at his dinner companions. "Well, it's not like I don't date. I just don't have anyone special."

"Sure," someone said with a snicker. "Then why have you suddenly turned into a monk? You were always the first one on the party line."

"Maybe he's not occupied, but *pre*occupied," Carole said. "Maybe she doesn't know he exists."

They all laughed at that.

Pat considered straightening them all out but decided it wasn't worth the effort. "I need to get back to the room and prepare for tomorrow's workshop," he said and dropped his money on the table. "Right now all I've got is three knock-knock jokes and a song from 'Sesame Street.'" He got to his feet. "Good night, all."

They were all wearing irritating little smiles, but Pat didn't let it bother him. He wasn't going to let anything bother him. He was going to work on his talk and go to bed. Without calling anyone. Without missing anyone.

And if tonight didn't do it, he had another week of travel to learn to be on his own again.

"Lucy, no. You're a bad girl." Trisha snatched the chunk of chicken breast away from the kitten, but like an unruly child, the little cat just glared back, its green eyes flashing like tiny emeralds. "And I don't need any back talk from you. I've had enough of it for one day."

And she certainly had. Angie had been a holy terror today. She and Rulli had started with their new tutor this afternoon—an elementary education major from the local branch of Indiana University. She was a very nice young woman but maybe, Trisha feared, a bit too nice.

Pat was better suited for the girl. He was able to keep a tight rein on her and, surprisingly, Angie accepted it. Except that Pat wasn't too available for the kids with all his traveling. It had been almost two weeks since the kids had seen him. And they were missing him.

Damn, Trisha thought. She was missing him. Was he really traveling all this time or was he just avoiding them? Her, as well as the kids? Suddenly the little chicken thief struck again.

"Darn you, Lucy," Trisha exclaimed. "You're really bad. Look at what a gentleman Sniffles is. Why can't you be nice like him?"

The chunky Burmese had a much calmer disposition, but right now his huge soulful eyes were saying, If I'm so nice, why does she have the chicken and I have nothing?

"Oh, all right. Here." Sighing, Trisha pulled off a piece of meat and threw it in front of the well-mannered cat. He accepted the gift graciously and began to chew it. "That's it for both of you."

The front doorbell sounded, precluding any further discussion.

"Can I trust you guys to stay out of this?" Trisha asked. The innocent looks on their faces were answer enough. "Yeah, right."

She put the dish in the refrigerator before hurrying to the door, wiping her hands on a towel as she went. The party at the door leaned on the buzzer.

"Hold your horses," she shouted.

Before opening the door, she looked through the peephole. It was Pat, looking rather rumpled and weary. Her heart smiled with relief as she pulled open the door; maybe he really had been away.

"Hi," she said.

"Hello." He looked almost uneasy, uncertain. "My flight just got in. I thought I'd drop by on my way home."

"Great." Though the South Bend airport was on the northwest side of the city and Trisha lived on the southeast side. Pat would've had to have practically climbed over his house on the way here. Not that she was going to question him. "Come on in."

"Yeah, sure." He shrugged. "Why not?"

Opening the door, Trisha stood aside to let him in. She wasn't absolutely sure, but she thought his eyes looked like Sniffles's did when he wanted something. "Sit down," she said. "Would you like something to drink? Have you eaten?"

"I don't want to put you to any trouble."

"Oh, don't be silly." It was so good to see him. He'd been gone ten days but it seemed like months. "I was about to have dinner."

"I'm sorry." He made a face. "You've probably had a hard day and here I come, barging in on you."

She didn't want him to leave. The time he'd been gone had dragged so and she must have a million things to tell him. "Have you eaten dinner yet?"

"They served some sandwiches on the plane." He started toward the door. "I'd better go."

"No, that's okay." She grabbed his arm. "I was just making a chef's salad. I have more than enough for two."

"You sure I'm not a bother?"

"Not yet," she said with a laugh. "But you're working at it."

He seemed to relax. A soft smile took hold of his lips. "I was just wondering how Angie and Rulli were."

"They're fine. Ornery as ever, but Rulli's studying his spelling. Worked on it with his new tutor today." She moved farther into the living room. "Come on and sit down. We'll have a bite and I'll fill you in."

"You know, we could go out someplace."

She put her hands on her hips and gave him a look. "You think I can't make a passable chef's salad?"

"No. No, ma'am." He shook his head, pretending fear. "Not me."

"Good. Sit down." She nodded toward the stools at the kitchen counter. "Get comfortable. Take off your coat and tie."

"Anything else?"

She turned to see that he had already dropped his coat on the sofa and was undoing his tie. "Your shoes, if you want."

"Okay."

"And if that's not comfortable enough, then tough," she said with a teasing laugh and went back to dividing the salad. "We're proceeding slowly."

"Is that a threat or a promise?"

Trisha smiled at him. It was going to be a fun evening, and maybe even a little more than fun. It must mean something that he had come here rather than go home. "Anything I can do?"

Lucy came running over to jump onto his shoulder. In a split second, she was curled up around the back of his neck. Pat looked stunned, and a little uneasy as the kitten sniffed daintily at his ear.

"What's she doing?" he asked.

"Getting to know you," Trisha said, secretly smiling at the sight of the cat with Pat. She wouldn't mind nibbling at his ear herself. Would he look that uneasy if she was doing it? She suspected he would. She was right when she said they were proceeding slowly. "Do you want French, Italian or Ranch dressing?"

"Italian is fine."

Sniffles had come to have a snack of his dry food and Lucy jumped off Pat's shoulder to join the other cat. Trisha got out some silverware.

"Want a glass of wine?"

"Sure."

She poured two glasses. "So, how was your trip?" she asked as they sat down to eat.

"All right. Long."

It had seemed long to her, too. "Get much accomplished?"

He shrugged as he poured dressing on his salad. "Probably not. Everything takes time."

Sniffles stopped eating, and jumped on the counter. He stopped just past the stovetop to watch them eat.

"How'd he get his name?" Pat asked, nodding at the cat.

"He has the sniffles a lot," Trisha said and went back to her salad.

Pat's look said that didn't quite explain it, so she went on. "I'd had a cat since grade school and, when he died two years ago, I went to a cat show to look for a kitten. I saw Sniffles there and it was love at first sight. I couldn't resist him, but then he came down with a runny nose the next day. The vet thought he'd caught a little cold, but it wouldn't go away and we eventually found out it was feline herpes."

He winced. "Is that serious?"

She shook her head. "Not life threatening, and not contagious to humans," she added quickly. "But he has a runny nose in the winter and a tendency to sneeze on you."

Pat stared at the cat, who stared defiantly back at him. "Don't they come with some sort of guarantee?"

"Sure." She tried to figure out how to explain it without coming off sounding sappy, then wondered why she worried. If she and Pat were friends, he wouldn't mock the soft, sentimental side of her. "I had the right to return him, but I couldn't."

Pat's eyebrow rose in question.

She just smiled. "I love him. You don't give back someone you love just 'cause they aren't perfect."

He shook his head in obvious confusion as he sipped his wine. "But he's just a cat."

"Love is love," she said. From the look on his face, she knew he still didn't understand. "Love is roses blooming in the middle of the desert. It's sunshine in the darkest part of the night. It's courage to stare down all your worst fears. When you find it, you don't let go of it. Not for any reason."

But his laugh said he didn't believe in love's power. "It's getting your legs broken by a speeding train," he said. "Hurts like hell, but cripples you so you can't escape."

She didn't know what to say. His pain hung there in the air, throbbing with agony, but his eyes forbade her to notice. He'd lost his mother to death, his father to alcohol and his brother to the streets. No wonder he was terrified of love.

"So what's the other cat's story?" he asked as if they'd been discussing the weather.

She tried to follow his lead. "Why does there have to be a story?"

"There is, isn't there?"

She stared down at her salad, spearing some lettuce with a bit more force than necessary. "Lucy was a gift from my father," she said.

"That doesn't seem like much of a story," he said. "Sniffles had a bit more drama."

"I never take gifts from my father," Trisha said.

Pat looked a bit taken aback, but she didn't know if it was her tone or her words that did it.

"I saw some Abyssinians at a cat show last spring," she explained slowly. "And I happened to mention to my brother how beautiful they were. A week later, Lucy arrived on my doorstep, air express from California."

"And this was a problem?" he asked.

Trisha bit back the annoyance that just thinking of her father awoke. "My father walked out on us when I was eleven," she said. "He was a doctor. Moved in with a volunteer from his free clinic. She was young, wealthy and pretty. Not long afterward he was opening up an office in a wealthy neighborhood of Chicago and acting like he'd never heard of us or the clinic. It closed soon after, even though my mother tried her hardest to get other doctors involved."

"And you're still angry."

She didn't like how Pat said that, as if he was judging her and finding her wanting. "And shouldn't I be?"

He held his hands up in surrender. "Hey, I'm not criticizing. I was just asking. I'm the last one in the world who would believe the 'love is roses in the desert' theory."

She felt slighted somehow though. If he wasn't criticizing her anger at her father, he was criticizing her belief in love. How silly she'd been to think she could—or should—open up to him.

"Never mind," she said, digging back into her salad even though her appetite had fled. She knew her voice was curt, but she couldn't help that. "The gist of it all was that I would have refused to accept Lucy from him, but it would have meant another cross-country trip for her. She had looked pretty miserable after the first one, and I couldn't do that to her." Trisha fixed Pat with a definite glare. "Even if that meant I wasn't following my own philosophy."

Pat sighed and put down his fork. "I screwed up, didn't I?" he said. "I really wasn't criticizing. If anything, I was thinking about you. I learned the hard way that anger like that only backfires."

"It hasn't yet," she said. But the look in his eyes made her feel better, made her annoyance slip away.

"Are you sure it hasn't?" he asked. "Why are you still single?"

His question seemed to catch her defense unawares, but all she did was laugh slightly. "Gee, why don't we get personal? I'm not married because I only trust males who have skinned knees and play on swing sets. Why aren't you?"

He relaxed and finished the last of his salad. "Are you kidding? I'm waiting for the woman that I'd walk barefoot in the snow for."

"Hope she owns stock in an aspirin company."

"No, seriously." He picked up his glass of wine and held it up to the light, staring at it. "I don't want anybody leaning on me. It sounds selfish, but it's not. I don't want to fail anybody the way I failed Angel."

"You can't keep blaming yourself," she said.

He grinned. "Sure, I can. If you can stay mad at your father forever, I can blame myself for Angel not doing more with his life."

She laughed, unable not to. "We are certainly a pair," she said. "Both avoiding relationships because of ghosts from the past. I guess we have nothing to fear from each other."

His eyes took on a new light, almost like hope or anticipation or maybe just relaxation. "You're right," he said. "It sounds like the perfect relationship."

And it did.

"Douglas, you just cannot do things like that," Trisha snapped.

"They're only Ping-Pong balls."

"That's not the point," she said. "If you smash them, they can't be used anymore. And that means that no one can play."

"It's a stupid game anyway."

"Then you won't mind not playing until you replace the balls you smashed."

"Jeez," the kid muttered. "You don't gotta get all hyper about it."

Trisha just held her hand out for the paddle. After a moment, he gave it to her and walked away. His pride demanded that he make some crack to his friends, at which they all snickered, but Trisha knew better than to pursue the argument. She closed her hand around the paddle and turned back toward the office.

It was this damned heat. Even though September was fading fast, it had to be close to ninety today. And that meant they had twice as many kids inside as usual for a Friday afternoon. Everybody was looking for someplace cool and nobody seemed to be leaving even though it was dinnertime.

"Miss Stewart," a little voice called. "The drinking fountain don't work right."

"I know, Wendy. We're getting it fixed."

"When?"

"When we can. You'll have to be satisfied with water that's wet, instead of wet and cold."

Trisha went into the office. Clarissa looked up from her desk, with a stack of message notes. Trisha felt something collapse inside her. She'd only been gone about ten minutes to take care of Douglas.

"Three tutors can't make it, as if we wouldn't have noticed by now." Clarissa flipped to the next message. "Michael Shaughnessy's had some business problems and isn't going to replace his computers after all, so we won't be getting his old ones." Then to another. "And your car won't be ready today. They don't have a part in stock. Hopefully, tomorrow."

Hopefully, tomorrow. Trisha took the messages and went into her office. Yes, she certainly hoped tomorrow would be better. She sank into her chair, her eyes closing. Yesterday had been so nice. At least, the evening had been. Pat hadn't stayed long; he was visibly tired after his trip. But they'd had a nice dinner. And even more important, they seemed to have taken a step forward in their relationship. They actually had sort of agreed to have a relationship, maybe.

"Knock, knock."

Trisha's eyes flew open and she found Pat in her doorway. He was dressed informally, just in jeans and a short-sleeved shirt, and his eyes were concerned.

She smiled at him. "Hi. What are you doing here?"

"Just dropped in to check with Angie and Rulli. He had only one wrong on his spelling test."

Trisha nodded. "I know. He was so excited."

But Pat's eyes did not lighten with the news. "You look beat."

She shrugged. "It's been a hell of a day." She leaned her arms on the desk. "It always gets crazy here when it's hot outside."

"Well, it is that." He came farther into the room and sat down. "I thought the weather was supposed to get cooler the later in September it got, but we'll probably be wishing we had this day all over again come December."

"Believe me, I won't want this day again," she said with a laugh, but it came out weary and weak.

"That bad?"

"Worse."

Clarissa came to the door. "Sorry to interrupt, but Mike Gentry just called."

"Not the grant!" Trisha cried. "We lost it?"

Clarissa shook her head. "They want more information. He's sending us some more forms that we need to fill out before we resubmit."

Trisha just felt beaten. "How many times can we resubmit before we've missed the deadline?"

"Think there's a plot in all this?" Clarissa asked.

"I just wish there was," Trisha said with a sigh. "That would mean that someone cared, even if negatively." She rubbed her eyes but the weariness just wouldn't rub away.

Pat leaned forward. "When do you get off?"

Clarissa looked at her watch. "She should have been gone an hour ago." Her voice was scolding.

Trisha just shook her head as if they didn't understand. "I can't leave with things so crazy," she protested.

"Why not?" Clarissa asked. "Jeff and I can handle it. We've handled worse in the summer."

"But I—"

But Pat had gotten to his feet and had taken her hand, pulling her to her feet. "Come on. You need a break. Hanging around here isn't going to do anyone any good."

"Wait a minute," she cried. She didn't like his highhandedness all of a sudden. Or was it that she didn't like how good her hand felt in his? "I have responsibilities here."

"And the main one is to stay mentally healthy for the kids," he said. "You can't do that as beat as you are. You need a break."

"Maybe I need to make my own decisions." Why was she putting up such a fuss? She'd spent time with Pat before. This would be no different.

"Maybe you ought to listen to someone else for a change," Clarissa snapped. "You aren't the only one with sense around here."

Maybe she *was* the only one with sense. The only one who saw the path she and Pat were heading down. Yesterday it had seemed perfect—smooth and pleasant. This afternoon it seemed scary—steep and treacherous.

"Look," Pat said. "I'll leave my home number. We'll grab a bite to eat and go over there. If Clarissa needs you, she can call."

It would look foolish to keep protesting. "All right," Trisha said finally, then turned to face Clarissa. "You have to promise to call if things get even a little more hectic."

"Honey, I'm no martyr." She pushed Trisha out the door. "I'll call if I need help, believe me."

"And I'll be in, first thing in the morning," Trisha said. "So—"

"It's going to be morning before we get out of here," Pat said. "I'm sure Clarissa knows what to do."

Trisha said nothing, just let him lead her out into the hallway and into the chaos.

"Miss Stewart," someone whined.

She started to turn, but Pat beat her to it. "Miss Stewart's leaving. Go see Clarissa."

"That might have been important," Trisha snapped at him.

"I would guess it's someone who wants to complain about something you can't change," he said. "Give it a rest, will you?"

By that time, they were to the door and, a few steps later, outside. The heat just seemed to sink around her, like a thick blanket she had to fight her way through.

"It's really awful out," she said. "No wonder everybody's inside."

"At least it's peaceful out here," he said.

She stopped and listened. There was traffic noise and radios blaring and people shouting, but they were all far away. No one was pushing at her or demanding anything of her. She sighed and let herself relax.

"Now, this isn't that bad, is it?" Pat asked as he opened his car door for her.

"No, it's very nice." When he got in his side, though, she fixed him with a glare. "Just this once, though. I'm not someone who likes to be bullied."

"Then I'd better take real advantage of my one chance," he said with a slightly wicked grin.

She eyed him uneasily as he started the car and pulled into traffic. He drove with a purpose, as if he knew exactly where he was going.

He glanced at her, catching her eyes on him and let his smile warm her heart. "Those clothes washable?" he asked.

"Huh?" She looked down at her cotton culottes and knit top. "Yeah. Why? Are they dirty?"

"No, I was just curious."

He drove a few more minutes in silence. They went through the downtown area, then across the river. He turned, pulling into a parking lot on the east side of the river.

"What are we doing here?" she asked, looking around. There were a few restaurants in the area, but they were more formal. Neither she nor Pat were dressed appropriately.

"We're going rafting," he said. "If your shoes can't get wet, you might want to leave them in the car."

She just sat there as he slipped his shoes and socks off. "We're going what?"

"Rafting," he repeated. "You know. We get in this rubber boat and let the current take us over the bumps until we get to the end."

"I know what rafting is," she said.

"Good." He got out of the car. When she didn't move, he leaned down to look back in. "You can't go rafting in the car, you know."

"Who says I want to go rafting at all?" she asked as she climbed out her side.

"Are you hot and sticky and tense?"

She shrugged, not really wanting to answer. "Kind of."

"Then this is the answer."

He reached out his hand and she seemed unable to do anything but take it. Together they walked across the lot, then onto the wooden footbridge over the East Race. Trisha stopped to frown down at the raging water beneath her. She was no expert in water sports, but she knew what "white water" was and that there was a lot of it down there.

A rubber raft came through the open floodgate beneath her, the people frantically paddling as the current threw them into a section of rapids. The raft bounced up, nose high into the air; then it plunged down amid the screams of the people in it. Suddenly the water tossed the raft aside, flinging the people into the water as easily as the wind scatters dandelion seeds.

"Oh, Lordy," Trisha muttered.

"They went into it sideways," Pat said. "You have to face the rapids."

"Is that like facing a firing squad?"

Pat just laughed and led her off the bridge. Trisha turned, watching as the capsized rafters swam to the side. Lifeguards were there to help them out as another one caught hold of the raft. Everyone was laughing.

"This is a perfect example of industrial development," Pat said. "Taking something no longer needed by one industry and changing it to be of use in another."

"Our local lifeguards needed more work?"

He gave her a look as they got in line for their tickets. "In the early days of the city, they diverted this mile-long section of the river to power the mills," he said. "Then, when coal and electricity came along, water power wasn't needed and the race lay dormant until about ten years ago, when the city revamped the area. They made the whole area here more park-like and added movable buffers to the race to change the current and floodgates to control the depth of the water. What resulted was a world-class course that draws kayakers from all over the country, and a recreational rafting area that draws from as far away as Chicago and Detroit."

"Suicidal people can be found in every locale."

He stopped just before the ticket window. "If you really don't want to do this, we don't have to."

"You mean if I don't want to drown, you're not going to make me?"

He just stared at her. "It's not dangerous. No one has ever drowned here and little kids go on it all the time." He paused. "I just thought it would be a great way for you to relax, but..."

His eyes were suddenly open windows to his soul. She saw his certainty that this would relax her turn into a gamble. She saw his disappointment, his feeling that he had misjudged her. Then just as quickly, those windows shut tight and he let a mocking laugh leave his lips.

"Hey, it's—"

Trisha stepped forward in line. "If I drown, my mother'll be mad at you, and so will Sniffles and Lucy."

"You won't drown," he said as he bought two tickets. "This is as safe as can be."

How safe? she was wondering a few minutes later when she and Pat were fitted snugly into a narrow rubber raft. But it wasn't drowning in the river that she feared now.

She was sitting on her feet, in between his legs. They each had a paddle and were paddling from the dock toward the floodgates. She was not as effective a paddler as he was, probably causing him extra work to maneuver their raft where it should be. But every movement he made, she could feel. And it felt very nice indeed.

She even found sitting in the raft a joy. The bottom of the raft was only a layer of rubber so that the gentle movement of the current seemed to brush against her. They slid through the floodgates as sweetly as ever, the current moving them at a steady pace, but not really all that fast. She felt that the river was a part of her, not something to be nervous about. Not something to—

"Oh, my God!" she screamed.

Through the floodgates, they were suddenly hurtling down a steep incline, heading toward raging white water. Gargantuan waves were going to swallow them up and hurl them to the bottom of the river. She'd never get the club a new van. She'd never get that federal grant to hire a part-time counselor. She'd never grow old and have children.

But Pat was right behind her, his arm slipping around her waist and pressing her back against him as their raft dived into the waves. He would keep her safe. His strength was something she could lean on. He was someone she could depend on. She closed her eyes and leaned back, willing his arms to never leave her. Water washed over them, drenching them both and filling the raft with water but, astonishingly enough, it bounced right back up.

She opened her eyes. "We made it," she gasped.

"You okay?" Pat's mouth was right next to her ear, his tone so gentle and sweet that she could only nod.

She looked forward and realized they'd gone only through the first of the rapids. Pat let go of her as he went back to paddling, fighting the current as he sent them down a gentle slope instead of the frothing one at the near side of the race. She got brave enough to help paddle a bit herself, though all too soon, they were at another patch of white water. One where there was no gentle path to take.

"Oh, Lordy," she breathed.

But Pat was right there behind her again, slipping his arm around her and holding her safe and secure. She had a sudden vision of him riding through all of life's storms, holding her safe whenever she got scared. She leaned back, closing her eyes as they rode through the rapids.

It was almost fun, she realized, as the water bombarded them, trying to upset the raft and dump them into the river. If she'd been alone, it would have succeeded, but with Pat behind her, with Pat to fight with her, she knew that the river could never defeat them.

Another set of rapids, wider and higher and deeper than the others, came up, but Trisha just laughed. She kept her eyes open, her heart too certain of success to cringe away. The raft plunged into the wildest part of the white water, but she only laughed.

"This is great," she said over her shoulder to Pat.

"Stick with me, kid," he said. "I'll never steer you wrong."

His words were carried on his laughter, but she felt their trueness deep in her heart. The water splashed over them, the current tossed the raft about, but still they sped forward. She had found someone so rare and true, someone she hadn't thought existed except in her dreams—a man to lean on.

Then suddenly they were at the end of the run. A lifeguard tossed them a rope and once Pat caught it, they were towed to the shore. Another guard gave Trisha a hand to help her out of the raft. She found her legs were shaky and her clothes drenched, but all she could do was smile at Pat.

"Well?" he said.

"It was great," she said as she tried to wring out her shirt. "Fantastic."

"Not hot and sticky and tense anymore?"

She just laughed and fell into his arms. He held her a moment, then with his arm still around her, they walked up the ramp to the sidewalk that would take them back to the parking lot.

"And to think that you didn't trust me," Pat murmured.

"Never again," she vowed, keeping her voice as light and teasing as his had been. But her heart knew it was the truth, not a joke.

"Try these," Pat said, handing Trisha a T-shirt and some running shorts he'd brought downstairs. Both had shrunk in the wash so they were closer to her size than his other clothes.

She took them with a grin. "Don't like me dripping all over your hardwood floors, huh?"

He let his eyes caress her slender form like a race car driver drives, slowing down where the curves were the best. Though she kept pulling her shirt away from her, it had gotten thoroughly soaked while rafting and was determined to cling to her. "Oh, you can drip over my floors all night if you want."

She just gave him a look, held the clothes in her arms and turned to the bathroom just off his kitchen. She stopped in the doorway. "Have you looked in all these?" she asked.

He glanced into the room over her shoulder. She was looking at the old, built-in cabinets over the bathtub. "What for?"

"The treasure." Her tone marveled that he even had to ask.

Sighing, he frowned at her. "There is no treasure."

She just shook her head as she went into the bathroom. "Oh, ye of little faith." She closed the door.

Pat allowed himself a smile as he went on up to his own room to change his clothes. He liked having her here. The house didn't seem nearly so old or quiet. Maybe they'd just stay here for dinner, order in a pizza or something. He wished suddenly that he had the time and the ingredients to make her a real dinner.

As he arrived downstairs, Trisha was coming out of the bathroom, carrying her wet clothes in her arms. His old clothes had never looked so good as they did on her, even baggy as they were. A sudden hunger filled every molecule of his body and he had to swallow hard.

"Do you want to throw those in the dryer?" he asked.

"I think they ought to be washed first."

"I've got a washer."

She shook her head. "If you've got a plastic bag, I'll just stick them in there and take care of them at home."

He felt strangely disappointed that she wouldn't use his washer, that she was keeping her life so separate. And that reaction was nothing short of ridiculous. Why should he care if she washed her clothes at home or here? He led her into the kitchen and found a plastic grocery bag for her.

"I ordered a pizza," he said. "That okay with you?"

"Sure. Sounds great."

He tried to find something to do while she took care of her clothes, but he found himself staring at her, at the sweet curve of her bare legs, at the softness of her cheek that seemed to beg for his touch. He cleared his throat and looked away.

"Want to see the rest of the house?" he asked.

"Sure. And you can show me where you've looked for the treasure."

He made a face and waved her ahead of him into the hall. "I've looked everywhere," he said. "Upstairs, downstairs, basement and attic."

"I'm sure you did." She turned to pat him gently on the cheek. "But maybe what the search needs is a woman's touch."

He wanted to grab hold of her hand and keep it pressed against his cheek, but she'd probably think he was crazy. Maybe he was. "I'm sure my grandmother looked everywhere, too," he said.

"Maybe," she replied. "Or maybe she wanted you to find it."

Pat just shrugged.

"Come on. Show me what's upstairs." She turned on her heel and started up the stairs.

"Just my bedroom," he said, following her up more slowly.

He was suddenly conscious of the worn rug and wished he'd replaced it. Or at least taken it off so that the bare wood would show. But when his eyes left the rug, they found her backside, so trim and firm. He wasn't able to turn away. Maybe this house tour wasn't a good idea.

"My bedroom is the first door on your right," he said, as they reached the top of the stairs.

The same worn rug ran down the middle of the hall, promising nothing of worth was up here. Why hadn't he painted up here yet? That would make the place livelier and more inviting. That would promise that good things could be found here. Trisha marched right past his partially closed door.

"Don't you want to look around in there?" he asked.

She didn't reply. With his shorts and T-shirt barely covering half her body, he was catching glimpses of places he'd like to look around.

"There are probably a lot of things in there that could use a woman's touch," he added.

But she just went down to the far door. The drab rug and dingy walls must have spoken to her. "What's this room?" she asked, her hand on the knob. "An empty bedroom?"

"Yep."

She opened the door, flicking on the overhead light. There was no furniture in the room. The wallpaper was yellowed and peeling in spots. Curtains covered the windows, but she could tell the windows hadn't been washed for a while.

"There are not too many places to hide anything," Pat pointed out.

"Is that a closet?" she asked, pointing to another door.

He nodded.

She looked inside and found the same thing he had—nothing. She looked so disappointed that he wished he'd hidden something there for her to find.

"If it was easy to find, it would have been found years ago," he pointed out gently.

"I know." She frowned into the closet, then closed the door slowly. "What we need is a good, methodical search. When we have lots of time to do the whole house at one sitting."

"In case the treasure roams?" he asked.

She just made a face at him. "You're such a skeptic," she said. "You don't deserve a treasure."

"That's probably my ancestors' theory. It's probably why I can't find it. They've decided that I don't deserve it and they're keeping it hidden until a truly deserving relative comes along."

She grinned at him. "What if one never comes along? Can I keep it if I find it?"

Her smile wreaked havoc on his good intentions and he was glad that she went back out into the hallway. He followed more slowly, but got there in time to see her peeking into one of the other bedrooms.

"Are all these rooms the same?"

"Pretty much. Mine's different." He paused. "Want to see it?"

She stopped. "You probably redid your room, didn't you?" she asked. "If anything was there, you would have found it."

"Maybe not," he said. "You said yourself that a woman looks at things differently."

"We'll cover it in our thorough search," she said.

Promises, promises. "And when will that be?" he asked.

She just closed the door to the empty bedroom and ran her hand lightly over the wide woodwork as if looking for secret panels. "I don't know," she said. "When's good for you?"

He was suddenly afraid that once she left, he'd never get her back. That if he didn't have a lure to hold out, she'd never want to come here again. And though his brain told him it didn't matter, his heart knew better.

"How about tomorrow?"

She looked at him with a laugh. "Tomorrow? And here I thought you didn't believe there was a treasure."

He felt vulnerable and exposed, as if she could see his real fears and would mock them. "I just don't want to impede your search."

"You're so kind."

Her eyes were searching, though, looking for hidden secrets that he worried she'd find. The doorbell broke the power of her gaze and she looked away.

"That sounds like dinner." She started down the stairs. "I've got a million chores to do tomorrow. How about Sunday?"

He tried not to feel the sudden surge of pleasure that raced through him, tried not to admit that it was due to the fact she was coming back. Coming back for a real visit where he could make her dinner, where her laughter would linger in these old shadows for longer than a moment.

"Fine with me," he said lightly. His pleasure was due to none of those things. He just liked showing off the house.

Chapter Eight

"Davey says Uncle Henry's gonna die," Rulli said.

Trisha put the stack of good books back on the shelf. "Is he that sick?" She tossed the two torn books onto the pile of discards.

Rulli just shrugged his little shoulders. He looked as if he was trying to be brave, but all she could see in his eyes was fear. "Aunt Rose was crying when the ambulance came."

"She could have just been scared," Trisha said. "You have to listen to what the doctor says about your uncle, not Davey."

Rulli pulled some more books off the shelves and handed them to her. "Davey says Aunt Rose is gonna move to a special kinda place where they'll take care of Uncle Henry. And that we can't come 'cause kids can't live there."

"Your aunt isn't going to desert you," Trisha said. She tossed one book with no cover and flipped through another. Someone had decorated the inside cover with a crayon, but it was still readable. She put it on the shelf. "You know she's been working with Mrs. Adamanti to find you and Angie a new home. She's not going to leave unless you and Angie are taken care of."

"Davey says nobody's gonna want us 'cause we're too old."

Trisha reached over to pull the boy into her lap. "Don't you listen to Davey. Someplace there's somebody who is really going to be glad to get you two. Mrs. Adamanti's really good at finding homes for kids, you'll see."

Angie flew into the study room with Pat right behind her. "Pat's here," she announced. "We can go now."

Pat looked decidedly startled and Trisha climbed quickly to her feet. "Angie, I haven't even talked to Pat yet. How about if you and Rulli carry those old books out to the trash for me?"

"All right, but I ain't staying here alone all day," the girl said. "It's just too boring."

Trisha flashed a smile at Pat as the kids left the room. "We've a little problem," she said.

"So I gather." His eyes were tight. "Angie had a little message for me when she opened the door. Something about her and Rulli coming with you this afternoon."

Trisha grimaced. This wasn't the way she'd planned the day would go. "I told her I was supposed to go to your place, but I never said they could come along. It's just that their uncle was taken to the hospital last night. They were left all alone and wandered over here even though we're closed on Sundays. I figured I'd just stay with them and we could do our search some other time."

He looked as if his would-be home run had just been caught by an outfielder at the fence. "No, it's okay," he said. "They can come. I've got plenty of food."

"Really, we can do it another time," she said quickly. She couldn't read just what his disappointment meant. "I never meant to force us all on you."

"Hey, it's a big house and you wanted an all-out search" He shrugged. "Now we've got more bodies to do the looking."

"Look for what?" Angie asked.

Trisha let her eyes search Pat's again, looking for some sign that he'd rather not have them all, but found none. Not that she could read much of anything in his expression. He had on his closed-up, politely distant look.

"A treasure," Trisha said slowly. "Pat's grandmother said there's a treasure in his house and we're going to look for it."

"Cool," Angie said.

But Rulli looked confused. "You mean like a pirate treasure? Did pirates used to live in your house?"

"Sure," Pat said, putting his hand on Rulli's back as he ushered them out of the room. "We've always been a wild bunch of guys."

Trisha followed them, closing up the club, with a warmth growing in her heart. The kids bickered good-naturedly with Pat as they trooped out to his car. She was sure he hadn't really wanted the kids to come, but he was being an awfully good sport about it. How many other men that she knew would have let the kids tag along?

Pat had the kids settled in the back seat by the time she got to the car. She sat with her back to the door so she could keep one eye on the kids and the other on Pat.

"Cool car," Angie said, her voice brimming with approval.

"I bet you can go really fast, huh, Pat?" Rulli said.

"Yeah." Pat pulled out of the parking lot. "If I pedal hard."

Trisha smiled but the kids let his humor sail right over their heads.

"This ain't fast," Angie pointed out. "Uncle Henry's old car goes faster."

"We're in the city," Pat said.

"Davey goes fast in the city."

"Davey probably has a load of speeding tickets, too," Pat said and continued along at the speed limit.

"Big wimp," Angie said, slumping back in the seat, the sense of approval totally drained from her voice.

"That's okay, Pat," Rulli said. "You don't gotta go fast. I don't want you to go to jail."

"Thanks, kid."

The kids grew silent, staring at the big, old homes that lined Washington Street. This outing would be just great for them. It would take their minds off their uncle and their precarious home situation. And Pat might even enjoy it. Trisha was sure she was going to. They pulled into the driveway next to Pat's house.

"Wow, this is a mansion," Rulli said.

"No, it ain't," Angie said. "It ain't got no big walls around it with guards and dogs."

Pat flashed a smile at Trisha as he opened her car door. "Trust Angie to put me in my place."

"We all have a purpose in life."

"Oh?" His eyes took on that fiery look. "And what's yours?"

"The same as all women." She moved her seat forward so the kids could get out. "To civilize the men around them."

"I might need a lot of work," he said.

"I don't give up easily."

The kids had run up on the porch. Angie was peering into a window while Rulli was walking a pretend tightrope along the edge of the porch. Pat took Trisha's hand as they walked up the stairs. It was going to be a good afternoon. The kids would add to the day, not detract from it. She was certain of it.

She was still certain once they got inside, even though the kids seemed to think the spacious rooms were an invitation to kick off their shoes and run around, turn cartwheels and slide in their stocking feet across the floors. Pat looked a little startled, but she knew the kids would calm down.

"Guys, come on," she called. "Remember, this is Pat's house. Let's behave."

"They are," Pat muttered. "They may be behaving poorly, but it's still behavior."

"Thanks. You're a big help." She turned back to the children. "Kids."

Rulli ran back over to her. "Let's look for treasure."

"Where's it hid?" Angie had screeched to a stop in front of a fireplace and peered up. "Maybe there's a secret room with bodies in it."

"I doubt it," Pat said. "We've never lost anybody in this house."

"Pirates murder people," Rulli pointed out.

"The people who lived here were nice pirates."

Rulli looked distinctly disappointed, but Trisha just waved them into the living room. "Let's do this right," she said. "We'll do a room at a time and everyone works together. Angie and Rulli, you look down low for anyplace something could be hidden. But be real careful not to break anything."

The kids darted off immediately. Angie started at the door and crawled around on the floor, looking at the baseboard and plasterwork; Rulli looked under the furniture.

"This is going to be very productive," Pat said.

"Hey, you don't believe in the treasure anyway," she pointed out.

"No, but somehow I figured this afternoon was going to proceed a little differently." His eyes gave her a hint at the kind of afternoon and evening he'd hoped to have.

She patted his hand. "You're a real hero to these kids. Rulli is scared stiff about what's going to happen to them, and Angie has to be, too. You're helping them forget for a little while."

His smile held little humor. "That's me. Role model. Hero. Next month I'm going to be featured on one of those Saturday-morning cartoon shows."

"Come on," she said with a laugh. "Let's look up high."

She took him by the hand and led him over to the fireplace, where she started looking for cracks and secret panels. She wasn't about to tell Pat, but she thought he was a hero, too. He was letting the kids into his life when they needed someone. Not everyone was so willing to share themselves.

"Hey, I found something," Rulli called.

Angie was the first one over, peering under the sofa with him. "It's just a pen," she said in disgust as she pulled a ballpoint pen out from under the couch.

"Well, I didn't say it was the treasure," he pointed out.

Trisha just exchanged a smile with Pat and went back to the fireplace. She'd found no loose bricks or little rosettes that turned or any other things that always revealed the hidden treasures in movies. The damper was soot covered so anything hidden above the fire would have been charred.

She moved on to the built-in shelves on either side of the fireplace. Pat brought her a step stool, but it didn't bring any great luck. An hour later, they were searching the parlor; a while after that, it was the dining room. But no luck anyplace.

"This is boring," Angie whined. "I mean, like really boring."

"I told you there was no treasure," Pat pointed out. "Want to help me fill my bird feeders outside?"

"Yeah," the girl said and got to her feet. "I'm gonna be a forest ranger when I grow up."

"Forest rangers have to work with bears," Pat said.

"I ain't afraid of bears," Angie said. "I ain't afraid of nothin'."

Since Trisha had heard Angie mouth those words often enough, she could have finished that line herself. Instead, she pasted a smile to her lips and sank onto a dining room chair. "What about you, Rulli? You going to quit, too?"

"Uh-uh," he said. "I like this."

She frowned at him. "We've got to go about this smarter, though," she said. "If you had a treasure, where would you hide it?"

He thought for a minute. "Under my bed."

"No, it can't be under furniture. None of this furniture is old enough."

Trisha heard Pat's voice and Angie's laughter as a screen door slammed at the back of the house. Suddenly she felt very lonely. This afternoon might not be going as he envisioned, but it wasn't as she had expected, either. She'd somehow thought she'd have to be fighting her fears about growing closer to Pat, not sitting here with Rulli.

"Let's walk around the house," she said. "Maybe that'll give us some ideas."

So she and Rulli toured the house on their own. The second floor had four bedrooms. Pat's was the largest one with a sitting room/porch off it. Then, in what Trisha had thought was a hallway closet, they found a narrow set of small, steep stairs leading up to the third floor and down to the kitchen. They went up to the huge dormitory-style room.

Rulli walked across the wide-open floor littered with old furniture and boxes. "I always knowed Pat was rich," he said in an awed voice. "But I didn't know he was this rich."

"I don't think Pat is rich," Trisha said.

"Yeah, he is," Rulli insisted. "He's gotta be to live in a humongous house like this."

Trisha would have said that Pat was comfortable. But this

probably would have been palatial to any kid who lived in a two-bedroom bungalow with six other family members.

"It's been in Pat's family for a long time," Trisha said. "He got the house when his grandmother died."

Rulli wandered over to the dormer windows at the far end. "Aw, neat," he exclaimed. "You can see Coveleski from here."

Trisha joined him at the window, her eyes glancing at the baseball stadium in the distance, then looking down at Angie and Pat in the backyard.

"Man, wouldn't it be great to live here?"

The pathos in Rulli's voice brought a lump to Trisha's throat.

"You could see all the games for free."

She put a hand on Rulli's shoulder and roughly cleared her throat. A good social worker didn't get emotional about her client's problem, not if she wanted to help. She focused her attention on the stadium. All she could see was the outfield.

"I don't think you could see much of the game from here," she said.

"I guess." She could feel Rulli shrug his shoulders under her hand. "But I bet you could see the fireworks real good."

"Yeah, I bet you could."

The huge emptiness of the house was impressive, but sad, too. This was a house made for a family, made to be filled with kids and love and laughter, not to be so silent and empty. Why wasn't Pat married and making this place a real home? Not that it was any of her business.

"Come on, big guy," she said. "Let's get back downstairs."

"Are these the kids' stairs?" Rulli asked, as he looked down.

"I think they were for the servants."

"Oh." He sat down at the top of the stairs. "Can I look for the treasure up here?"

Her eyes flickered over the dusty items scattered in the room. It didn't look as if anyone had been up here for ages.

"Yeah, okay," she said. "Just don't mess anything up."

"I won't. I'll stay by the stairs."

"That's fine," Trisha said, stepping around Rulli and moving sideways down steps that were about as deep as the width of a man's hand. "I'll be on Pat's porch."

She walked through Pat's bedroom and onto the porch where she sat in a wicker chair and watched Pat and Angie in the backyard. They were talking and laughing as they cleaned out some birdbaths. Angie seemed to be ordering Pat about, but he looked to be taking it well. She obviously needed a strong hand but Trisha hoped that wherever the girl landed, that strength would be tempered by gentleness.

There were so many needy kids in this town. And then there was Pat, with so much to give, yet so determined to remain apart. Trisha closed her eyes. She wished she could find the treasure in the house, just to show him that it was all right to believe.

"Miss Stewart!" Rulli called as his little feet thumped down the stairs and across the hall. "I found it! I found it!"

Trisha jumped to her feet as Rulli came flying through Pat's room. He had a grungy-looking wooden box about the size of two cigar boxes.

"I found it!" He put the box on the wicker chair and raced over to the porch railing. "I found it!" he called out to Angie and Pat. "I found the treasure!"

As Pat and Angie came running, Trisha took a look at the box. Her heart was racing with excitement. The box was certainly old. The wood was dried and dusty, the brass trim on the box was badly tarnished. It didn't seem to be locked, but Pat should be the one to open it. It was big enough to hold all sorts of exciting things.

"It was under the window seat," Rulli said, then hurried back out into the hallway as the back screen door slammed. "It was under the window seat in the attic," he called down the stairs. "It thumped funny when I jumped off. The treasure was under it."

Angie flew onto the porch. "What is it? Is it lots of money?"

Pat wasn't far behind, but he slowed down when he saw the box. His eyes grew soft, not with disappointment, but with familiarity. "Well, what do you know?" he said. "I haven't seen that for years."

"You've seen it before?" Trisha asked.

"It ain't the treasure?" Rulli sounded crushed.

Pat shook his head and squatted down slowly next to the box. "Depends on what you mean by treasure." He ran his fingers in the dust on the cover. "It's an old box that my brother and I used to keep stuff in." His voice softened until it was barely audible. "Our treasures."

"How'd it get under the window seat?" Rulli asked.

Pat shrugged. "I probably hid it there and forgot."

He pulled it open. The box was filled almost to the top with papers and photos and little trinkets. He took the top papers off and unfolded them.

"This is a story I wrote in first grade," he said with a little laugh. He passed it along to Trisha. "Man, did I ever slave over it."

The kids looked over her shoulder at the shaky block letters telling about a bunny. "You must have really been proud of it," she said.

He had already picked up the next papers. "I kept it because I figured I could use it the next time I had to write a story. I wasn't going through all that work again."

Angie snickered. Obviously a kindred spirit.

"I wrote a bunny story," Rulli said. "It was in second grade."

"Oh, yeah?" Pat looked up from the papers he was looking at. "We're bunny buddies, then."

"Yeah." Rulli looked pleased at the idea.

"I think bunny stories are dumb," Angie said, and leaned on the arm of the chair to peer over Pat's shoulder. "What's that?"

"My report card from third grade."

"Uh-oh," Angie said with a giggle in her voice. "You got a *D*."

"What in?" Rulli was trying to stand on his tiptoes to see.

Pat looked anything but pleased. "Spelling." He glared at Rulli as he tucked the report card under his bunny story. "I had a run of bad luck."

Angie snickered as she ignored the glare that was now turned on her. Trisha struggled to keep a serious look on her face.

"Hey, look at this," Angie cried as she pulled something from the box. "It's a pocketknife."

"That was my brother's." Trisha could clearly see the shadow that crossed his face. She could feel her heart go out to Pat. "I got it for him for Christmas one year and he thought it was the greatest thing he'd ever gotten."

"It's cool," Angie said, pulling the blades out.

They looked about as sharp as a butter knife, so Trisha figured Angie's fingers were safe. But was Pat? He was looking off toward the backyard, obviously lost in the past somewhere. She wished there were a way to help him accept the past, to remove that burden of guilt he seemed to always carry with him. But she knew of no way. Maybe all she could do was give him a little space.

"Look at these," she said, pulling out an envelope of old photographs.

They were faded and curled with a brown tinge to them, but even without such clues, she would have known they were old from the people in them. They were group photos, taken on the front porch of what was now Pat's house. The women were in white, frilly long dresses, the men in suits with starched collars. It must have been taken in the early 1900s.

"Who are they?" Rulli asked.

"Pat's relatives?" From the corner of her eye Trisha saw him nod. "This older couple was what, great-grandparents?"

"Great-great-grandparents," Pat corrected.

She glanced up at him. His eyes were still shadowed with pain, but it was a more distant hurt. He pointed to a younger woman amid the group.

"That's my great-grandmother."

"Was that taken on the front porch here?" Angie asked.

"Yep. My great-great-grandfather built the house."

"Wow."

The house seemed to be in all the pictures, from ones in the front yard of kids and a wagon decorated for a Fourth of July parade in the 1920s to ones of Pat with his infant brother on a porch swing. There were shots from Christmases in the living room, Thanksgivings in the dining room and just random shots of family life scattered through the place. As Pat sorted the pictures by age, Trisha could see the people grow old, but the love and happiness in the pictures didn't change.

"This is my grandfather," Pat said, stopping at one picture. "He had the loudest voice of anyone I've ever known."

Rulli peered at the picture. "Did he yell all the time?"

"He never yelled," Pat said. "He was a little deaf so he talked loud, but he never got angry or mad or yelled."

For the next several hours, Pat went through the box, telling them stories about his family. How that man fought in World War II in France, and that woman helped organize the union at the Bendix plant in town. How this was the Christmas that the turkey caught fire and how a cousin's baby was born in the house during a blizzard in the 1950s.

The kids sat as if hypnotized. They were fascinated by Pat's collection of buffalo nickels and the arrowhead that his mother had found while digging in the garden here. Trisha just sat back, watching and listening. Nothing Pat said was all that extraordinary or revealing, yet she'd never felt so close to a man.

Little by little the story of his family was coming out. His great-great-grandfather's success as a wheelwright at the end of the last century, then the gradual changing of the business as transportation modes evolved, and finally the business's rapid decline when it failed to mechanize at the right time. The family went from privileged to ordinary, from shopping in Chicago to shopping at rummage sales. Through the tale, the house in the pictures reflected the changes.

Trisha looked around at the porch. Pat was taking the house back to the old days, the better days, when it had been a showplace. If only it could in turn give him back the happiness that it had held over the years.

"Hey, look at the time," Pat suddenly said. "I need to get dinner started."

"Let's have pizza," Angie cried.

Pat was gathering up the papers and pictures and stuff from the box, but stopped to give Angie a look. "I've got a good dinner planned."

"Pizza's good," Angie protested.

"I mean good for you," Pat replied.

"Yuck," Angie said with a sneer. "You mean like that stuff they make us eat in school?"

"That's okay, Pat," Rulli said. "We like stuff that's good for us."

"I'm making food that's good to eat as well as being good for you."

"Yeah, right," Angie muttered.

Trisha quickly jumped in. "Okay, kiddies. No more arguing." Both Angie and Pat glared at her. "We're all going to pitch in and help." She herded everyone before her. "Pat, what do we need to do?"

"The potatoes need to go in the oven, a salad has to be made and I'll get the barbecue fired up."

"What are you putting potatoes in the oven for?" Angie demanded. "Cookies go in the oven. Potatoes get mashed or fried."

"I want my potatoes baked."

"Miss Stewart," Angie whined.

"Baked potatoes are good and good for you."

"Kids." Pat's voice was getting firm again. Very, very firm. "Angie, baked potatoes are good—trust me. You can put butter and sour cream on them and they're just great."

"What's a barbecue?" Rulli asked.

"It's a thing where I cook the meat outside," Pat replied. "Come on. You can help me."

"Oh, no," Angie wailed. "Miss Stewart, they're gonna get bird poop all over my hamburger."

"I am not," Pat snapped back. "And I'm not making hamburger. I'm making steak."

"How come you don't have hamburger?" Angie demanded. "Somebody rich like you should have enough money to buy something good."

"All right, knock it off." They all turned to stare at Trisha. She smiled at them. "Thank you. Now, Rulli, go help Pat. Angie, stay here with me. And nobody argues with nobody."

There was a long moment of silence, before Pat whipped his arm up in a snappy salute. "Yes, ma'am."

Suddenly his eyes were dancing as they met hers. A kind of electric charge filled the air between them. This simple sharing of joy awoke other needs within her, reminded her there were other ways of sharing. The heat of desire filled her body. Trisha felt herself leaning in toward Pat.

"Miss Stewart."

Angie's whine brought her back to earth so hard that it almost took her breath away.

"Yes, Angie?"

"I got a stomachache. Can I go lay down?"

"You're just hungry, dear." Trisha put her arm around the girl's shoulders. "Now let's get started with dinner. The sooner we finish, the sooner you can eat."

"Swell," Angie muttered, as she dragged herself toward the kitchen.

Pat looked around the crowded Harrison School gymnasium, a feeling of panic filling his stomach. Paper pumpkins dotted the walls, cornstalks and real pumpkins were strategically placed around the floor, and in the center was an Indian tepee. Parents and grandparents, intermixed with a few older siblings, filled the bleacher seats before him. He didn't belong here.

"Hi," Trisha said, coming up behind him. "You just get here, too?" She squeezed his arm. "There's some seats up there."

Without waiting for a response, she led the way up to one of the top rows of the bleachers. Was she so certain he'd follow that she didn't even have to look back and check? She sat on the bench, scooting down to make room for him. He sat down.

"I get nosebleeds up this high," he muttered.

She just laughed. "The kids are really excited about your coming. It's all they could talk about all week."

He grunted some sort of response, still not certain when he'd agreed to come. They'd been having dinner last Sunday, Angie grumping about the lack of real food, when Rulli had told him about the school program. Though Pat didn't remember ever actually saying he'd come, Angie had seemed to take for granted that he'd be there.

"If it weren't for you," Trisha said, "I'd be the only one here for them, and I don't count because I'm here for all the other kids, too."

Pat reached up and rubbed his eyes. He couldn't believe it. Here he was, a footloose and fancy-free bachelor, playing daddy to a couple of kids whom he really didn't know. How in the hell did he ever get pulled into something like this? He didn't even fit on these stupid bleachers.

"Hello, Trisha. It's so good to see you again." A tall woman in a gray pantsuit was standing in the aisle down from them. The tag on her lapel said that she was Mary MacGregor, Principal.

"Oh, I'm glad to come," Trisha replied. "The kids always put on such a nice show. You and your staff do a great job with them, Mary."

The principal stared at Pat.

"I'm with her," he said, pointing at Trisha.

"Mary," Trisha said. "This is Pat Stuart."

"Oh, the jobs man." Mary MacGregor's professional smile turned genuine as she stuck her hand out. "I'm pleased to meet you."

The best Pat could do was a weak smile in return, but he took her hand.

"Pat's here for Angie and Rulli," Trisha explained.

"Oh," Mary MacGregor replied. "Are you related?"

"No." The word came out with such force that Pat suddenly felt the heat of embarrassment filling his cheeks. "No," he repeated, in a softer and more normal tone. "I work with them a little bit when I have time. At the Boys and Girls Club."

"Pat's a volunteer," Trisha said.

"Wonderful," Mary MacGregor said. "We could use more adult volunteers in our children's programs. Especially men."

"Yeah, I know." His smile felt stiff on his face and Pat wished the principal would go away so that he could drop it. "The boys need a role model."

"It's not just the boys," Mary MacGregor replied. "Girls need an adult male in their life just as much."

Pat nodded. He and Rulli got along fine, but he wasn't sure what he was doing for Angie. They couldn't spend five minutes together without getting into an argument. In fact, he wasn't sure that the girl even liked him. Although if she didn't like him, then why did she want him at this little shindig?

The principal wandered off, greeting other guests as the schoolkids filed into the gym with their classes. Pat scanned the lines of kids, but didn't see Angie or Rulli.

"How's their uncle?" he asked Trisha.

"Still in the hospital, but getting better. They expect he'll be home tomorrow or Sunday."

"Kids must be relieved."

Trisha shrugged. "Rulli is. He thinks everything's fine, but Angie knows better. Their uncle has emphysema and a bad heart. They want to get him into one of those retirement communities where care is close at hand, but the kids couldn't live there."

"They must have other family around."

"Not any that are in shape to take on two kids."

Pat just stared out at the scoreboard across the gym. He didn't know if she was hinting what he thought she was, but it was out of the question. Sure, Angie and Rulli needed a helping hand. But it didn't have to be him.

He was a bachelor who traveled all the time. Kids like Angie and Rulli needed someone who would always be there for them. Not someone to drop in now and then. Besides, he knew nothing about kids and family. Hell, the last person he had tried to take care of was Angel, and that had been an absolute and total flop. Suddenly the dull beat of tom-toms filled the gymnasium.

"Look, there's Rulli," Trisha cried and waved.

Rulli was dressed in jeans and a plaid shirt with a straw hat on. Pat guessed he was supposed to be a farmer since the kids around him were dressed like crops to harvest. Rulli's eyes were on him, so Pat waved before Rulli turned to follow his classmates to their places.

Pat turned to Trisha, but forgot whatever it was he was going to say. Her eyes were bright, her face was flushed and her mouth was open in a wide smile.

"Look at them all," she said. "Aren't they cute?"

She was what Angie and Rulli needed—a person who understood kids and knew how to care for them. More important, she was there and available. All day, every day.

He forced his eyes back to the kids and found Angie walking in. Like her whole class, she was dressed as a Native

American. When she spotted him and Trisha, she waved wildly, making sure everyone around her knew that she had someone in the audience.

Pat waved back, but didn't feel too good. When Angie turned away, he stared across the gym at the far wall with the stupid pumpkins and moons.

This wasn't where he belonged. He should just make a stand and that would be that. Trisha belonged here. Not only was she capable but she enjoyed getting involved in other people's lives.

Sure, Trisha was stretched thin, but she just needed more help. There were other people like her in the world.

His eyes drifted down to the kids where Angie's class was getting ready to do a dance. The girl kept looking their way, her face radiating all the pride and hope and possession that he'd learned the hard way to avoid.

He didn't belong here. These kids needed and deserved a long-term commitment. They needed more Trishas at the club.

He wasn't doing the club any good sitting on his butt here in the bleachers. He was just wasting his time. He should be out doing something he was good at—like raising money so they could buy a new van. So they could hire more Trishas. So they could take care of more kids.

So he wouldn't be a square peg stuck in a round hole because he didn't know how to gracefully extricate himself.

"You're pretty quiet tonight, Pat."

Pat looked across the table and shook his head. He was sitting with Walt Butcher in a nightclub on Chicago's near-west side. A band was playing, a singer was wailing and the crowd was laughing, talking and dancing. The place was so damned noisy that Pat wondered how the heck Walt could tell that he was quiet.

"What did you say?" Pat shouted, a wry smile on his face.

"You know what I mean," Walt shouted back.

A waitress came by and Walt signaled for two refills. Pat's drink was still almost full, but he'd known Walt long enough not to argue. Walt would just say that he needed some new ice cubes.

Walt Butcher was the CEO of a venture capital firm and Pat always dropped in to visit him when he was in Chicago, to keep in touch with the money men. Sometimes finding the dollars to finance a move was the biggest help Pat could lend a firm wanting to move into his patch.

The only real problem with Walt was that he considered himself a ladies' man, having already been married—and divorced—twice. And he was now looking for wife number three, which was why they were sitting in this trendy club at 2:00 a.m.

The waitress came by with the drinks. She removed Pat's full glass after she'd placed the new one down. Walt lifted his glass to Pat and took a healthy sip. Pat lifted his glass in turn and touched it to his lips.

"So tell me about this new girlfriend of yours."

Pat stared at Walt. "I don't have a new girlfriend." Sure, Trisha was a girl who was a friend, but she wasn't a girlfriend.

A smirk slowly eased onto Walt's face. Pat definitely was not going to get into a conversation about Trisha with Walt. "I go out," Pat insisted, "but I'm not serious about anyone."

Walt turned to look out on the dance floor, taking another drink from his glass. Pat felt himself drifting into a blue funk. He didn't belong here, either. It didn't feel the way it used to.

He slowly let the air out of his lungs. His trouble was that he was letting the kids get too close. It was okay to give them money, maybe help the relatives find a job or make sure that they had a good tutor at the Boys and Girls Club. But there was nothing of a personal nature that he should be doing for them.

Fortunately, he had recognized the problem before he had let himself get in too deep. Now was the time for him to back out. Not entirely, of course. He would still do fund-raising for the club. A lot of it.

He felt himself feeling better already. He felt sorry for people having trouble making ends meet and yet he wasn't doing the thing he did best—contributing to their financial health. That would be the biggest help he could give Trisha and all the Angies, Rullis and Douglases.

Once he had helped Trisha get the club back on its feet, he could back out gracefully. That didn't mean he and Trisha had to part. Well, they couldn't really *part,* since they didn't have that kind of relationship. They were friends. And there was no reason for that to stop. He just didn't want everyone to be leaning on him. He just wasn't cut out for close relationships.

"Hey, Pat, old chum. See those two little ladies there?"

Pat looked at two youngish women near the dance floor. Their dress and makeup bordered on the exotic.

"What say the four of us go someplace a little more private?" Walt said. "You know, maybe hit a blues joint on the south side, have a little breakfast later."

The women were apparently operating with their antennae full out for they looked Pat's way and smiled. They appeared young, vital, filled with sensual energy. All signs indicated they knew how to have a good time. There wasn't a single thing about them that said "major commitment required." But Pat couldn't.

"I really ought to get going," he said.

"Going?"

"I have a breakfast meeting tomorrow morning," Pat replied. "Eight o'clock. Over at the Hilton by the airport."

It was all right to have a little evening's fun, but he wasn't here on vacation. He was here on business. And he was a mature, responsible businessman. One who had his priorities in order. One who knew how much rest he needed in order to be able to operate with a clear head.

"Maybe some other time," he said, standing up and reaching for his wallet.

"Forget it," Walt said, waving off his offer to pay.

"Hey," Pat protested. "I'm not a charity case."

"You can pick up the tab next time," Walt said.

"Yeah, next time." Pat put his wallet away. "I'll give you a call when I come in again."

"Sounds good."

"And I'll arrange my schedule a little better."

"Great."

Walt's voice didn't quite match his words. Pat could see a sagging around the corners of his eyes. Pat quickly turned away and hurried toward the door.

It wasn't as if he were leaving Walt alone. Heck, Walt wouldn't be alone long at all. Probably no more than five minutes. Besides, if he really wanted a foursome, he should have warned Pat ahead of time. He wasn't a college kid anymore. He had responsibilities. Others were dependent on him. Like the city he worked for.

Not specific individuals. He didn't do one-on-one. That wasn't his forte. But when it came to groups he was one of the best. That was his strength. And that was where he should concentrate his energy.

Chapter Nine

"Miss Stewart."

Trisha looked up from her desk to see Angie standing in the doorway to her office. "Yes, Angie. What can I do for you?"

"Is Pat coming in today?"

"I don't know. It depends when he gets back from his trip."

The young girl came into Trisha's office and plopped herself down in a seat, half lying, half sitting—a position Miss Manners would have never approved of.

"Is there anything I can do?" Trisha asked.

"Naw."

Poor Angie, Trisha thought. She was such a bundle of contradictions. She had the smile of an innocent and the mouth of a street thug. She was bossy, demanding and could be more than a little mean. Yet she was also loving and caring. She was always looking after the little kids and was a champion of the weak in any group.

"Rulli wants Pat to check his spelling homework."

"I can do that," Trisha replied.

"So can I." Angie swung her feet out in front of herself, banging the heels together. "I mean, he's got like third-grade words, you know?"

"Yes, I know."

"That's what I told him. I said, let me look at that stuff." Angie made a face and shook her head. "But, no. I can't, he tells me. He says Pat's gotta check his stuff."

"I see," Trisha murmured.

"It's like maybe only a guy is smart enough to check his work." Angie shook her head again. "I tell you, Miss Stewart, that boy's getting a little too bigheaded. He's looking for a good whap upside his head."

"Now, Angie. Rulli is growing up, and if you really want to do what's best, you'll go ahead and let him."

"Yeah." The girl's face twisted itself into a multiwrinkled frown, but even that wasn't enough to compromise the soft, angelic features. "I guess."

Trisha smiled down at the girl. When Pat had talked about his brother, he'd mentioned how hard it was to let go. And that was exactly what Angie was going through. Poor kid.

"How are you doing in school?" Trisha asked.

"Pretty good."

"Getting into any fights?"

"Nah." Angie shook her head. "Not what you'd really call fights."

Not really a fight? That was an interesting way to put it, but Trisha thought it was better not to probe. Angie hadn't been late for the club's late-afternoon study session for three weeks now. That meant that she wasn't being kept after school. If she was getting into anything, it couldn't be all that serious.

"Anyways," Angie said, "when is Pat gonna come in?"

"I'm sure it will be sometime in the next hour or so," Trisha replied. "Like I said, it depends on how soon he gets in."

"How come he's away so much?"

Trisha felt a twinge in her heart. It looked as if she wasn't the only one getting used to having Pat Stuart around. "That's his job, honey."

"So why don't he get a different job?" Angie asked.

"All jobs have good parts and some not-so-good parts," Trisha replied. "I would guess that, most of the time, Pat likes his job."

Angie made some more faces and contemplated the toes of her shoes for a while before she stood up. "Okay," she said.

"I'll tell Rulli that Pat is supposed to be here. But if he don't come by suppertime, then, like it or not, I'll look at his dinky little spelling homework."

"He might not want you to."

"Yeah, he will." Angie smiled. "All I gotta do is twist his arm. Then he does anything I tell him to do."

"Angie."

"I only twist it a little." Angie rolled her eyes heavenward. "It's not like I go around breaking his arms off, you know."

"That's very kind of you," Trisha said.

"Hey," Angie replied with a shrug, "he's my brother."

"Go do your homework, Angie."

"Sure."

Angie smiled, just as sweet as honey, and silently walked out toward the study room. Trisha shook her head and smiled. That was one female who wouldn't need any assertiveness training. Although, she was only ten now. One never knew how things would turn out as she grew older.

Trisha turned her eyes back to the paperwork in front of her; unfortunately her attention didn't follow. She'd thought Pat was coming in today. At least she'd hoped he would. She hadn't asked, but there was no reason that she should. It wasn't as if she owned him. Or as if she wanted to.

For a moment—the briefest of moments—an image danced before her eyes. A tall man with light brown hair, bare chested and muscular, with a heavy leather collar around his neck and a chain hanging from that.

"Damn it, Pat," she muttered under her breath. "Get over here."

"Hello."

Trisha looked up and screamed.

"Well, thanks a lot," Pat said.

"I'm sorry," Trisha said. "You startled me."

"You were talking to yourself."

"I was concentrating on my work," she said. "A lot of people do that."

She tried glaring at Pat but that resolve quickly melted away as she saw the stress lines at the corners of his eyes. Poor guy. His out-of-town trips were so filled with meetings that he rarely got a good night's sleep on the road.

"I'm glad to see that you could get here," Trisha said. "A lot of people have been asking for you."

"Who? Has my secretary been calling here?" He slumped into a chair and wiped his face with his hands. "There's no reason for her to do that. She has the number for my pager and for my cellular phone."

"No, silly." Trisha felt a lightness about her and laughed. "Angie's been looking for you."

"Great."

"Oh, don't worry." Trisha laughed again, feeling an almost uncontrollable urge to get up and hug him. Her hands wanted to smooth the worry lines from his face. "She's not angry with you."

"Lucky me."

"Actually, Angie's not looking for you for herself. Rulli wants to see you."

"What does he want?" Pat's tone was that of a man who had won millions in the lottery and had just been told that a distant cousin had called.

"He'd like you to check his spelling homework." Trisha could feel a tiredness creeping into her voice. "He's apparently taken your little talk to heart and is determined to improve."

"Why should I check it?" Pat asked. "Is his tutor a no-show again?"

"This doesn't have anything to do with the tutor. He won't even let Angie check it." Trisha paused a moment, searching Pat's face for even the tiniest sign of compassion and care. Was any there? She felt her stomach tighten, rapidly working its way toward knot status. "He thinks you're interested in him and his work."

Pat shook his head. "Maybe I should straighten him out."

"Oh, hell." Trisha had gone straight from worry and concern to anger. She did not stop at annoyance. "Maybe you should just go home."

"Look," he said sharply. "What's important is for him to be interested in his work."

"I know that. But Rulli's just a kid."

"That's what's important." Pat went right on, obviously choosing to ignore her words. "Not whether I'm interested, or

Angie, or you—or Santa Claus. No one is there for the tough times except the person that you build inside yourself. Just you. No one else."

"I understand all that." Her voice was growing louder and Trisha stopped to take a deep breath. "But there are times in everyone's life when they need a helping hand. And right now, that's where Rulli's at."

"Great." He turned away from her and looked out toward the club's study room. Tension radiated from him like heat from a sunlamp. "Great."

Trisha took another deep breath. It appeared that Rulli wasn't the only one needing a helping hand. "Why don't you go home, Pat? Come back when you feel better."

"There's nothing wrong with me," he snapped.

"I didn't say anything was wrong. You just appear to be tired."

"I'm tired of being pushed into areas where I don't want to go. Where I don't fit."

He seemed exceptionally irritable today. Had something gone wrong on his business trip? Or was it more of a personal matter?

"I don't understand," Trisha said. "What do you mean, 'don't fit'?"

"Ah, forget it." Pat stood up. "If I have to explain it, you wouldn't understand anyway."

"Thank you." Trisha could feel her own irritation rising to meet Pat's. "Since I'm too dumb to understand, perhaps we shouldn't be having this conversation."

"Where's Rulli?" he asked, looking out over the study room. "I'll check his damn paper and then I'll go home."

She was about to tell him to just go home, forget about Rulli, but he was already out in the study room. For a moment she considered running him down and getting him out of the club. But nothing would be gained from making a scene. Instead, she just kept an eye on him.

As she watched, Rulli turned, his face lighting up when he saw Pat. Trisha steeled herself to see disappointment cross it when Pat made some curt remark, but it never happened. Rulli's smile stayed bright.

Pat sat down next to him, his hand mussing the kid's hair slightly in what had to be a fond gesture. Trisha just stared, a puzzled frown taking hold of her lips.

Pat unlocked the door and trudged into his house. It was dark and smelled as though it resented being closed up for the past two days. Great, just what he needed—a house with an attitude. He tossed his briefcase on a table in the foyer, then stooped down to collect the mail from the floor under the mail slot. A few bills, a few magazines and more than a few ads. He tossed them next to his briefcase and went on up the stairs.

For a moment, he wished he had someone there to greet him. Someone who was glad to see him, regardless of his lousy mood.

Jeez, what a wish. He loosened his tie and went into his room to change clothes. He didn't need somebody or something there to lean on him. About all he could handle would be a ghost, though with his luck, it would be his grandmother and she'd scold him night and day.

Pat grimaced as he tossed his suit coat on the bed, then followed it with his tie, shirt, then belt. No, today especially, he had no urge to run into his grandmother. She would give him holy hell.

He'd acted like an ass. A first-class one at that.

He sat on the bed to take off his shoes, but instead just lay back and stared at the wavy pattern on the plaster ceiling. He'd had no reason to snap at Trisha, no reason to be so ungracious.

Except that he was so damned scared.

No matter what he was doing, Trisha and the kids were on his mind. They were haunting him more thoroughly than any ghost could. Never having been haunted before, he wasn't sure how to react. So he reacted like any normal, red-blooded man—he struck out and showed everybody how tough he was. Now he felt even worse.

Well, what are you going to do about it? he could almost hear his grandmother ask.

What was he going to do about it? Was he going to lie here all night, thinking up excuses, or was he going to be a man and apologize?

It wasn't Trisha's fault he had been so weak lately. It wasn't her fault that he couldn't get her eyes out of his thoughts, or that he heard the sound of her laughter everywhere. He just had to be a man about it and ignore it.

He knew all the shadows that lay in his soul. He knew that no one should ever lean on him, and it was up to him to make sure no one did.

Wearily, he sat up and pulled his shirt back over his head. No sense in letting Trisha's anger ferment into something even bigger. He'd go over and explain. He'd just tell her that.

Tell her what? That he was infatuated with her? That she danced through his dreams, both waking and sleeping? That when he was near her all he wanted was to take her in his arms and make mad, passionate love to her?

No. He'd tell her he'd had a headache from too little sleep. And jet lag—that was plausible. And maybe even a touch of air sickness—those little planes flying over Lake Michigan could cause that real easy.

Yep, that was what he'd do. He go over there like a man and lie to her.

"Hey, you two," Trisha shouted. "Cut that out."

Lucy had bitten Sniffles on the butt and now they were facing each other down with ears back and tails flicking.

"What is it with everybody today?" she asked. "Is it something in the air?"

Neither cat paid the least bit of attention to her, since it would mean taking their eyes off their companion. Trisha went to the sink, wet her hand and splashed them. That drew a snarl of protest from both and they ran into the dining area, where they sat glaring at her.

"Fine," she told them. "Now you both can be mad at me. It'll give you something to do besides biting each other."

She turned away from their sullen faces and gave her attention to final preparations for her dinner. It looked pretty much done so she turned off the heat on the electric skillet and put a cover on it. All she had to do was slice the tomato for the salad and she could sit down to eat. But as she was reaching for the knife, the buzzer for her front door sounded.

"Swell. Just what I need—somebody else to bug me." The cats raced her to the front door. "Get away from there. I don't want either of you dashing outside."

Their attitude indicated they were going to do what they darn well pleased. Trisha glared at them before looking in the peephole.

"It's Pat." Neither of the cats looked particularly impressed. "I wonder what's wrong now."

"Hi," he said, as she swung her door open.

"Hello."

As they stared at each other, Sniffles leaned against Trisha and howled.

"I guess he's mad at me, too," Pat said.

Pat was wearing his crooked, aw-shucks grin, but Trisha had no intention of being taken in by it. "I never said I was mad at you."

"That's right, you didn't." He paused to look down at both cats, who were now sitting on their haunches looking up at him. Then he looked back at her. "Are you?"

Her inclination was to pitch him in the river across the street, but he was one of the money men in this town. And her kids needed a lot of money. "Is there anything I can do for you?"

"Well," he replied. "I was thinking that if you were mad—"

"I said I wasn't mad at you," she snapped.

"Oh." He looked down. "That's too bad."

The hell with the money. She should just go ahead and pitch him in the river, then stand on his neck to make sure his head stayed under water.

"Because I was thinking that if you were mad at me—"

She considered screaming, but she didn't think it would have any effect on him. His skull appeared to be three inches thick and surrounding a pea brain.

"—I could bring you a peace offering." He bent toward the side of the door and picked up a box, showing her the top. "Like a cheesecake, for instance."

She felt her anger slipping away, like a slowly leaking tire. Desperately her mind raced around trying to find the leak and patch it. She'd been nurturing her irritation all evening and she didn't want to let it go.

"And—" he held a can up for her to see "—I brought along some cherry topping."

Trisha clenched her fists. The man didn't fight fair at all.

"Have you eaten yet?" she asked.

"No."

"All right, then. Get in here."

"Yes, ma'am."

Pat stepped quickly into the room. He'd barely closed the door when Lucy leapt onto his shoulder and began nuzzling his ear. He blinked in surprise but didn't do anything to dislodge her.

"Lucy," Trisha snapped. "Get down." She snatched the cat off his shoulder and dropped her on the floor.

"Don't worry about it," Pat said. "She was just saying hello."

Trisha turned and stomped off into the kitchen. She knew exactly what Lucy was doing. She just didn't like a traitor.

The cats raced her to the kitchen and hopped up on the counter. Pat shuffled along after them, looking reasonably subdued. Unfortunately, the man was very sneaky, so Trisha knew that she'd have to maintain her guard.

"I just threw some hamburger and vegetables together."

"Great."

"I've used up the lettuce," she said. "But we can stretch it with tomato, cucumber and green pepper."

"Whatever," Pat said. "Don't go out of your way for me."

"I'm not," Trisha said. "I'm doing it for the cheesecake."

"That makes sense."

Trisha kept her face set firm. There was no way she was doing anything for him. She had enough taking care of kids during the day. She didn't need to expend energy caring for him.

And she didn't need that Boy Scout smile, either, so he'd better be careful. Let him start joking with her, trying to make her laugh in any way, and he would be wearing a generous portion of hamburger stew around his ears.

"You cut the vegetables for the salad," she said. "I'll set the table."

"Yes, ma'am."

"And don't start anything," she said as she snatched out napkins and silverware. "Not if you know what's good for you."

"I'm really sorry about this afternoon," he said.

She glanced over at him, trying to read what lay behind his words, but his eyes were on the tomato he was slicing.

"It was a long trip," he said.

He'd only been gone a few days, not like last time when he'd been gone more than a week.

"Jet lag, you know." He did glance at her then, but his eyes darted away. "Then we hit a lot of turbulence over the lake."

"I see." It had been a warm, windless day, but then that didn't mean that there hadn't been turbulence, she guessed.

He cut a few more wedges of tomato in silence, as if the task needed great concentration, then looked back up at her. His eyes were cloudy, as if the turbulence was resting inside.

"Hell, the trip was fine and the flight was smooth," he said, a trace of his earlier curtness in his voice. "It was just that I kept thinking about you guys. Wondering if the kids were doing all right in school, you know. I didn't even have a chance to drop in at the office before I came out to the club."

Was this supposed to make her feel warmer toward him? That cheesecake had better be damn good. "You didn't have to come if you didn't want to," she pointed out. "Nobody's holding a gun to your head."

"Damn it, that's just it," he snapped. "I did want to."

She stopped getting the plates out, holding them in midair as she turned toward him. "So why are you so angry?"

He looked away, his anger seeping away as his shoulders sagged almost in defeat. "Because I did want to come," he said, "I'm not good at relationships. I never have been, yet I seem to be getting sucked into this one whether I want to or not."

She turned, getting the plates out and then the wineglasses. "Well, all I can say is that you certainly are a silver-tongued devil. I would never guess that you have trouble maintaining relationships, not with such flowery phrases at your disposal."

He was behind her then, his hands on her shoulders and turning her to face him. His eyes bespoke of an inner torment that wanted to tear at her heart.

"I don't know what to do," he said. "In the past I've always ended up failing the people I care about. They need something from me I haven't been able to give."

"That can't be true," she said, shaking her head.

The touch of his hands on her seemed to befuddle her thoughts, make her mind work in slow motion. The anger that had been her protection was gone. She felt alone and vulnerable, exposed to all the wild winds of his hurt.

"I failed Angel," he said. "I couldn't make him see his life was going nowhere."

"That's one person, supposing what you say is even true."

"I failed my father. He needed more than I could give him to make him stop drinking."

"He made his own choices. He was an adult. You were a kid."

"I was seventeen when I left."

"You were a kid." She slipped her arms around his waist, pulling him closer to her, closer to the heart that wanted to give him solace.

He seemed ready to take it. His arms pulled her even closer and he laid his head against hers. "I just don't want to hurt you or the kids."

She closed her eyes. His heart was beating so close to hers, racing along with an urgency that was soon echoed in her own. "How could you hurt us?" she whispered.

"I don't know." His voice held a desperation. "I just don't want to take a chance."

She pulled back slightly so that he looked down at her. His lips were so near, so tempting. She reached up and lightly brushed them with hers. "You have to stop worrying so," she told him. "No one's asking anything of you."

"Yes, they are. That's what a relationship is."

She loosened her hold on him slightly so that her hand could slide over his chest. She could feel how strong he was, how much a man. Yet there was a fear in his voice, a worry in his eyes that came from the little boy he once was.

"So what am I asking of you?"

He frowned. "Work with the kids. Help at the club."

Her hand stopped its roaming, instead playing lightly with the top button of his shirt. "No, that's the other me. The club director. I'm talking about me the woman, right now."

His eyes met hers and seemed to drink deeply of all the messages that lay there, but he just shook his head. "I'm not sure," he said.

She just laughed and laid her head against his chest. "Neither am I," she admitted. Sometimes the tenderness in her heart betrayed her, led her onto paths she wasn't certain she should take. His embrace turned comfortable, a place of refuge from the contradictions of her soul.

"So what are you asking of me right now?" he asked.

"To stop grumping," she said.

"Okay. Consider me stopped."

She looked up into his eyes. A gentleness rested there that tore at her peace of mind. It was so tempting, just to walk softly and bask in that sweet caring.

"I want you to hold me for a while," she said.

"I can do that."

A need flickered in her heart. A boldness crept into her desires. "I want you to keep the demons away for just a night."

His eyes darkened with sudden shadow.

"Not for forever," she whispered. "Just for tonight. I don't want to be alone."

She wasn't sure where the hunger had come from, or the fear suddenly of being alone. The fear that, even for a night, she would not find love.

"Is that really what you want?" he asked, his voice hoarse.

"The demons always come back," she said. "The fears. The worries. I just want tonight."

"I can give you that."

It was somehow enough and somehow everything. Where had this hunger come from? Where had these hidden needs sprouted from? She had been so content, so at ease with her life, and now suddenly, at the touch of his hands, her heart wanted to explode. She had to feel his warmth around her, had to live in his touch.

Pat's lips came down to claim hers, setting her heart afire. She pressed closer to him, as her own mouth begged answers from his soul. As her spirit tried to find reason amid the madness of her desire. But his nearness only caused the flames to leap higher and higher, consuming any last shred of sanity that lingered.

"This is insane," Pat murmured. His lips had moved from hers and were dancing across her cheeks, lighting flames along her forehead and breathing warmth and yearning into her soft curls.

"I know."

And it was. But wonderful insanity. She had no fear in her heart, no worries about tomorrow. Just for a night, she needed to belong. She needed to trust and believe and throw off her fears.

"What do you say we get more comfortable?" she suggested and slipped loose of his arms, but only long enough to pull the plug from the electric frying pan.

"That's getting more comfortable?" he teased, but his voice betrayed the heat raging in him.

His hunger was intense; she could feel his needs in the urgency of his touch, in the way his lips claimed hers once more in a blinding torrent of desire. It was as if she had suddenly awakened a ravenous lion or a forest fire that needed to consume everything in its path.

His touch lit a fire that she could not stop or even slow. There was nothing but Pat, nothing but the two of them and the night that lay ahead of them with sudden promises of joy.

"Maybe we really should get comfortable," she said.

"Got another pot to unplug?"

"Watch it, fella," she said with a laugh. It came out shaky as her voice quavered, but her sense of rightness and power and surety lent a strength to it also.

Trisha took Pat by the hand and led him into the bedroom. She silently closed the door and stayed leaning against it. Her eyes slowly caressed him, reveling in the certainty of her delight.

He took a step closer, his eyes glowing with his hunger even as his arms opened to her. She wasn't aware of moving, but she was suddenly in his embrace and her heart was full. His hands owned her, moving with magical possession over her back, slipping under her blouse and unhooking her bra. There was a freedom in his passion that allowed hers to rise and dance with him in the heavens.

"Oh, sweet Trisha," he murmured into the night.

But his hands on her bare skin were anything but murmuring. It was as if they were shouting of the wonder the two of them could create. Of the splendor that their embrace in love could bring. She closed her eyes, letting the magic swarm over her and swallow her up with its promises.

"Are you sure we ought to be doing this?" he asked.

She let her eyes open and slowly drank of the needs in his eyes, mixing them with the hungers of her own soul. "How can we not?"

"Easy. I go home and lie in the freezer." His laugh was weak. "You can keep the cheesecake."

She just reached up and began to unbutton his shirt. "Silly man," she said. "Of course I keep the cheesecake. You gave it to me."

"Did I?"

But his words were lost as their lips met again. They clung and drank and whispered phrases of love even as their hands built the fires into a raging storm that would not be denied. They moved as one toward the bed, leaving clothing as a trail to be followed back to sanity. But only if one wanted.

When they finally fell together onto the bed, their hearts were ready. His hands had taken possession of her soul, stealing it away so that she was able to answer only the dictates of her body, of that mindless hunger that wanted Pat to complete the missing half of her being.

She opened her heart to him and her body, taking him into the essence of her soul and letting his fire devour them both. His hands could not—would not—stop their glorious caressing. Together they soared higher and higher until they were above the night, above the world and its petty ties, above the fears that kept her awake in the darkness.

They were magic and wonder. They were splendor and rightness. Together their hearts were life itself, filled with a power that could know no bounds. Then the stars exploded around them, their souls danced and laughed and sang of magic, before slowly gliding back to earth on the gentlest of breezes.

Trisha closed her eyes and was more than content. She was happy.

Pat's eyes flickered as he danced on the edge of wakefulness. Suddenly his breath stopped. He wasn't in his own bedroom and it sure as hell wasn't a motel. There was a soft ambience in the air that—

In the dim light sneaking around the closed blinds, he saw two golden eyes staring at him from about two inches away. No, they were glaring at him.

He edged back slightly and found that the eyes were attached to a cat. A cat? Where had a cat come from? He'd never heard of a ghost in the house, let alone a feline one.

Suddenly the cat moved and caught the light differently. It was Sniffles. And he didn't seem approving.

Memory came washing back along with wakefulness. Pat was at Trisha's apartment. He'd come over to apologize. She'd invited him for dinner, only that had gotten a little delayed. Then after dinner and a slow savoring of the cheesecake he'd brought, they'd fallen prey to those treacherous emotions again. A fact that didn't seem to have slipped by Sniffles's notice.

Pat turned gently on the bed so as not to waken Trisha. "All right, all right, I get the message," he said under his breath to the cat. "This is your spot, not mine."

As he turned, he caught a glimpse of the clock—3:40.

Oh, hell. He had barely an hour to get back home, take a shower and be on the road. He had a breakfast meeting in Indianapolis at eight o'clock.

He slipped out of bed, causing another protest as a sleepy little cat sat up where his legs had been. Lucy yawned, then muttered a squeaky complaint. Great—one was mad because he stayed, another was mad because he was leaving. He couldn't make anybody happy. Story of his life.

Yet he was pretty sure he had made Trisha happy last night. He knew she'd sure turned his world upside down. The sex had been pretty near perfect.

Pat picked up his clothes, frowning into the darkness. That word sounded so clinical, as if Trisha were a nonperson. As if he'd been dancing with a stranger in one of those old-time, dime-a-dance clubs. Meet, touch, then never see each other again.

"We made love," he whispered to Sniffles and grabbed his shoes.

But his heart quailed at the words. They seemed to imply an emotional union that sex was only a small part of. And he wasn't ready for that. Certainly not now. Probably not ever.

He sneaked out into the living room and turned on a light. Both cats had followed him out. They did not bring any great wisdom with them.

"You guys didn't have to get up, you know."

Sniffles just glared.

"Hey," Pat grumbled as he put on his jockeys. "It isn't like I just had my way with her."

Sniffles continued glaring, as if in disbelief. But Pat knew it hadn't been just him wanting the closeness.

He picked up his shirt and slipped it on. "It was mutual desire. We both wanted it."

Lucy began washing her face while Sniffles looked away.

"Who are you to complain, anyway?" Pat picked up his pants. "You're just a cat. A pet."

If looks could kill, Sniffles would have struck Pat dead in a second.

Pat pulled his pants on. "I mean, she likes you and all, but she might want more in her life, you know."

The cat's glare increased about a hundredfold, but Pat barely noticed. What if she did want more in her life? Just what did that mean? And was he prepared to be what she wanted? He decided that when he came back from his trip he'd start cutting ties, not make new ones.

He sat down to put on his shoes when a blur sped by him and became a light weight on his shoulders. Lucy had come aboard.

"See, Sniffles. Lucy likes me."

The male cat looked away, and somehow Pat felt bound to explain things to him.

"I would never hurt Trisha," Pat promised. "I care about her. I really do, and I wouldn't hurt her any more than you would."

Sniffles seemed to snort as if he'd been in on Pat's thoughts over the past few days. As if he knew that the best way for Pat not to hurt people was for him to stay away from them.

"Hey, I know what I've been thinking," he assured the cat. "That it would be better to pull away some. But that was with the club stuff. This is different. And I'll be real careful not to let things get out of hand. That shouldn't be too hard with me on the road so much.

"Speaking of which—" he glanced at his watch "—I'd better get off my butt or I'll never make my breakfast meeting."

Pat moved quietly back to the bedroom door. "Come on," he said, motioning to the cats. "Keep your lady company." He held the door open while both cats trotted in; then he went to Trisha's side of the bed.

"Trisha." He touched her shoulder gently. "Trisha."

"Hmm?" She turned toward him and slid her arms around his neck, but he wasn't sure if she'd opened her eyes.

"I gotta go."

"Unnn."

"I have to. Remember, I have that meeting in Indy?"

She moaned softly, deep down in her throat, causing Pat to look quickly at the clock. Then he shook his head. No way. He'd never make that meeting.

He bent down and kissed her, deep and long, then let her go. "I'll call you later. Maybe we can have dinner if I'm back in time." He stood up, and walked to the door.

"Pat?" Her voice was barely a breath on the night air.

He stopped, his hand on the door. "Yeah?"

"Drive safely."

"I always do, kid. I always do." Then he quickly—very quickly—made his way outside. It was a good thing he didn't have to walk away from her every morning. He'd never get to the office, much less take a trip out of town.

Chapter Ten

Life was certainly interesting lately, Trisha thought as she munched on a french fry. Across the table from her, Pat was frowning in distaste as he nibbled at his hamburger. Next to them both, Angie and Rulli were wolfing down their dinner.

"I'm going to get a refill on my tea," Pat asked. "Can I get you anything?"

"No, I'm fine. Thanks," she replied.

She watched as he walked back to the counter of the fast-food restaurant, unable to keep her eyes from following him. Her emotions had been on a roller coaster the past few days. One minute she had been missing Pat while he was away, the next she was hurt and angry because of his attitude when he'd returned. The wonderful ecstasy they'd shared last night had been followed by gloom and uncertainty this morning. But when he'd called her late this afternoon about dinner, she'd forgotten everything except how much she was learning to care for him. That knowledge should have been scary, but somehow it was too right to be.

"Pat and Trisha sitting in a tree . . ." Angie sang out.

Trisha turned to smile at the girl. "What's this? Dinner entertainment?"

Angie wasn't to be deterred. "So what's going on? You got the hots for Mr. Stuart?"

Trisha tried to keep the blush from washing over her cheeks, but knew she was unsuccessful. "Mr. Stuart and I are friends," she said.

"Uh-huh."

They were, regardless of that knowing look in Angie's eyes. Last night hadn't changed that. Maybe it had strengthened the friendship, deepened the bond, but it hadn't changed the basic relationship. Trisha didn't think she was up to explaining that to Angie though, even supposing she wanted to. She was glad when Pat sat back down.

"Hey, Pat," Angie said.

He looked across the table at her. "Yes, my dear?"

His voice was teasing, but Angie's smile quickly turned to a frown. "You see any horns on my head?" she asked.

"No," Pat replied carefully, cautiously, as if he were fearful of where he was suddenly treading. Rulli knelt up on his seat to stare at Angie's head.

"That's 'cause I ain't a deer," she said. "Bambi's a deer and you know what happened to him? He got shot."

Pat's eyes reflected a touch of tension. "I thought it was his mother that got killed."

"Well, if he didn't get shot, then something ate him," Angie said. "That's the way it works if you're a deer."

"Lady deer don't have horns," Pat said.

"I ain't a lady, either," Angie pointed out. "I'm a woman."

Trisha tried to catch Pat's eye, trying to warn him to just back off, but his gaze was on Angie. There was no winning these discussions, Trisha knew, but Pat so hated to let Angie have the last word.

"What's the difference?" Pat asked.

Angie paused to suck in a mouthful of milkshake. "Ladies kiss butt. Women kick butt."

Pat looked at Trisha but all she did was laugh. "You had to ask."

"And people say men are violent," he grumbled.

"But when we kick butt, we do it different," Angie went on. "When we're done, we smile and say stuff like 'excuse me' and 'have a nice day.'"

"Finish your french fries," Pat said.

Trisha laughed again and patted his hand. He looked so cute when Angie got the best of him. "You're getting quite an education here."

"I am indeed fortunate."

"Can I have some pie when I'm done?" Rulli asked.

Trisha just looked at Pat. This was his treat. He just shrugged as if he didn't know what the big deal was. "Yeah. You finish your fries, you can have whatever you want."

"Can I have your car?" Rulli asked.

The two kids squealed in laughter, falling back in the seats as if they were suddenly too weak to sit up.

"Good one, Rulli," Angie said.

"Yeah." He nodded his head, eyes shining like an eager little puppy. "I know."

Trisha couldn't help but laugh with the kids. At times, Pat was such an innocent. For all his tough west-side background, the kids seemed able to worm their way around him awfully easily.

He frowned at her, no doubt because of her laughter. "I really appreciate your help," he said.

"This is a rough world, fella." She picked a french fry out of the package in front of him, warm comfort surrounding her like a shawl. She had never felt so much a part of something, so content. "If you don't learn to take care of yourself now, you never will."

"Like I said, thanks."

"Don't mention it."

She smiled at him and his eyes softened; his lips curved into a smile that was powerful enough to curl her toes in her shoes. There was fire in his gaze that said he remembered their passion of last night. And that hunger was lying restless just under the surface. That whenever she wanted to rekindle that flame—

"Hey, Pat, I'm ready for my car."

Pat blinked, looking as if he'd just awakened from a deep sleep.

"I mean, my pie," Rulli said, going off into hysterical laughter.

Angie joined him. "Good one, Rulli," she said after a moment.

"I know."

Pat looked at Trisha. "I feel like retching."

"It'll be easier to pay for the pie," Trisha replied.

He reached for his wallet and gave each of the kids money for dessert. They dashed off to the counter as he slowly returned his wallet to his pocket.

"They're certainly high tonight," he said, turning to watch the kids wait their turn impatiently.

"They were going home to an empty house again," Trisha said. "It was a surprise that they could talk you into taking them, too."

"For me, too." He turned back to her. "To be honest, when I came to pick you up and the kids were around again, I wondered whether it was a ploy to avoid being alone with me."

Trisha reached over to take his hands in hers. His eyes seemed to swallow her up and, for the moment, she let them. But there were things he needed to understand. Last night hadn't changed much of anything in her life. Except that little part that she gave to him. "The club is part of me," she said. "That's just who I am. I can't put the kids aside when it's my time to leave for the day."

"So I'm learning."

There was something in his voice that she didn't understand. Something that almost made her afraid. "You didn't have to take us all out," she said, her heart pulling back slightly. "Or I could have paid for the kids."

He made a face at her. "You don't really think I'd begrudge the few dollars for their dinner, do you?"

"No."

"In fact, I would have gladly spent more to go someplace that served real food," he said. "It's just that a dinner for four wasn't my plan for the evening. I was thinking of the two of us at a more intimate little restaurant. Tablecloths, delicious food, plenty of wine."

She tightened her hold on his hands, needing for him to accept her as she was. "We can do that some other time."

Something inside him seemed to give way and he nodded. "Sure. Some other time."

Trisha leaned forward with a sigh. "The kids really needed this," she said. "They had a meeting with Jessie Adamanti this afternoon."

"The social worker?"

Trisha nodded. "She's hoping not to have to put them into foster care where they could get split up and tossed from home to home, but there aren't too many couples looking for older kids. There is one that's a possibility, but she's afraid Angie may be a bit too much for them."

Pat's eyes grew stormy. "Angie's a good kid. She can be a pain, but she's a good kid."

Trisha shrugged. "But she's not everybody's idea of a perfect little girl. She's not into ruffles and lace. She's doing well if she combs her hair—curling it would probably cause her pain. And she wouldn't be caught dead with a doll."

Pat glanced over to the counter where the kids were contemplating their purchases as if they were vital to national security. "They don't seem too worried."

"Rulli probably doesn't know and Angie wouldn't show fear if she was dying."

He kept on watching them. They made their choices and were paying for the desserts. He turned back to Trisha. "Would they really separate the kids?" he asked.

"If there was no other choice."

He seemed to share her worry. His eyes were quiet, his mouth a tight little line. "Angie's a tough kid," he said. "She's going to make it, I know. But not if they take Rulli from her."

"Unfortunately, it may not be in anyone's control."

"Maybe if I talked to this Adamanti woman," he said. "You know, explained things to her about the kids..."

Trisha just shook her head. "Jessie doesn't need things explained to her," she said. "She's a good, caring person. She knows the kids and knows what they need."

"Yeah, but—"

"This isn't a contest where, if you act the toughest or the fastest, you'll get your way," she said.

"I know that. But the squeaking wheel gets the grease."

"The wheel is already squeaking the loudest," Trisha said. "And it's getting all the grease there is. If that one couple doesn't work out, Jessie said she'll feature the kids in the

'Sunday's Child' column. They have good results finding homes for kids with that.''

Pat seemed to relax. "I just want things to work out for them.''

"We all do.''

He nodded. "Yeah, I can see that.''

"Hey, what are you guys doing?'' Angie asked. She had a chocolate ice-cream cone and was devouring it as if she thought it might vanish.

"We're just talking,'' Trisha replied.

"What about?'' Rulli asked. He had a cherry pie and red was smeared around his mouth, making him look as if he were grinning.

"Oh, nothing much,'' Trisha said.

"Yeah, right.'' Angie licked her cone, all the while staring at Trisha and Pat. "If you were talking about nothing, then how come you're holding hands?''

Trisha glanced down and found that their hands were indeed still clasped. She pulled her hand back quickly.

Rulli snickered. "Good one, Angie.''

"Yeah, I know.''

"About the other night,'' Pat said as he took a left on Western Avenue. "I didn't mean for it to happen. That wasn't my plan when I came over.''

Trisha turned from the window. His voice had been careful and controlled, as if he'd rehearsed his speech. "I never thought it was.''

"I just wanted to make sure you knew,'' he said.

She let her eyes dance over his face, at least the part that she could see, but it didn't give her insight into his sudden confession. "I thought it was something spontaneous.''

"It was.'' He shrugged. "But we never got a chance to talk about it and I didn't want you to think—''

Trisha just laughed. He was so sweet. "Do you think I'd be sitting here in the car with you if I thought you'd taken advantage of me? I would not have abandoned cleaning my closets for you, even if it is a gorgeous fall afternoon.''

"Well, I didn't know.'' She was sure he was trying to hide it, but she couldn't help laughing at his little hurt sound.

A hint of guilt covered her sun and she leaned over to slip her arm through his. She laid her head on his shoulder. "Don't pout," she teased. "It was very nice of you to clarify things. It's the mark of a true gentleman."

"I'm not a true gentleman," he snapped.

She sat up, frowning at him. "It's not an insult, you know."

"It's a misnomer," he said, sounding irritated.

"I see." She didn't understand where this all was going. Was he back in his grumpy mood of the other day? "You're not a gentleman, you're not a hero, and you're not a role model. Anything else you aren't that I should know?"

"Probably lots." He sounded so tense suddenly, so serious.

"And I suppose it's just a coincidence that all those roles involve someone admiring you. Involve someone approving of your behavior."

"I just think everyone has strengths and weaknesses," he said. "And my weaknesses aren't anything to do with inter-personal relationships. I'm much better working on a busi-ness level. You know, negotiating a deal, finding the fi-nancing—that sort of thing."

"Impersonal things," she said.

"It's better to know who you are and be honest about it, than to lead people on."

Suddenly everything became clear. He needed to know she wasn't about to slip chains on him. "You haven't led me on, if that's what you're worried about," she told him. "I'm en-joying our friendship, but I'm not looking for it to be any-thing more. Honest. I barely have enough time for the life I have now. I can't take on anything else."

"I feel the same way."

"I'd like to go on as we are," she said. "As friends."

"That sounds perfect."

He reached down for her hand, and squeezed it. There seemed to be no reason to let go, so she didn't and just laid her head against his shoulder once more. She felt so comfortable with him, so much as if they belonged together. Though she did have some misgivings about this little shopping trip.

"So, as my friend," she said after a moment, "one whose strength is in financing deals, do you really think we should be doing this? I mean, before we even have the money?"

"We're just looking today," Pat said. "We need to get an idea of what we're talking about so we'll know how much money we have to raise."

"I just don't want to get my hopes up," she said. "We might find out we can't buy anything for months and months."

"It won't be that long."

"That's what you say," she said.

"Boy," Pat said. "You have a very cynical outlook on life."

"It must be the company I'm keeping."

"Swell." A car was pulling out of a spot in front of the dealer's door and Pat pulled into it. "I knew I'd get blamed sooner or later."

"Good." She released her seat belt. "Then I didn't disappoint you."

Suddenly his arms were around her and he was pulling her to him, tilting her chin up. "I don't think you could ever do that," he murmured before bending down and kissing her.

The world and all its burdens disappeared. There was nothing but the two of them, nothing but the fire raging in their hearts and the needs that his touch awoke in her. Together they could find a world of wonder and beauty, a world where only joy existed and only sunshine ever reigned. His arms tightened around her, and her heart cried out its delight. This surely was heaven. There could be nothing more perfect.

Slowly they pulled apart. Trisha found it hard to breathe and gazed ahead at the building. She remembered herself that they were just friends, but the racing of her heart seemed to mock her. So what? There were different kinds of friendships, that was all.

"That man's staring at us." A white-haired, older man was standing behind the big glass doors, smiling at them. Trisha grinned at Pat. "I guess they don't get too many people parking here to make out."

"We weren't making out," Pat said. "I just gave you a little kiss."

"Same thing."

He gave her a look. "If you think it's the same, you had very sheltered high school days."

"My high school days were just fine, thank you." She flashed him a knowing smile. "Maybe not as exciting as yours, but just fine."

"Since my high school days consisted of working and studying, a saint's was probably more exciting." He opened his door. "Want to have dinner tonight?"

"Sure."

He'd brushed aside his high school days as if they'd hardly mattered, but Trisha couldn't let them go as easily. Her teenage years had been fun if she subtracted her anger at her father. There had been parties and friends and secrets passed in the hall between classes. Mainly it had been a time of trying on all different personas, of being safe because she had her own little clique, and of planning the future from a protected distance. Pat came around to her side and opened the door for her.

Maybe this was why he was so serious. Maybe he'd never learned to have fun. Was that something that you could learn later? She wished she knew how to bring joy into his life.

Pat helped her out of the car. As he was closing the door behind her, the salesman bore down on them.

"Good afternoon, folks." The salesman's grin grew wider as he stuck his hand out. "Jerry Barber."

Pat took the man's hand. "Hi, Jerry. Pat Stuart."

"A pleasure meeting you, Pat. What can I do for you and the little woman?"

The little woman? Pat had turned to introduce her, but Trisha just shook her head. A devilish urge had taken hold of her.

"We'd like to look at some vans," Pat said.

"Sure thing." The man's eyes lingered for a split second on Trisha's stomach—checking for signs of pregnancy? "How about a minivan? We got a lot of young folks like you buying them. Then, when the family comes, they're all ready."

"No, that won't do." Trisha smiled sweetly at the man. "We need a standard-size van."

"I see." He laughed heartily, obviously trying to show that he was a with-it guy. "Expecting a lot of kids, are we?"

"Yes, we are," Trisha said. "Six or eight. Although we might end up with as many as twelve."

"Twelve?" He appeared to pale, then smiled. "Right, right. Sometimes you give the neighbors' kids a ride."

"No," Trisha said. "No neighbors."

The salesman blinked a few times. "Yeah, that's the way it is these days," he said. "The kids you live near aren't the ones your kids want to play with. No one goes to a neighborhood school anymore."

"Oh, mine will. I—we—" she flashed a smile at Pat "—we firmly believe in neighborhood schools."

"Ah ..."

Was he actually at a loss for words? "So," she said, "do you have large vans or not?"

"Oh, yes," the salesman replied, waving them toward the south edge of the lot where a row of shiny new vans stood. "We sure do, Mrs. Stuart."

Mrs. Stuart. Suddenly her urge to tease the man fled as his words echoed in the breeze, shimmering in the air and smiling at her. They felt remarkably nice, like a taste of chocolate when you were expecting only the bitterness of coffee. Mrs. Stuart.

She shook her head. Hadn't she been listening to her big speech a few minutes ago? About how they were friends and she had no time for anything else? Or her words from several weeks back about not trusting a man without skinned knees? Maybe she needed to make recordings and play them often.

"Twelve, huh?"

She struggled to come back to earth and found the salesman facing her as they walked across the lot. "Maybe," she said. "You know how it is. One comes, then another and before you know it you've got ten or twelve."

"Uh-huh." He gave Pat a forced smile, then waved at the vans ahead of them. "I'm not sure you could seat twelve in them, but eight would be no problem." He hurried ahead to whip open the side doors of several.

Pat bent his head close to her ear. "Are you always this nasty?"

"Hey," she protested, "what was nasty? He's the one who called me a 'little woman.'"

"I just have one question. Are you going to say 'excuse me' or 'have a nice day' when you're done?"

For a moment, Trisha was puzzled; then she remembered Angie's definitions last night and burst into laughter. "I just might," she said.

His arm slipped around her. "Boy, I'd better be careful what I say."

"At least you were warned." She couldn't help but move a touch closer, to feel his strength just a bit more around her. "You have Angie to thank for that."

The salesman was standing beside the door of a blue van. "Now, this is a really nice model," he said. "Leather seats, automatic transmission and power windows and locks."

A million things for the kids to break. "I think we need something a bit more basic," she said.

"Well, we have a nice one just over here without the power package."

"Hey, don't aim low," Pat said. "Pick exactly what you want and we'll find the funding."

"I want practical," she said as they followed the salesman over to a red van. "The kids would kill power windows in a week playing with them."

"Maybe they'd surprise you," he said.

She wouldn't doubt it. Everything lately was a surprise. It was as if she were living in one of those glass balls and someone had shaken it up. But instead of snow falling, happiness was.

"Table for two?"

At Pat's nod, the woman led them to a table in the far corner. A candle flickered on the table, its glow supplemented slightly by the dim lighting in the room. He was glad to see a linen tablecloth and napkins on the table. That should mean that real food would be available. And that would mean that he could show Trisha a good time. It was about time.

"This is very nice," Trisha said, looking around them. "I don't get out to eat too often, and sure never have time to drive up to Michigan for it."

"It is nice," Pat agreed, but his eyes were on her.

After shopping for the van, he'd dropped her off at her place and then had gone home to change. He'd told her to dress casual, that he wasn't going to wear a suit on a Saturday, but even casual looked good on her. Her snug-fitting pants did vicious things to his peace of mind, and her navy silk blouse only added power to the punch. If he hadn't been sort of involved with her before, this outfit would have pushed him into it.

"Good evening, folks." A large man in a white apron came toward them. "I'm Charlie." He shook hands with Pat and bowed toward Trisha. "You are newcomers to Charlie's Dining Room, right?"

"We are," Pat replied. "But you come highly recommended."

The chef acknowledged the praise with a quick, short nod. "How about a glass of white zinfandel? On the house."

"Sure," Pat replied.

"That's very kind of you," Trisha said.

"Not really. It's just good business."

"True," Pat agreed. "But if our meal turns out half as good as I've been told, we'll most certainly come back anyway."

Charlie laughed, a deep sound that echoed in his body. "I was thinking bigger than another meal." He waved his hand toward the back of the restaurant. "I've got a nice little banquet room. When you're ready, I'll take care of you."

Pat was puzzled and just a touch worried. A number of his acquaintances had spoken highly of this place, but no one had mentioned that the owner was a bit strange. "I'm from South Bend," Pat said slowly. "I'm not sure I can bring many business meetings up here to Michigan."

"No, no, no." Charlie's laughter boomed out, the sound waves filling the room and rattling the pictures on the walls. "I'm talking about your personal business."

Pat and Trisha exchanged quick, puzzled looks. She didn't appear to have a clue, either, as to what the man meant.

"You're a nice young couple," Charlie said. "You're going to spend time together. Then you'll want to spend more time with each other. And more. Until one day, you'll want to join your hearts. Then I want you to come up here and ask me to cater your wedding reception."

Pat just stared at the big man. First of all, how did he know they weren't just friends? Or married already? Or relatives?

"And you know a lot of people, my friend." He dropped a huge paw on Pat's back. "So it'll be a big reception."

This was just all too weird. "How do you know we're not married already?"

"Because you aren't." The chef shook his head. "You have a glib tongue, but numbers do not lie."

Pat stole a glance at Trisha. She was staring at the man, a small smile on her face. Or maybe it was fear. It was time to put an end to this nonsense. "That's very interesting, but—"

"I saw your license plate when you pulled in," Charlie said. "Then when you two walked in, your aura followed you."

"Yeah," Pat said. "I noticed it was a little foggy in here."

Charlie went on as if Pat hadn't said a word. "It'll be a winter wedding. The weather will be cold but the food will be hot. Almost as hot as your love for each other. And many people will come."

This was getting to be too much. "I'm hungry," Pat said and turned to Trisha. "Aren't you?"

Trisha didn't respond. She was still staring at the chef. It had to be because her mother had raised her to be polite, not because she was buying any of this nonsense.

"You shall have many children and a lifetime of happiness."

"That's good," Pat said, trying again to bring them back to real life. "But what I'd really like right now is some menus."

"I feel a struggle," Charlie said.

"Not unless I have to wrestle you for a menu."

"Your numbers are clear and sharp, written in the stones that define the path of your life. I see the number seven."

Pat frowned and glanced Trisha's way. He wished he could tell what she was thinking.

"Seven?" she said with a slight laugh. "You sure it's not twelve?"

Pat laughed, his heart relaxing.

Charlie just shook his head, not impressed apparently with their frivolity. "No, seven is your number."

This was getting too weird for words. "Well, it is close to seven o'clock," Pat said. "Does that count?"

Charlie suddenly reached over to the nearby counter, then handed them each a menu. "My specials are on the board in the corner. *Bon appétit.*"

The chef turned and slowly walked away, leaving behind a huge, silent vacuum. Pat tried focusing on the menu but the letters just danced before his eyes.

"Here you go." A tall waitress with a snake tattooed on her left forearm placed glasses of water and wine before each of them. "Now don't let Charlie spook y'all."

Pat looked from the waitress to Trisha and back again. "Spook? We're not spooked."

"Charlie's heavy into this numerology thing." The waitress, like her boss, didn't seem to listen too well. "I guess it's using numbers to tell the future. I don't know." She shrugged. "I'm not into that kind of stuff myself."

"Neither am I," Pat said firmly.

"Well, I'll be back in a minute to take your orders."

As she walked away, Pat brought the words on the menu into focus. "How about you?" he asked Trisha without looking up. He thought her joke had been answer enough. He thought they had gotten a lot settled this afternoon, but maybe he ought to be certain where he stood before he went rushing off into the quicksand. "Do you believe any of this numerology stuff?"

"Oh, I don't know."

He looked at her. He had meant his promise to Sniffles that he wouldn't hurt her, and he didn't want some kooky chef to break it for him.

"Don't worry," she said, a chuckle bouncing in among her words. "I'd never get married in the winter."

She was studying her menu, so he couldn't see her eyes. She was joking. At least, he hoped she was. He would assume she was.

"Yeah," he agreed. "Me, neither. Your hands would go numb so you couldn't put the ring on. Your nose would run. And your lips would freeze together when you kissed." He shook his head. "Horrible."

"Horrible," she agreed.

The heaviness in the air dissipated as Pat took a sip of his wine. It was delicious. The evening lay before them, all its magical promises still intact. "I think I'll have the goulash," he said.

"I'm going to have the chicken paprika," Trisha said.

"Great. Maybe we can sample each other's food."

"That would be fun."

They smiled at each other. She was beautiful, she was fun to be with and she was so levelheaded. Pat took her hand and raised his glass to her. "To a pleasant evening and fun."

"Hear, hear," she answered. "To fun."

They crossed the state line from Michigan into Indiana, where the commercial development was heavier and the lights were brighter. He glanced at Trisha out of the corner of his eye.

The changing amounts of light played on her face, bringing out a different aspect of her beauty every few moments. Trisha was like a diamond. Every time he looked at her, he saw something new and more beautiful.

"It's still kind of early, isn't it?"

"Uh-huh," she replied.

Pat felt his cheeks warm as he realized how high schoolish his remark had sounded. "Want to drop by my place?" he asked.

"Are you going to want me to pay for my meal?"

"N-no," he stammered. "Of course not."

"Oh, good." She turned toward him, putting out a smile he could have read by. "I thought you were going to make me rake leaves."

They shared a laugh and he reached out to hold her hand. "I wasn't going to make you do anything," he said. "I did think we might watch a movie and have some popcorn. But you can close your eyes and refuse to eat if you want."

She just laughed and laid her head on his shoulder. It felt so right, it almost hurt. How had he gotten so lucky to find someone so perfect for him? Someone who was so easy to be with and expected nothing in return?

They rode in silence because no conversation was necessary to fill the edges. Once he pulled into his drive, he went around quickly to help Trisha out her door. His grandmother would approve of his manners, or was it just that he didn't like Trisha's hand out of his for longer than absolutely necessary?

"You actually could use some help raking leaves," she said, shuffling her feet through the pile that had blown up on the sidewalk.

"I'll call you if the guys I hired don't show up."

"Okay."

They held hands and walked up the steps and across the porch to the front door. As he pulled his keys out, Pat hesitated just a moment. He'd never had a woman over to his house like this and the evening seemed special. As if he ought to break out the champagne. He unlocked the door. Trisha would think he was nuts.

They went inside and he flipped on the lights. The house looked surprisingly warm and welcoming. He led her back to the small parlor where he kept his TV.

"Can I get you something to drink?" he asked.

She shook her head. "No, I'm fine."

She certainly was that. More than fine. He watched the slow sway of her movements as she walked over to the sofa. He followed, drawn as if she were a magnet, and sat beside her.

"What's on?" she asked.

It took him a long moment to realize she meant on television tonight. "I don't know."

Didn't care, either, but he hadn't asked her here with any purpose in mind other than to share her company. He looked around and found the remote control. He flicked on the set, then flipped through the channels.

"Oooh, that's a good one," Trisha said as some old film came on.

He had no idea what it was but tossed the remote to one side. Whatever she wanted was fine with him. "What is this?" he asked.

She settled in on the sofa, sliding down slightly so that her head was on his shoulder. "Some old movie," she said.

He let his arm go around her, just to let her know his shoulder was hers for the using. "I knew that much. Does it have a name?"

"Who needs a name?" she said. "These old movies are easy to figure out. See, now that girl is one of the bad guys."

The light fragrance of her cologne was surrounding him, teasing him with her nearness, like strawberries in February teased you with the promise of spring. He tried to concentrate on the movie. "Have you seen this before?" he asked.

"No, but she's wearing a daring dress and too much makeup. In the old days, that spelled trouble."

"So I'm safe because you're not wearing much makeup?"

She turned and gave him a pretend glare. "Maybe my makeup is more subtle."

"So I am in trouble?"

"It remains to be seen." She turned back to the movie, much to his disappointment. "Let's see what role you're suited for."

A man walked onto the set. "How about him? Who's he?"

"That's the hero," she said. "See how conservative his suit is and how open and trustworthy his face is."

"That must be me, then," he said. "Hero material."

She gave him another look before turning back to the screen. Another man came on. "Now that's you. Suit's a little too snazzy, and his eyes a little shifty. The guy's obviously a rat."

"A rat?" he cried. "I'm a rat?"

"Hey, you've told me you aren't a hero," she pointed out with a definite smirk in her voice.

"Yeah, but I never said I was a villain."

She turned so that she was effectively in his arms. "Yeah, but villains are more fun."

It was hard to think coherently when she was looking at him that way. When her softness was there in his arms, ready to be held and touched and explored. He leaned in and kissed her softly. "Whatever the lady wants, the lady gets," he murmured into her lips.

"Ooh, what a nice attitude," she teased, but when his lips strayed from hers, she moved to bring them back.

It was getting harder to think, harder to remember why anyone would want to. She was so soft, so inviting. Her lips drove him insane. He wanted to drink in all of her, to feel alive in ways that only she could make him feel.

His hands moved over her silk blouse; the smooth, slippery fabric only tormented him, though, for it wasn't as sweet as her skin. He pulled it from her pants so that his hands found the real silk, the real softness. He roamed over her back, pulling her closer so that his lips could taste deeper and deeper of her magic.

When her hands began to return the explorations, all hope of sanity was lost. The world was on fire, and all rejoicing with it. He needed her with a driving hunger that swept all else from its path. Nothing existed but her and the needs she awoke in his heart. He'd felt so alone and with her he felt whole.

The night slipped away as they gave their hearts free reign. First, there in the parlor, locked in her arms, he found heaven as he had never dreamed it existed. Sweeter and hotter and more driven than the other night at her apartment.

Then later, when he couldn't bear to take her home, they found passion again, safe in the warmth of his bed. But the night was so much more than shared desires, than moments locked in fervor.

The magic was in lying together, close so that their hearts beat as one, as they fell asleep. It was in waking briefly in the night to find he wasn't alone, and falling back asleep with her tucked safely in his arms as if she'd never leave. It was peace in the deepest, darkest corners of his soul.

Chapter Eleven

Trisha balanced the tin of brownies in one hand, a container of soup in the other, and pushed the car door closed with her foot. After skirting around the other cars in the street, she reached the sidewalk. The neighborhood where her mother lived was beautiful at any time of year, but it was especially gorgeous today. The colors of the changing leaves were vivid against the blue sky, the river seemed to be singing as it raced along and jack-o'-lanterns grinned happily from doorsteps and porches.

Trisha couldn't believe that Halloween was almost upon them. The past two months had gone by so fast, thanks to Pat.

"Trisha!" Her mother stood at her open door, waving Trisha in. "About time you got here."

"Hi, Mom." Trisha hurried down the walkway toward her. "How are you?" She gave her mother the food and a quick kiss to the cheek.

"Have I got a surprise for you!" Her mother pulled her inside.

"You've decided we're not going to rake leaves today?"

Her mother closed the door. "Oh, don't be such a smarty-puss." She took Trisha by the hand and dragged her into the living room. Trisha's brother and his family were there.

"Hi, Tish."

"Bob. Susie. Great to see you guys." Trisha hugged first him, then his wife. "And Kelly and Trent," she said as she bent down to hug her niece and nephew. "Boy, have you two grown."

Trisha laughed as she stood. "And to think I vowed years ago I would never say that to a kid."

Her mother just chuckled. "That's what happens when you get old. You find yourself doing all the things you vowed you'd never do."

Bob started to laugh. "Does that mean Tish is going to get married?"

"You never can tell," Trisha's mother said. "She has been seeing someone for a while now."

"Ooooo, really?" Susie cooed. "Tell all!"

Trisha felt her cheeks heat up. "There's nothing to tell. I've gone out a few times with a volunteer at the center, that's all." That's all? Those two nights of passion flashed through her thoughts and the blush in her cheeks deepened.

It didn't escape her brother's notice. "Oh, ho, Tish. What are we hiding?"

She just smiled sweetly at him. "Nothing. Absolutely nothing. Now, aren't we supposed to be raking leaves?"

"I'm sure we'd rather hear about your love life, dear," her mother said.

"Except I have nothing to tell." Trisha turned to the kids. "Want to go outside? We've got lots of leaves to play in."

"All right!"

The kids raced ahead of Trisha to the door, where she turned back to the others. "If I remember rightly, Mom has lots of rakes."

Bob groaned. "Well, that hasn't changed. She's still watching to see if everybody does their share."

They followed her out to the backyard. Trisha got a rake from the garage and started raking under the old oak in the corner. It was a glorious day. Just the right nip in the air, just the right amount of sunshine. Susie joined her.

"All kidding aside," Susie said, "have you found somebody?"

Trisha raked the deep red leaves into a pile for moment before answering. "He's a friend."

"That's a great start."

"No, I mean that's all we want to be," Trisha explained. Avoiding Susie's gaze, Trisha carefully pulled a twig from the tines of her rake. "Neither of us has time for a big-deal relationship."

"That's not always something you choose."

"It can be," she said. "If you're careful."

Trisha stood for a moment, letting the slight breeze ruffle her hair. On the other side of the yard, Bob was chasing the kids, trying to toss handfuls of leaves at them. He wasn't even coming close, but the kids were squealing in pure delight.

Trisha glanced at Susie and saw she was watching Bob and the kids, too. Yet her eyes were not reflecting laughter; they were filled with love—total, unabashed adoration of her husband and kids. Trisha felt almost as if she were prying, watching such devotion.

What would it be like to love someone so much? To feel that you were such a part of their lives? Trisha felt suddenly left out. As if she were watching a play that she'd never have a part in, and it saddened her. She turned slowly back to her raking and Susie joined in her efforts.

By the time they had a reasonable pile raked up, Bob and the kids had joined them. Bob had his own rake, but the kids were more interested in jumping into all the piles. Trisha's heart ached a bit as she watched them. Would she ever have a love to hold her through the night? Kids of her own?

"They can be a real handful," Bob said.

Trisha looked up to find her brother watching her. And reading her mind apparently. "Oh, I know they are," she said. "I'm around kids all the time, remember?"

"It's different having your own."

"I suppose." This was the one thing she'd found most annoying about her brother—the fact that he was an expert on everything.

"I always pictured you as having a lot of kids," Susie said to Trisha.

"I do," Trisha replied. "We have almost a hundred members in the West Side Boys and Girls Club."

"No, I mean your own. You know, like seven maybe."

"Seven?" Trisha's voice was more of a squeak, and she rushed to clear her throat. "That's an odd number. And a lot for this day and age."

Susie just laughed. "Oh, I figured you'd have a few, adopt a few and gather a few more in other ways."

"I see." Trisha went back to raking, more industriously this time. Seven? It was just a coincidence. They happened all the time. Nothing to get all hyper about. Nothing to pay any attention to.

"So what are you guys doing in town?" Trisha asked brightly. "I thought you usually timed your visits around the Christmas holidays."

"Actually, we're looking for a house."

"Not here," Susie said quickly. "In the Chicago area."

"I'm joining a small accounting firm in Chicago," Bob said.

"Great," Trisha said.

"We'll be a couple of hours away from here," Susie said. "And not too far from my folks in Springfield."

"They'll be glad of that."

"And so will Susie," Bob said. "She didn't like California."

"Not a bit." Susie shook her head. "I like the changing seasons. I want to see a real winter."

"You're my witness, Tish," Bob said. "I'm going to need help the first day we get a windchill of minus forty degrees."

Trisha laughed, then laughed even more as Susie took off after Bob with a huge handful of leaves. He shouted his protests as the kids yelled their encouragement. Trisha just watched as Susie caught him and dumped her leaves on him. He retaliated, catching her so that they both lost their balance and fell into the leaves, laughing.

"They seem really happy, don't they?"

Trisha turned to find her mother at her side. "Yeah, they do."

"Sometimes I used to worry," she said slowly. "You know, that your father's and my divorce would sour you two on marriage. But it didn't seem to affect Bob."

Because he barely noticed, Trisha thought sourly. He was almost out of high school at the time and lived with Trisha and their mother only for that last year. Then he was off to college. Between visits to their father and summer internships, he had never really called their home his after that. He had never been there when their mother was struggling to make ends meet, working one job while taking night school classes to get a better job.

"I think everything that happens in our lives affects us," Trisha said slowly. "The good stuff and the bad."

"But I never wanted to make you afraid of marriage."

Trisha forced a laugh. "Afraid of marriage? Where did you get that idea? I'm not afraid of it. I just don't have the time."

Her mother's eyes were not laughing with Trisha. "And how would marriage take up more time?" she asked. "Instead of sharing your life with your cats, you'd share it with a man."

Trisha went back to raking. "I like my cats."

"You ought to have a man you like more."

"Hi, Ben."

"Pat, good to see you." The president of the chamber of commerce came around his desk to shake Pat's hand, then, putting a hand on his shoulder, directed him to a sitting area in the far corner of his office. "To what do I owe this visit? You got another piece of good news for the city?"

"Not today." Pat shifted in the chair. "I'm here with my hat in hand. I need some money."

"Personal or business?"

"It's for the West Side Boys and Girls Club."

"I understand that's become somewhat personal for you."

For a moment, Pat stopped in surprise. Was that a twinkle in Ben's eyes? "The club needs a new van," he finally said.

"Have there been problems sharing yours?"

"No." Pat shook his head. "We've had no problems with sharing. The problem is that my department's vehicle isn't suitable for the club. It doesn't provide enough seating for the kids."

Ben just nodded, that little smile still in place as if he were seeing some private joke.

Pat tried to ignore it. "I've negotiated a price with Oberlin Motors," he said. "What I need now is twenty thousand dollars."

"Has Trisha checked for the availability of grants?"

"No," Pat replied. "I'm doing this on my own."

"I think Trisha is more familiar with the grant request process than you are," Ben said.

"I know." Pat shifted in his seat. "She did an informal check before. She got the word that things were fairly tight, especially since it was so close to the end of the year."

Ben nodded. "She'd probably have a good chance for next year. If she submits now, people can enter the request into the queue."

"I was hoping to get it done this year," Pat said.

"That could be a problem." Ben put his hands behind his back and leaned back. "It's too close to the end of the fiscal year for most agencies."

Pat liked Ben. The older man had been a strong friend in the three years that Pat had worked in this town, but today he felt a growing irritation build within him.

"Twenty thousand isn't all that much," Pat said.

"Depends on who you talk to," Ben replied with a shrug.

"You know we could get this van thing taken care of today. You kick in ten K and I put in another ten. One, two, three. It's all done. Finito."

Ben just shook his head. His eyes had lost their twinkle. "I like going through regular channels."

Pat looked away for a moment. He'd thought he was coming here man-to-man. Friend-to-friend. Instead, he was feeling the way he had the day he'd gone to see Angel's second-grade teacher and she kept brushing him aside, saying she wanted to talk to their father.

Damn it, though. Pat wasn't eleven anymore. He could handle things himself. "Trisha could—" He stopped and took a breath. "I mean, those kids could really use that vehicle now."

Ben leaned forward. "You're making this kind of personal, aren't you?"

They exchanged stares, unblinking.

"It's okay to take a personal interest in Trisha Stewart," Ben said. "But you have to be careful about letting that attitude get in the way of your business dealings."

"What the hell are you talking about?"

"Come on, Pat." Ben tilted his head to the side slightly, a smirky kind of grin on his face. "This is a small town."

Pat just glared back. How much did Ben know? On the other hand, since his relations with Trisha were personal, what the hell business was it of anyone's?

"No one's saying that you're doing anything wrong," Ben assured him. "There's just a feeling around that you're partial to Miss Stewart's projects." He shrugged and his smile grew slightly. "Actually, that you're partial to Miss Stewart, period."

"Yeah, so what?"

"I didn't say anything was wrong," Ben protested softly.

"I volunteer at the club and work with a couple of kids." Pat found himself growing more irritated. "And we've had dinner a time or two."

"Pat." Ben leaned forward on his elbows and looked him in the eyes. "You're both young and unattached. What you folks do with your own time is no one's business but your own."

"Damn right," Pat snapped.

"But when it's personal," Ben said, "you have to be careful about how hard you twist arms for Miss Stewart's club."

"It isn't her club," Pat snapped. "It belongs to the neighborhood."

"You know what I mean." Ben leaned back and looked away a moment. "I guess things got off on the wrong foot here. I'm sorry. Maybe I was out of line. But you really need to let this grant request go through normal channels."

Pat was about ready to explode with anger, but knew that would accomplish nothing. He stood up. "You're probably right."

"It's a good cause, Pat. And early next year Trisha will have her new van. I promise."

"I thought the vehicle would belong to the club."

"Come on, you know what I mean. She's been there a few years now so Trisha and the club kind of get interchanged in people's minds."

Not in his mind. That kind of mix-up would never happen. The club was an organization. Trisha was a warm, loving, beautiful woman. The club had a charter. Trisha had a warm body.

"Let her keep using the development committee's vehicle," Ben said. "I'll make sure she has a new one by January. February, at the latest."

The way these things went, that meant maybe March but certainly April. Pat felt his lips tighten. "Well, thanks for your time," he said.

"See you at the chamber luncheon next week?" Ben asked.

"Yeah, sure."

He walked Pat to the door. "How you coming with that new warehouse over in the airport industrial park?"

"They plan to make a decision by December 1." Pat shrugged. "I think we have a good chance."

"That's good. Real good." Ben opened the door. "What was that going to be, about sixty or seventy new jobs?"

"Something like that."

"Well," Ben said, putting an arm on his shoulders, "we all appreciate the good work you've been doing for the town."

Normally Pat was well-disposed to hear good words from Ben. He'd always thought the man was a straight shooter, but today... today Pat just wanted to get out of there.

"Thanks." He slipped away from under Ben's hand and hurried out the door.

"Oh, Pat."

Gritting his teeth, he turned.

"She's a fine, young woman. Intelligent, charming, and everybody likes and respects her."

"Shouldn't you be telling that kind of thing to her board? She doesn't work for me."

Ben grinned. "Have it your way, but just make sure you take good care of that little lady. We're all very fond of her."

Pat could only nod his head, then hurry down the hallway. Once around the corner he leaned back against the wall and slapped it once with the bottom of his fist.

Take good care of her. What the hell was going on? He and Trisha didn't have that kind of relationship. Why was Ben telling him to take good care of her?

Take good care of her. The words echoed in his head. They didn't have that type of relationship. Or did they? Was everyone else seeing what he was too blind or stubborn to see?

Take good care of her. The refrain seemed more stubborn than the most annoying ad jingle. He couldn't be responsible for taking care of her. He couldn't be responsible for taking care of anybody.

The balloon exploded with a blast that killed off the chatter and laughter in the study room. And added an extralong cut to the mouth of the jack-o'-lantern Trisha was carving. She looked over at Pat. He was pulling the neck of the burst balloon off the tank nozzle, a look of extreme annoyance in his eyes. She went over.

"You okay?" she asked.

"Why wouldn't I be okay?" he asked and reached into the box for another balloon. "It was just a stupid balloon."

They were decorating the club's study room for tomorrow's Halloween party, and ever since Pat had arrived about half an hour ago, she'd thought something was wrong. He seemed distant, silent and unsmiling. She'd thought he needed a mindless task such as filling balloons with helium gas, but now she wasn't so sure.

"It was just a defective balloon, that's all." He slipped another one on the tank and filled it.

"Maybe we should have someone else do that for a while," she said.

He pulled it off and knotted the neck. "I only broke one balloon," he pointed out wearily. "If your budget's that tight, I promise to buy replacements for all of them that I break."

He sounded so tired, so lifeless. "It's not that," she insisted. "I thought you might want a rest. These jobs can get boring."

He shrugged. "Life can get boring."

Maybe letting him work alone wasn't a good idea. She could cheer him up easier if he were by her side. Besides, she liked having him near.

"Come on." She slipped an arm through his. He remained as stiff as a board but did come with her. "You can help me hang the streamers."

"I'm supposed to blow up these balloons," he said, indicating the box full of balloons.

"I'll have Jeff do them."

"Why? Because I can't?"

"No," she replied, putting on the cheerful tone she used for the little children who got whiny. "I just want to give someone else a chance to do it."

He made a slight face and looked at her.

"Hey, that's a very desirable job." She pressed a finger to his nose. "There were a lot of complaints that I was playing favorites when I gave it to you."

"Who was complaining?" he asked. "Jeff?"

Trisha laughed and hugged his arm to herself. "I need a strong body to lean on," she said.

"Maybe what you need is a telephone pole."

"You can't hug a telephone pole," she said.

"Of course you can. They're what? About eighteen inches in diameter. That shouldn't be any problem for you to put your arms around."

Normally these were the kinds of words they used in their verbal byplay, but tonight's tone wasn't right. There was no laughter in his voice.

"I want to string some streamers," she said. "I need someone to hold the ladder. It's a bit wobbly."

"Yeah, okay. I can do that."

"You sure?"

He stopped and stared at her. "I just stand there and hold the damn thing. What's so hard about that?"

"I just didn't know if you were feeling well."

"I'm fine." But his eyes didn't meet hers, darting away like a little kid afraid of getting caught.

"Okay," she said slowly. She let her arm slip out of Pat's and he made no move to retrieve it. Come to think of it, he'd made no effort to keep it there earlier, either.

Trisha stopped at the ladder and picked up the roll of crepe paper. "I was just going to drape this along the edge of the windows and doors," she said. "Or do you have any other suggestions?"

He just shrugged. "Whatever," he said. "Looks all the same to me."

She sighed, her eyes willing his back to her, but his gaze continued to roam. She climbed up the ladder and taped the end of the paper to the window frame, then came back down. When Pat just stayed there, unmoving, she tapped the ladder.

"Could you move it down a few feet?"

He did as she asked, no words needed. She taped another section of the streamer, then came back down. This time Pat moved the ladder on his own, but it didn't really signal an improvement in his mood.

"Is something wrong?" she asked.

He looked at her as if she'd inquired about the health of his cobwebs. "No."

"Have a hard week?"

"No harder than normal."

She climbed up to hang some more streamers only because she'd run out of questions. Or maybe chickened out of them.

"You don't have to come tomorrow to help," she said when she'd come back down.

"That's okay."

What did that mean—that he was coming or not? She didn't have the guts to ask. One more climb up the ladder and that section of windows was done. In silence they moved to the next one.

"How's that warehouse project coming?" she asked.

"Okay."

"Doesn't it get discouraging to work on these projects and then have them go someplace else?"

"Sometimes."

Didn't it get discouraging to try to find out what was wrong and not get anywhere? Extremely. This was a small window and done too quickly. They moved on to two more doors and then they were done. And she was no closer to cheering Pat up. In fact, she'd picked up a share of his gloom.

"It's starting to look pretty good, isn't it?" she said, looking around the study room.

A couple of workers were tying the balloons to the backs of chairs. Another was arranging cornstalks and uncarved pumpkins in the corners. A giant spiderweb made out of yarn had been stretched across the back wall, and earlier in the week, the kids had painted Halloween scenes on the office windows that looked into the room.

"Yeah, great."

But there was about as much excitement in his voice as in her heart. It was probably just his job, she told herself. He had a stressful job with lots of traveling. It had to wear him out at times. Maybe she should feel good that he was relaxed enough with her to let go when he was tired.

Her heart thought she was stretching it a bit, but her mind refused to mull over it anymore.

"Well, let's get to the jack-o'-lanterns," she said. "I think they're all that's left to do."

Chapter Twelve

"Miss Stewart. Hey, Miss Stewart," Angie called out.

Trisha glanced up to see a witch and a hobo bearing down on her. "Yes, Angie," she said, returning her attention to the task at hand. She was trying to repair a paper crown for a young king who had gotten into a shoving match with an Arabian princess. "What do you need?"

"Clarissa says we need the tubs," Rulli said.

Trisha nodded as she fitted the crown back on the king's head.

"You know, the ones we're gonna use when we bob for apples."

"Yes, I know what you're talking about, Angie." Trisha patted the still-sniffling king on the back and gently pushed him back toward the crowd. "There you go, Robbie. Now don't start anything more with Amanda. You know how she is when she gets angry."

Two little girls came skipping over. "Look, Miss Stewart. We're princesses, too."

Trisha looked down at her own Gypsy costume. Perhaps it was a bit outdated. "Isn't that wonderful?" she said.

"Miss Stewart," Angie repeated, tugging at her sleeve.

"Oh, yeah." Trisha reached in her pocket. "You want the key to the storeroom."

"No," Angie replied. "We want the tubs for the water."

"I know. And the tubs are in the storeroom, which is locked, which is why you need the key."

"But somebody's gotta carry the tubs for us."

"How about Kevin?" Trisha asked.

"He can't," Rulli said. "Harry Gordon's got a bloody nose and he's tryin' to make it stop."

Trisha sighed. She couldn't leave her post; at least she shouldn't.

"Maybe Pat can get the tubs," Rulli said.

"Nah," Angie said with a sneer. "He's a grump. He don't wanna do nothin'."

"Maybe he don't feel good," Rulli said.

Trisha glanced toward her office where she had last seen Pat and found him still there, one of the few adults here not in costume. He was leaning against the wall and frowning out at the sea of little bodies undulating around him.

"I'm sure he'd be happy to carry tubs for you," Trisha said. Well, maybe *happy* wasn't the right word. But she was sure he'd do it. "Go ask him."

Trisha had hoped his mood last night would just be a temporary thing, that it was just the result of a bad day or not enough sleep or eating the wrong thing at lunch. However, he'd arrived just as sour today.

No, that wasn't fair. It wasn't that he was really crabby and snapping at everyone. It was more that he was apart from them all. As if he'd built a wall around himself and would let no one close.

She watched as Angie and Rulli made their way through the crowd to where Pat stood. He took the key from Angie, but there was no lightening of his expression. In a few minutes, he was back with the tubs, carrying them over to the tables that Clarissa had readied. Angie and Rulli were bouncing around, full of energy and excitement, but Pat seemed to be in a different world. Once Clarissa started filling the tubs with a hose running from a maintenance room, Pat went back to his post by her office.

Staying along the walls where the kid density was the least, Trisha was able to get to his side. "Hi," she said, wanting to take his hand in hers, but he was so stiff, so forbidding. She shoved her hands in her pockets. "How are you doing?"

He looked at her. "All right." He looked away again.

She wished he would hold still for a minute so that she could see into his eyes. She needed to find reassurance there. She needed to learn that whatever was bothering him had nothing to do with her. That in an hour or so, or even a day or two, he'd be fine. But every time she tried to pin his eyes down, his gaze darted away.

"Your costume's great," she told him above the noise.

That caused him to glance down at his jeans and short-sleeved shirt.

"Your standard businessman-after-work getup," she explained.

He didn't crack a smile. "I was never much into Halloween."

Was that at the root of the problem—did this party bring back bad memories? She could understand that about Christmas or his birthday, but Halloween? What kind of bad memories could be associated with it?

She leaned in closer so she didn't have to shout. "Halloween's always been one of my favorite holidays," she said. "I loved pretending to be someone else for a few hours."

"So I gathered." His gaze swept across her Gypsy costume. "You look like one of the kids."

There was no fooling herself that he meant this in a positive way. She bristled slightly and looked away herself. "Well, I don't need anybody to walk me home," she said loudly. She could play the game as well as he. "Or tuck me in at night."

"That's good to hear." There was no emotion in his voice, no anger, no impatience. They might as well have been discussing crop rotation in Outer Mongolia, for all the interest his voice conveyed. If he wanted to be left alone, why couldn't she just leave him alone?

She couldn't. Did that make her pathetic or caring? She wasn't sure she wanted the answer. "Another hour and we'll start clearing them out. Most of the kids'll be ready to go home, but there are always a few diehards."

"I imagine," he said.

"Miss Stewart." A devil had come running over. "My horn's falling off."

Trisha pulled out the hairpins that had been anchoring the horn to the little girl's hair.

"Maybe I should go outside and take a look around," Pat said.

Trisha looked up from her repair job. "Ray will take care of that."

"Ray?" He frowned at her. "Ray who?"

"Ray Kazur. He's an off-duty cop. He helps out at all our parties." She finished pinning the horn back on. "There you go, Stacy. Good as new."

The girl bounced off, allowing Trisha to let her breath out slowly. Did Pat really want a breath of fresh air or did he just want to get away from her?

She looked over the room. The face painting in the corner seemed to be winding down, but the apple bobbing was going full tilt. The noise level wasn't lowering any. Maybe that was what was getting to him. She could barely hear herself think and she was used to the noise.

"If you want to step outside a minute, go ahead," she said. "We have enough adults here to cover things."

"That's all right."

"Now's the time to take a break," she pushed. Maybe he needed a short time-out. "We have less than an hour to go, but then there's cleanup."

"I'm fine."

"Cleanup shouldn't take long, though," she added, then took a deep breath. She felt like a novice about to go off a high dive. "Maybe we can go out afterward? Someplace quiet."

Pat's eyes searched the crowd for a century. Her stomach grew tight, her hands sweaty.

"I think I'll take a rain check," he said. "I'm a little tired. I wouldn't be good company." He pushed himself away from the wall. "I think I will take you up on that fresh-air offer, though."

Trisha stared at his back as he made his way to the door and out of her sight. She turned away to stare out over the party, but she was teetering on the brink of tears.

Well, he certainly was tired. There was no doubt about that. The question was of what—her, the kids, or all of the above?

"Sounds like they're raising the roof in there."

Pat started at the voice and turned from his contemplation of the night. It was a cop in uniform. "I take it you're Ray?"

"Yeah." The officer stuck his hand out. "Ray Kazur."

Pat shook his hand. "I'm Pat—"

"Pat Stuart." The man chuckled. "Hey, everybody knows you."

Pat didn't say anything. His face had decorated the local paper and news channels a lot lately, but he wasn't really comfortable with the notoriety.

"You were the quarterback on the '81 Washington team," Ray said. "You really took Adams to the cleaners for the city championship, passing for two touchdowns, running for one yourself and tackling that defensive back that made that interception. Man; ain't nobody ever gonna forget that game."

Pat felt himself relax. Those were some of the good times, before things went all to hell with Angel. "Yeah, things went well for us that night."

"I'll say." Ray laughed. "We really stuffed it to those east siders."

Pat just smiled.

"You remember Corrigan was their coach that year?"

"Yeah." The city's current mayor had been the Adams High School football coach back then.

"Well, sometimes he comes to the station and gets on his high horse about something. And when he does, me and some of the other west-side boys remind him of that game."

"Brings him back down to earth, does it?" Pat asked.

"Like knocking the rungs out of his ladder."

They shared another laugh and Pat took a deep breath of the cool night air. It had been a good idea to come out here. Get away from things and talk about the past. They paused a moment while Ray scanned the parking lot. It was quiet, with nothing moving as far as Pat could see.

"Nice of you to help out like this," Pat said.

Ray leaned against the stair railing, still facing out toward the lot. "Yeah, but guys like you, you're the ones that make the real difference."

Pat froze as if an Arctic wind had suddenly blown through. It wasn't what he wanted to hear. "I just come here once in a while," he said.

"Don't matter." Ray shook his head. "You're a real hero to these kids. There are little ones playing flag football who pretend they're you."

A horror crept through Pat's soul. "That's crazy," he said. "It wasn't that big of a deal."

Ray just laughed. "You been away too long, man, if you really think that. The kids here think you're a hero, big-time. And it's not just the football. They know what you're doing now—a big-time executive, flying around the country, making sure folks have jobs."

"I don't want to be anybody's hero," Pat protested.

"Sometimes you don't have a choice," Ray said. "Besides, what did you expect once you started working at the club? You've been like a big brother here for all the kids to look up to and lean on."

"But that's not what I wanted," Pat said, his spirits sinking so low, they'd need a ladder to see a worm's belly. "Nobody should be looking up to me, leaning on me, or anything like that."

"You think they ought to be looking up to some crud selling drugs on the street corner?"

"No. No." Pat took a deep breath, trying to still the panic in his gut. "It's just that I don't think I'm much of a role model. I've screwed some stuff up in my time."

"So? You think the rest of us haven't, too?" The cop pushed himself away from the railing. "Well, I'd better take a tour of the parking lot. Don't want nobody dinking around with the cars."

The officer walked briskly back into the lot and Pat felt his insides totally collapse. He really had no one to blame but himself. He should never have come back here. He'd been doing well in Oakland. There'd been no reason to leave. Certainly there'd been nothing here for him. The past was dead and buried. He could have hired an agent to sell his grand-mother's house and just gone on with his life.

But no, a chance to return to South Bend had come up and he'd jumped at it. And if he was really honest with himself, he'd have to admit that it was like returning to the scene of the crime. Like pulling at a scab to see if it would still bleed. Angel was gone, and Pat had to convince himself that the pain was, too. That he was free of the guilt.

Only now, here he was, with a passel of other people leaning on him. People that he would surely let down because he never knew the right thing to do. He'd done it before. What right did he have to think he wouldn't do it again?

"Pat," Trisha said.

He turned and looked into a beautiful pair of green eyes. They were too beautiful and he had to look away. It was time to reconsider that offer from Toledo. Leaving would be the best thing he could do for everybody.

"People will be coming to pick their kids up soon," Trisha said. "Could you stay here by the door and keep the kids in? They shouldn't leave here unless they're accompanied by an adult."

"Okay."

Trisha was about to go back into the building when she paused. "Are you sure you're all right?"

"I'm fine." He smiled at her. "I just had a little upset stomach. Probably something I had for lunch."

"We might have something in the medicine cabinet. Want me to check?"

"No, I'm feeling better now."

She looked at him a second before nodding and going into the building. Pat stepped just inside the door, breathing deeply as he willed himself to relax.

He'd give those Toledo people a call first thing Monday morning and see if they were still interested. He could tell everybody it was time to move on. That South Bend was getting back on its feet, and Toledo had some special challenges he thought he could meet. Sure, he'd miss things here—certain people especially—but it would be for the best. He knew that, even if they might not initially agree.

"Hey, where's Ray?" Angie said, bouncing up to him. Rulli was right behind her like a shadow. "Ray always watches the door at our parties."

Pat smiled at the two kids. They'd be two of the ones he'd miss. Somehow they'd wormed their way into his heart, but they'd get along all right. Trisha was looking out for them and she was better at that than he was.

"He's out patrolling the parking lot. You want me to go get him?"

"Nah," Angie replied.

"Don't worry, Pat," Rulli said. "You'll do okay."

"Yeah," Angie said. "Just make sure nobody don't go home with no strangers."

That stopped him. "Hey, how am I supposed to know who are the proper adults?" Pat said. "You'd better get—"

"Can't," Angie replied. "We gotta go."

She was out the door before Pat caught up with her, grabbing her arm before she totally dashed off. Rulli came outside after them.

"Our aunt Rose is here," he explained.

An elderly woman was hurrying across the parking lot. "Am I late?" she asked, puffing hard as she came up. "I'm sorry. I was—"

Suddenly she stopped and stared openmouthed at Pat. "Oh, my God," she wailed.

Trisha was suddenly at Pat's side. "What's wrong?"

"I have no idea," Pat said.

"Oh, my God," the woman just kept repeating.

"Mrs. Harris," Trisha said. "What's wrong?"

The woman pointed a shaking finger at Pat. "You're Patrick Stuart," she said. "You're Angel's big brother."

"Yeah," Pat said slowly. What was going on?

Ray was hurrying over, other people were spilling out of the club and people were coming from newly parked cars, attracted by the woman's cries, no doubt. Kids, adults, other volunteers. But no one seemed to have any idea what was going on. They were all just staring at the elderly woman.

She began to weep. "Thank you, God," she called out, looking up to the heavens. "All I can say is, thank you, God."

Trisha went over to the woman and put her arm around her shoulders. "Mrs. Harris, are you all right?"

The woman turned to Trisha. "He's Angel's big brother," she said. When this brought no response, she went on. "You know. Angel. Angie and Rulli's father."

"What!" Pat cried.

He took a step forward, then stopped. His mind and his body were frozen with shock. Angel had kids? Pat turned slowly to look at Angie—at her wide innocent eyes that were indeed so like Angel's. And little Rulli, with his wide smile that should have reminded Pat of his mother.

"It can't be," Pat said, even though he knew it to be true.

"But their last name is Ingram," Trisha said.

The woman just shrugged. "That was Maggie's last name. They were young and thought they had all the time in the world to get married." Her voice turned harder, more defiant. "But Angel's name is on the children's birth certificates. He was their father."

Pat just stared at the woman, a million questions flying through his head. None of this made any sense. "But what about Angel's funeral?" Pat asked. "You weren't there." He waved at the kids, almost afraid to look at them again. "They weren't there."

"Maggie and Angel were living in Plymouth," the woman said. "He had work there and they had a nice little house they were renting. But when he was in the accident up here, all the police found was his old driver's license."

"With his South Bend address on it?" Trisha asked.

The woman nodded. "They called Angel's grandmother but she hadn't seen him in years, either, so she just called you," the woman said to Pat. "Poor Maggie didn't know what had happened. They had had a fight, and she thought Angel was still mad. It wasn't until a week later that she found out he had been in a car wreck." The woman wiped at her eyes. "Maggie never got to tell him goodbye."

The crowd murmured its sympathy, but Pat felt numb. This was like a dream.

"I remember you from the Washington football games," the woman continued. "Angel, he always went with Maggie—they met in junior high—and he was so proud of you. He kept saying how you were his big brother. He told everyone.''

So proud of you. Pat had to turn away, his eyes awash with tears. Angel had been proud of him? Was this the same Angel who had turned so bitterly on him just a few months later? Pat couldn't speak, could barely breathe.

"And now," the woman went on, "my prayers are answered."

"What prayers?" Trisha asked.

Pat turned back.

"For these little tykes," she said, indicating Angie and Rulli standing nearby, their eyes as wide as saucers. "Now they got somebody to take care of them."

Pat found their eyes all turning to him. His heart wanted to leap for joy at finding that Angel wasn't truly gone, at having the chance to make things right after all this time. But Pat's soul turned heavy as he thought back to that last argument. Angel wouldn't want him to have anything to do with his kids. Pat had no doubt about that; Angel's words still echoed in his head after all these years.

"We wouldn't be no trouble," Rulli said. "Angie makes my breakfast so you don't gotta get up early."

Pat turned to the kids, stooping down to look in their faces. What could he say to them—your father hated me and would never let me have you if he had a say in the matter?

"I don't have a way to take care of you kids," Pat said slowly. "You know, I work long hours and travel a lot. You can't be by yourself that much."

"We ain't afraid," Rulli said. "And you could get a dog to guard us."

The want in the boy's eyes matched the need in Pat's heart. But it wasn't that simple. Even if he ignored Angel's wishes in the matter, would it be the best thing for the kids? Angel had said Pat didn't know how to love, and what if he was right? Could Pat risk Angie and Rulli's happiness on the chance that Angel had been wrong?

Angie was pulling her brother back. "He don't want us, Rulli," she said, her tone harsh and unforgiving.

"It's not that at all," Pat protested. And it wasn't. "I'll support you two. Money's no problem."

"Maybe we could—" Rulli began.

"Rulli," Angie snapped, cutting him off. "We don't beg. Remember? Daddy wouldn't want us to."

Pat swallowed hard, the lump of pain in his chest making it almost impossible for him to breathe. "You remember him?"

Angie gave him a look. "Sure I remember him. And I remember he didn't like you, neither."

It was as if a knife had gone through Pat's heart. Angel had never forgiven him. He slowly stood up as Angie grabbed Rulli's hand.

"Come on, Rulli. It's time to go home." She dragged him down the steps to where their aunt stood. The three of them turned and walked across the parking lot.

Pat just watched them go, vaguely aware that the rest of the crowd was dispersing, too. All he could hear were Angie's words echoing in his head. *He didn't like you, neither.*

"It'll be so easy," Trisha was saying, the excitement inside her bubbling over as she tore down streamers from the study room. "You can hire a housekeeper. You have so much room she can live in. We'll even help you find the right person."

The club was empty; all the revelers had gone home. Clarissa and some of the other workers had helped clean up and had finally left. Trisha and Pat were the only ones there, tearing down the last few decorations.

"Why, offhand, I can think of a half-dozen women who would be just wonderful," she went on. "Ones you could really trust with the kids."

"It's not that simple," Pat said. His voice sounded weary.

"But it's not that hard, either."

His reply was to yank the plastic garbage bag out of the can and twist the top sharply. He looked so tired that Trisha wanted to take him into her arms and hold him through the night. She wanted to make him feel safe and warm and protected, just as he would make the kids feel. But they had work to do first.

"Why did she wait so long to tell me?" he asked.

Trisha started on the streamers around her office door. "She didn't know that was you in the news. She doesn't belong to the chamber of commerce. You and she move in different circles.''

"I guess." The stumble in Pat's voice said he was still in shock. "It's just so hard to take in."

"I know." Trisha's laughter floated across the room. "It's like a dream come true."

"Not hardly."

She stopped her cleaning to frown at him. "I don't understand. This is your chance to make it up to Angel. He would want you to care for his kids."

Pat laughed then, a long and bitter sound. "I know exactly what Angel would want," he said. "For me to stay the hell out of their lives."

"That can't be true!"

Pat gave out a weary sigh. "This isn't the movies, Trisha. Everything doesn't necessarily work out neatly in the end. You heard Angie—Angel didn't like me. Even his kids knew it."

Trisha shook her head. "I also heard Rose say he went to your games and was proud of you."

"That was school spirit, not family pride," he said.

"Angie must have been two when Angel died. I doubt she remembers him, let alone his feelings about someone she'd never met."

"Maybe those feelings were really strong," Pat said. He leaned against the wall, his eyes looking far into the past. "The last time I saw Angel was at our father's funeral. We were both juniors—me in college, him in high school. I'd wanted to go to school locally so I could keep an eye on him, but he'd turned me down real thoroughly. He wasn't going to live with our grandmother, wasn't going to switch to a school district with a better college prep record, wasn't going to leave his loser friends."

"Maybe they weren't losers to him," she pointed out.

Pat came back to the present to shrug. "Whatever. He pretty much told me at that time to go to hell. I went to Texas instead on a football scholarship. I came home the first summer but it was like we were strangers. He didn't care if I was around, so I stopped trying. No use beating your head into a stone wall. But when Dad died, all I heard was how I'd abandoned them."

Pat paused and took a deep, ragged breath before going on. "He said I had no feelings. That I was cold and selfish and thought only about money, and not about people, and he was never going to be like me. That people mattered to him, even people who weren't rich and successful, but drunk half the time."

Trisha winced at the words, and at the raw pain in Pat's voice. "He was upset," she tried to point out.

"He was right," Pat said. His voice was dead, as if so much inside him was, too.

"No, he wasn't," Trisha cried out. "You have lots of love in you. Maybe too much. Every time you lost someone you loved or they seemed to reject you, you built up more defenses. You're like that now and you have to have been like that as a kid. You had too many hurts."

"This is crazy," he said and stood. "You've only known me for a month or two. Take my word for it, I'm not good with relationships."

"I don't believe that," she said. "And I never will. No matter what Angel said to you, he would want you to take care of his kids."

"I will take care of them. I'll set up a trust fund for them. They'll be financially secure until they're fully educated adults."

"Money isn't the important thing," Trisha said.

Pat stood there staring at her. "No, it isn't," he said slowly. "And this isn't about money at all. It's about truth. The truth is that if I stay around, I'll only end up hurting you and the kids. Angel knew me better than anyone else on this earth and I'm not willing to gamble anyone's happiness that he was wrong about me."

She frowned at him, confused by the sudden turn of the conversation. "What's this 'hurting me and the kids' nonsense?"

"Trying not to hurt others isn't nonsense."

Her stomach was suddenly in knots. This had nothing to do with the kids. Fear tried for the upper hand, but she grabbed at annoyance instead. He was trying to dump her! Well, she'd see who dumped who.

"Save your dramatics," she snapped. "The macho martyr role doesn't suit you. I've heard it too many times to be impressed."

He stiffened up even more. "I'm sorry my attempts to spare you pain are boring."

"Spare *me* pain? If that isn't just like a man!"

Her irritation was growing by leaps and bounds, but it was mostly with herself. She should have seen this coming. His moodiness the last week, the sense that he'd become suddenly distant—they all pointed to his pulling away from her. But she'd denied it, refused to admit that there was trouble in paradise.

"What's just like a man?"

She would not let him see the pain that was creeping along, stealing every shred of happiness that was ever in her heart. "Oh, never mind," she said and turned away, stripping the crepe paper streamers from the doorway with a vengeance. "It wasn't like this was an all-time-and-forever thing anyway. Neither of us wanted that. It was an Indian summer romance and Indian summer's over at Halloween. Very fitting."

"I must say you're taking this well."

She managed to smile at him just for a second. "Sure, why not? I'm a big girl. I know when something's over, it's over."

"I see."

She stuffed the last of the decorations into a garbage bag, the festive trappings all crumpled and smashed like her heart. "Want to drop these in the Dumpster out back on your way out?"

She didn't wait to see him grab up the two bags before he left, but went back into the study room. Her footsteps echoed hollowly in the emptiness as slow tears wove their way down her cheeks. She wasn't sure what had happened. She must have pushed too hard. Or not hard enough.

Maybe he wanted somebody taller or shorter. Blonder or darker. Maybe she was too serious, or too rooted to the area. Maybe he was allergic to cats.

Hell, talk about being lousy at relationships. She was downright pitiful. It was just as well that he wanted to end it now. Any longer and she would have had her heart all entangled. Then it really would have hurt.

Chapter Thirteen

"Here," Mrs. Harris said. "Look for yourself."

The old woman pushed the official-looking papers across the scarred kitchen table toward Pat, but there was no reason for him to look. He knew what he was going to see.

"See? Maggie was their mother. But you see here? In the box for the father?"

"I know, Mrs. Harris. I never doubted that Angel was the father," Pat said.

The old woman nodded and pulled back the papers, a tear running down each cheek. Pat wished that Trisha were here. She was good at handling people when their emotions were on the edge.

But she wasn't here to help him and wouldn't be again. It was for the best.

"Angie really looks like him, you know," Mrs. Harris said. "Rulli, he kinda takes after our side."

Pat cleared his throat. "Actually, he resembles my mother," he said. "His grandmother."

"That so?" The old woman scraped together the photographs spread over the kitchen table. Some were of the kids as they neared their present age, but most were of Angel, Maggie and the two babies. For Pat, it had hurt to see them, see their happiness and know that Angel hadn't thought enough of him to share it with him even slightly.

"Angie and Rulli." Mr. Harris paused for breath. His emphysema seemed well advanced. "They're really good kids."

Pat's stomach did a two-and-a-half forward twist. "I know," Pat said. "I can tell."

"They ain't had a lot, but they never complain," Mr. Harris went on softly.

"I'm going to make sure they get the best from now on. The best care and the best education." Pat looked down and found his finger playing with a scratch in the tabletop. He had to remind himself what Angel would have wanted. If it was the last thing Pat did, he was going to follow Angel's wishes.

"I had a meeting with the social worker this morning," Pat said. "We're going to work together to get things all straightened out. You know, find a good home for the kids. She said it shouldn't be hard, especially since I'm going to set up a trust fund for them."

Mrs. Harris's eyes glistened. "This is such a good thing you're doing."

Then why did he feel so lousy?

"We love 'em and all," Mr. Harris said. "But what could we give 'em?"

All the things that Pat couldn't. Pat tried to swallow and found he couldn't. Hacking roughly, he cleared his throat. "You gave them a lot," he said. "And I hope that you'll stay in touch with them, Mrs. Harris."

"Call me Rose, Pat. We're family, ain't we?"

"Yeah." He nodded. "We're family." He paused a moment and tried to will the ache in his throat away. "I really want what's best for Angie and Rulli. They're going to get all the advantages life has to offer."

"You're a good man, Pat," Mr. Harris said. "A real good brother."

It was time to go. Not cut and run—he'd abandoned his plan to call Toledo about that job offer. He was going to do his best for the kids, but it was time to get out of here before Mr. and Mrs. Harris started fitting him for a halo.

"Well," Pat said, making a show of looking at his watch. "I really need to be going."

"Yeah," Mrs. Harris replied, nodding slowly.

"I wanted to let you know if there's anything the kids need now—"

She shook her head.

"Or there's anything that needs to be covered," he said, trying for a diplomatic way of offering to pay for past care.

But again Mrs. Harris shook her head.

"Okay." Pat stood up and put his business card on the table, the one with his home and business numbers. "If you need anything, just call."

Mr. Harris ignored the card. "Rulli, you know he gets earaches a lot."

"I didn't know," Pat said. "I'll call around for a good doctor to have him checked out."

"And that Angie," Mr. Harris went on. "She's a nice kid, you know, but sometimes she ain't that easy to get along with. She's got a real mouth on her. Big enough to flatten a couple big guys, once she gets her dander up."

"Yeah." A smile flickered on Pat's lips, then just as suddenly he felt sick. Now was not the time to get sentimental about things. "Let me know if you or the kids need anything. You can call me any time of the day or night. My people can always get ahold of me."

Then he hurried out of the house as fast as he could. He had never felt so miserable in his life.

Angel should be happy at last.

"What are you drawing, Rulli?" Trisha asked.

"Nothin'."

She looked down at his paper and found that Rulli was telling the truth. The only thing on his paper was a scrawl of circles and zigzag lines.

"I guess you don't feel like drawing today. Want to play Ping-Pong?"

"Nah."

Poor little guy. Trisha was feeling rather lost herself. It hurt almost more than she could bear, this sudden loneliness. But she was an adult. She could handle it. Besides which, she knew the break from Pat was for the best. And if she forgot that for a weak, silly moment, she reminded herself as fast as could be.

It's not as if she and Pat had been going anywhere. And they hadn't been suited, not really. They'd both been too dedicated to their jobs also. They'd been friends, good friends even. But neither of them had been looking for anything permanent. So it had worked out just fine, as her heart would realize one of these days.

Just as Rulli would. He couldn't conceive that his life was about to change for the better. All he knew was that he wasn't going to live in Pat's big house and was disappointed.

"We have new books," she told the boy. "Would you like to look at them?"

"Nah." He got up and went across the room, joining a crowd watching two of the older kids play Ping-Pong.

As she was staring at Rulli, another body bumped into her. She looked down to see Angie's smiling face. Obviously, she wasn't suffering from the same depression Rulli was. "Boy, you look pretty chipper today."

"Yep," Angie said. "I'm gonna take care of everything. I'm gonna get me a plan."

"Oh?" Trisha didn't know if that should worry her.

"Yep. Pat can really be a butthead sometimes," Angie said. "But he's our butthead now."

"I guess," Trisha said cautiously.

"So whether I want to or not, it's time to do something."

This didn't sound good. At least not for Pat. "And what's that mean?"

Angie shrugged. "That me and Rulli are gonna live with him—he just don't know it yet."

Trisha frowned at the girl. "Pat has reasons why he thinks it would be better for you to live with someone else. A two-parent family would be able to give you both the support you need."

Angie gave Trisha an odd look. "If you married him, you guys would be a two-parent family."

A strange mixture of emotions washed over Trisha. Terror at the idea of a lifetime commitment, of trusting someone with her happiness forever. Ecstasy at the idea of sharing her life with Pat.

An idea he did not share. Reality came back just in time.

"That's not going to happen, young lady," Trisha said briskly. "Maybe you should focus on all the good that will happen now."

Angie shook her head. "Rulli's got it in his silly head that living with Pat is what he wants, and that's what we're gonna do."

"Sometimes, no matter how much you want something, you can't have it," Trisha said. Those seemed like words for her to remember.

"That's pig barf," Angie said. "You ain't never wanted something bad enough."

Trisha just stared at the girl as she stomped away.

"Angie sharing her wisdom with you?"

Trisha tried to force a smile as she walked along with Clarissa. "Why do I have the feeling that girl knows more about life than I do?"

"Maybe life has had time to teach you about all the things you don't know," Clarissa said. "Angie's still got some lessons ahead of her."

"I get the feeling she's going to learn them differently from me."

"Don't we all learn our own way?"

Clarissa was too philosophical for Trisha. She just walked back into her office and sank into her chair, frowning at the growing stack of paperwork on her desk.

Clarissa followed, sitting across from her and kicking off her shoes. "Those kids don't have a clue how good life's going to get."

"Angie's plotting something."

"So what else is new?"

"She's determined that she and Rulli are going to live with Pat."

Clarissa made a face. "I think the kids are probably better off with somebody else. I don't think Pat has the slightest idea what's up with kids. They'd run him ragged."

"True."

"Don't think he had the slightest idea what was up with you, either," Clarissa added.

Trisha pulled a form off the stack and began to study it intently. "Oh, I don't know about that. I think we understood each other very well."

"Then why'd he take off?"

"Who said it was his decision?" Trisha asked. "Maybe it was mutual."

"Sure. And getting the flu's a mutual decision between you and the bug."

"We both had our own lives and it was time to lead them."

"So why are you moping around like a kid who lost her dog?"

"I'm not," Trisha pointed out, then glanced out her window. "Uh-oh."

Clarissa turned also. "It's just your mother."

Trisha's mother marched into her office. "You poor dear," she said and seized Trisha in a giant hug.

Suddenly Trisha felt like a ten-year-old who'd scraped her knee and had run to the sanctuary of her mother's arms. The scrape didn't go away magically but it felt better. Everything felt better.

Everything felt worse. She had the sudden urge to burst into tears and cry on her mother's shoulder for years. She wanted to sob about how hurt she felt and how alone. And how she had no idea why he'd left like that.

But she was a grown woman and grown women didn't admit to being dumped.

"Hi, Mom." Reluctantly, Trisha pulled herself out of her mother's embrace. "What are you doing here?"

"Visiting." Her mother sat down in the chair next to Clarissa. "Is there some kind of a law against a mother visiting her child?"

There was a lump in Trisha's throat and her lip was borderline quivering, so she thought it best not to trust her mouth to words. Silently she shook her head.

"Good," her mother said, then turned to Clarissa. "And how are you?"

"Just fine, thank you."

With the pleasantries out of the way, the three of them leaned back and let a silence swallow them up.

"So, has he come to his senses yet?" Trisha's mother asked suddenly.

"Nope," Clarissa answered as if Trisha weren't even there. "Men can be such fools."

"Tell me about it." Clarissa sighed.

"They seemed like such a perfect couple."

"He seemed more human around her. Not such a stuffed shirt."

Trisha waved her hand in the air. "I am here, you know."

"He must have run scared," her mother went on.

"My thought entirely. Got to liking the coziness a little too much and it scared him."

"Maybe it was a mutual decision," Trisha said for the second time that afternoon.

"He'll come back," her mother told Clarissa and got to her feet. "Just needs a little time."

"You think so?" Clarissa shook her head. "I don't know. He might need a boot in the butt first. He's a pretty stubborn fool."

"Maybe I don't want him back," Trisha said loudly. "Maybe I don't have the time for a relationship like that. Did you ever think this is what I want?"

They turned to stare at her then. But only for a moment.

Clarissa shook her head as she followed Trisha's mother out the door. "I bet if she went to see him, he'd fall in line like a homesick puppy."

"What's with this puppy nonsense?" Trisha called after them. "I'm a cat person, remember?" Besides, she was not going to go see Pat. It was over.

Pat pulled the shiny, new van up near the door of the Boys and Girls Club. He turned the ignition off and leaned back a moment, savoring the vehicle's new-car smell.

But as much as he tried to hold on to that scent, reality came stomping in, crushing the pleasant softness surrounding him beneath large, unfeeling feet. He should have let the dealer deliver the van. Then he wouldn't have to see Trisha.

Shaking his head, he almost laughed out loud at that thought. That was how this whole mess got started. A van was delivered to the wrong address and before he knew it, Miss

Trisha Stewart—her smile, her laughter, her womanly scent—had claimed ownership of his life.

If that hadn't happened, he wouldn't be in the pain he was in now. But then, neither would he have found Angel's kids, so he couldn't be totally sorry.

He looked around the parking lot and the surrounding streets. It was four in the afternoon. Everything was empty around him. There was no one here to see him. And Trisha was probably inside.

That meant he could probably sneak over to the door, ease it open, throw the keys in and run. But that was more than a little cowardly.

Maybe what he ought to do was leave the keys in the van, walk over to Western and catch a bus downtown. Back at his office, he could call Trisha. Though there was a chance that the van would get swiped, there was a smaller chance he'd get caught.

Which made it even more cowardly than the first option. No, he was a man and he should act like one.

He took the keys out of the ignition and put them in his coat pocket. Then he took a deep breath, straightened his tie and walked in the door.

The scene was typical, everyday. Some kids were playing Ping-Pong while others sat with tutors and studied. Angie and Rulli were in the study room and when Rulli looked up, Pat waved. Instead of returning his wave, the boy turned back to his studies.

For a moment, Pat's firm resolve danced on the edge of crumbling, but he told himself that maybe Rulli hadn't seen him. The kid probably needed glasses. And even if he had seen him and still rejected him, he would just have to deal with it. Pat was doing the best he could.

He looked toward Trisha's office. She was inside and Clarissa was just outside her door, looking for something in a filing cabinet. Holding his head high, he strode over. "Hi, Clarissa."

The woman looked over her glasses and examined him carefully, as if he might be an impostor. "Hello, Mr. Stuart," she finally said. "How are you?"

"I'm just fine." His voice was vigorous and confident, thanks to the sales training his job had given him over the years. "Is Miss Stewart available?"

Clarissa took her glasses off, letting them hang over her ample chest, and put her head in Trisha's office. "Are you available for a Mr. Patrick Stuart?"

"What does he want?" Trisha asked without looking up.

"What is the nature of your business, sir?"

This was a tad stupid, but he could play the game as well as anyone. "I have a gift that I would like to present to Miss Stewart."

"He's got something for you."

"Actually it's for the club. But I want to present it to Miss Stewart as a representative of—"

"Oh, for heaven's sakes," Trisha snapped. "Just get in here and quit wasting our time."

Pat considered pointing out that he hadn't started this little charade, but he was old enough to know that women were not enamored of logic. He stepped into the office and sat down.

"All right, Mr. Stuart," Trisha said. "How may I help you?"

"Actually I'm here to help *you,*" Pat replied, as he dropped the keys on her desk. "They're for your van."

"I don't remember asking for it." She looked out the door. "Maybe Clarissa—"

"I said *your* van."

She turned back to stare at him.

"Your very own van," he said. "That you don't have to share with anybody. Unless you want to."

Her glance flickered down at the keys. "You were able to secure funding?"

"Here's the title." Pat leaned forward and laid the document on the desk next to the keys. "It's all yours."

"You didn't answer my question."

"Don't worry about it." Pat unfolded the title document. "The van's registered in the club's name. There are no liens on it. You guys own it free and clear."

She stared at him a long moment, then down at the keys and document on her desk.

"I had it fitted out just like you wanted," he said. "Bench seats, easy-clean fabric, seat belts—everything. All the stuff you picked out when we—" He paused a moment to swallow. "It's just the way you wanted it."

"Thank you."

There was nothing more to say. He should just turn on his heel and walk out, but he didn't. He was finding it harder and harder to breathe, though. It was as if the oxygen were being sucked out of the air and no more was coming in.

Suddenly the phone rang and Trisha snatched it up, obviously wanting to get it before Clarissa could. From the conversation it appeared to be one of Trisha's board members.

"I'm going to look in on Angie and Rulli," he murmured.

Trisha continued to concentrate on her phone conversation.

Shrugging, he made his way out into the study room. He would have preferred to run. Get out and find himself a nice bar and test those depths of alcohol where his father had found solace.

But the kids were his responsibility and he had to keep in touch with their progress. Besides, he wasn't like his father. Never was and never would be.

"Hi, guys," Pat said.

Angie looked up and a sudden smile covered her face. "Uncle Pat," she cried. "Hi."

She flew out of her chair to grab him in a clumsy hug. Pat was stunned, but recovered enough to return the embrace. What was she up to?

She let him go enough to turn to her brother. "Rulli, look. It's Uncle Pat."

Rulli frowned at his sister. "I thought we didn't like him anymore."

Angie laughed and came pretty close to sincerity. "He's our uncle," she said, her voice almost sweet and reasonable. "And kids always like uncles. Uncles are nice."

"Oh." Rulli turned to Pat. "Hi, Pat."

"Hi, kid. How's it going?"

Rulli just shrugged and looked back down at the math paper he was working on. "Okay."

"Rulli got an *A* on his science test," their tutor said.

"Good job, Rulli."

"Hey, Uncle Pat," Angie said, tugging on his arm. "Look what I got." She held out a scrap torn from the newspaper. "It's a coupon. You buy one cheeseburger dinner and get another one free. And I got two of them. What d'ya say we all go out to dinner? You know—you, me, Rulli and Miss Stewart. It wouldn't cost you hardly nothing."

Except his peace of mind. "That place is a grease pit," he said instead. "Your arteries will be clogged shut by the time you're thirteen if you eat there."

"Okay." She stuffed the coupon back in her pocket. "So where do you want to go?"

He'd thought she'd been accepting defeat too easily and he sighed. "Nowhere. I've got plans and your aunt is probably expecting you for dinner."

"You got plans?" Angie's thin veneer of joviality was gone and her usual belligerence was back. "What d'ya mean you got plans? What kinda plans?"

"I have a life, you know," he pointed out. He was not about to tell her his plans were a carryout pizza and a rented video.

Angie took a deep breath and recovered a bit of her former sweet self, but only a bit. If Pat hadn't known better, he'd have thought her eyes had looked almost scared for a moment there.

"Sure," she said. "I know you got a life, but we're related. If you're going to give us an aunt, you should tell us first."

Ah, light dawned, but with it came a small niggling of pain as he answered. "I'm not going to produce an aunt. You don't need to worry."

"Hey, who's worrying? So how about tomorrow? That good for you?"

Her maneuverings were about as subtle as a Mack truck, but he didn't mind. Up to a point. He wanted to spend time with them. "Sure, tomorrow's fine. The three of us can go get some dinner. Maybe even—"

"No, the four of us," Angie corrected. "Miss Stewart's coming with."

"She's busy," Pat said.

"No, she's not," Angie said. "All we gotta do is ask."

"No, we don't have to ask. I know. It'll be the three of us."

She sagged back into her chair. "Gee, that'll be a lot of fun."

"It could be," he pointed out.

"So could getting a shot, but it ain't." She pulled her book over toward her. "I got homework to do."

"So, are we on for tomorrow?" Pat asked.

"I am," Rulli said. "How about we go for spaghetti?"

"No, we ain't," Angie said and glared at Rulli. "It's a school night and we gotta study."

Pat just sighed. At least things were back to normal with her. "Well, maybe over the weekend, then," he said.

"Sure, Pat," Rulli said. "That'd be great."

"We'll see," Angie added darkly.

Chapter Fourteen

Pat sat there and stared at the frozen-food meal before him. The barbecued chicken dinner was no more edible than the pizza he'd bought for dinner last night. It all tasted like cardboard—bad cardboard at that.

It was probably the damned rain. He turned his irritation toward the dark, gloomy scene framed by his kitchen window. The weather had been nice for about a week after Halloween, but early this morning, the rains had hit, bringing a bone-chilling wetness to the area. The forecast called for at least two more days of the same. Hot dog.

He took a sip of his tea, then made a face. Hell, even that tasted like dishwater. Maybe he was coming down with a cold. Well, he picked a good time to have one. He was going to be in town the rest of the week.

Just as he pushed his plate away, there was a loud banging on the front door. "What the hell?" he muttered in the silence.

He went to the door, turned on the porch light and looked out the sidelights before quickly pulling the inside door open. "What in the world are you doing here? I thought you never went out on a school night."

"Let me in," Angie shouted at him as she gave the storm door a good, solid kick. "I'm drowning out here."

He opened the storm door and stood back as she came in, shoes squishing loudly and clothes dripping enough water to form puddles wherever she walked.

Worry took over. "What are you doing out on a night like this? Is something wrong? Where's Rulli?"

"Rulli's home." She kicked off her shoes, pulled off her socks and dropped them on the floor, then dumped her coat on top of them. "You're my uncle, remember? Can't I drop by for a visit?"

"You ever hear of a phone?" Pat asked. "It's a marvelous invention. You can talk to people without going out in the rain."

Instead of paying attention to him, Angie was sniffing the air like a bird dog on scent. "What's that smell?"

"And you should have my number," Pat said. "I left my card with your aunt Rose."

"Are you making dinner?"

Pat shook his head. Women. The kid was ten years old and she was already controlling the conversation, answering only the questions she felt like answering.

"Yeah, I made dinner."

"Did you eat it all up?"

"I just had one bite."

"No good, huh?"

"It's fine," he snapped. "It's something I usually like. I just wasn't hungry tonight."

"How come?"

He closed his eyes a moment and wiped his brow. What had he done to deserve this? "I don't have an appetite. I think I'm coming down with the flu or a cold."

"Don't breathe on me." She brought her arm up across her mouth and nose. "Germs travel through the air, you know. I learned that in school."

"That's good," Pat said. "Too bad you never learned what happens when you walk around in the cold and wet."

But Angie was already gone. Pausing to clench his jaw tight, he followed her into the kitchen. She had seated herself at the table and was enthusiastically digging into his barely touched dinner.

"This is awful stuff," she said around a mouthful of food. "You eat this all the time? You need somebody to cook for you."

"I'll put that on my list," he said.

"You do," she said. "You need to get married. I read that married men live longer and are healthier. Me and Rulli don't want you kicking off. We ain't got no other relatives."

"I'm touched that you care," he said. "But once I get the trust fund set up, you'll be taken care of, no matter what."

She frowned at him. "Money ain't the only thing."

She was serious, and sincere. It surprised him more than he wanted to admit. And touched him, too.

"No, it isn't," he admitted.

That apparently covered, she glanced around her. "Got any pop?"

"There's tea in front of you."

She looked in the cup and made a face. "How about hot chocolate?"

"I have milk. Take it or leave it."

"If you had a wife, she'd buy some pop when you ran out," Angie grumbled.

"I can buy my own soda, thank you."

After pouring her a glass of milk, Pat returned to the table and put the glass in front of Angie. He sat down across from her. There were just a few scraps on her plate in spite of her complaint that it was awful. Then she picked up the glass of milk, looked at it and made a slight face before draining it.

"All right."

Angie wiped her mouth with her sleeve as she glared at him with those hard little eyes set in a face of angelic innocence. Pat swallowed hard. God, she looked exactly like Angel. How the hell could he have missed that?

"Now we're gonna talk."

Pat bowed slightly.

"I guess I'm supposed to like you because you're my uncle," she said.

He took a deep breath and slowly let it out. "You don't have to."

"Yeah, I know, but rules are rules." She paused to rub her nose with the back of her hand. "Anyway, Rulli already does and so does Miss Stewart. And they're both real unhappy about the way things are going."

"Look." Pat leaned forward, his forearms on the table. "I'm sorry about everything. But I can't—"

"I'm talking," Angie pointed out.

Man, oh, man. He could feel all the muscles stiffen up in his body. Angel might have been a bit mouthy, but for pure, all-around bossy, his kid had him beat, hands down. Pat stifled his inclination to pitch the kid out into the rain and leaned back to listen.

"And on top of everything, you're the meanest man I know."

"Thank you," Pat replied stiffly. "I've always been a high achiever."

"Using big words all the time don't change nothing."

Pat sighed. "Let me take you home, Angie."

"I bet you got picked on all the time when you were a little kid. That's why you don't live where you used to. You're afraid that people will beat up on you."

"I'm not afraid of people beating up on me."

"You are, too. And the only reason you let people come to this big old house is so you can show off."

He considered pointing out that Trisha had brought her and Rulli over, that he hadn't invited them at all. But he didn't want to get childish. And most of all, he didn't want to get into a conversation about Trisha.

"Come on," he said, standing up. "I'm taking you home. You must have homework to do."

"Well, I don't care about your stupid old house. And I think your old pictures are dumb."

Oh, Lord, he thought as he stared into her little face. The kid was going to cry. Angie was about to do something that, Pat was willing to bet good money on, she hadn't done in a long time.

Damn. He wished Trisha were here. He couldn't handle these emotional confrontations. He hadn't been able to handle them when he was dealing with Angel, who was a guy. And he sure as hell couldn't handle them when they involved a little girl. He stared off down the darkened hallway for a second and then dared a peek back at Angie.

She was peeking back at him, no closer to tears than he was. Her glance darted away again, but not fast enough. Damn. She was playing another game. Yesterday's was to be sweet and cute. Today's must be to be sad and cute.

He leaned back in his chair, his arms crossed on his chest. "Let's cut out the games, Angie. We'll deal much better with each other honestly."

She glared at him, obviously not pleased that he had seen through her. "How come you got to keep this house?" she demanded.

"I don't know." He shrugged, not about to voice his suspicions. "Maybe because I lived here with my grandmother."

"How come my father didn't get to live here?"

Pat turned away. "He didn't want to."

"Yeah, right." She didn't believe him.

"Damn it," Pat snapped. "He didn't. I asked him myself. A whole bunch of times. And he always said no."

"And that's what me and Rulli would say, too," she said. "Even if you asked a million times."

"I see." Pat took a deep breath and softly cleared his throat. "Well, I agree with that. I think there are better places for you guys to be."

"Yeah, and you know why?"

"We really should be getting you home." Pat didn't want to know her reasons. He was sure they would involve all his many flaws. "Let's get your shoes and socks back on."

He started them moving slowly back down the hallway.

"I know the stuff is wet," Pat said. "But I don't have anything your size to wear."

"We don't want to live in this house 'cause there ain't no happy left in it."

Pat was picking up Angie's sneakers and socks. He should have put them in the clothes dryer. Maybe he could still do it. Suddenly his mind caught up with her words.

"There's no happy in this house?"

"That's right." She glared up at him, hands on her hips. "You 'member all those happy people in the pictures you showed us?"

He nodded.

"Well, they're all dead. And they took all the happy with them."

He stared at his little niece. So cocky. So know-it-all. What the hell did she know?

But then he suddenly saw she did know it all. The happy *was* gone from this house. That had been the treasure his great-grandmother had talked about and it truly was all gone.

"But my dad, he had lots of happy and he gave it to me and Rulli," Angie went on with a smug little smile. "And we don't hafta share any with you if we don't want to."

"No, you don't," Pat said slowly.

"If you want any, you're gonna hafta stop being such a butthead," she said. "You gotta stop thinking about only what you want and stop hurting people 'cause you're still afraid of getting beaten up."

"I'm not afraid," he said, but his voice was weak and un-convincing, even to himself. Rulli and Angie did have happi-ness in their lives. In spite of all the troubles, they were happy.

And in spite of all his successes, he wasn't. Not really. The only happiness he'd had lately was what others had shared with him. Angie and Rulli and especially Trisha.

But it was too late. He'd burned his bridges and there was no going back, even if he wanted to. And he suddenly wanted to.

Pat scooped up the mail from the foyer floor and tossed it, along with the newspaper, onto the kitchen table. He had no desire to look at any of it. Based on the way his week had gone, it would be all bills and bad news. The only good thing hap-pening was that the wet rain of the past few days had turned to snow. It was miserable enough to match his mood.

He pulled a cup from the cabinet, filled it with water and stuck it in the microwave to heat. His mother used to make him some kind of lemony tea when he had a cold and it had al-ways tasted so good. He wished he had some of it now. Maybe it would take away that ache inside him.

But then, it probably wasn't the tea that held the cure. Lord knows, he'd tried to duplicate it often enough over the years and had always fallen short. It just didn't work without loving hands tucking you into bed, without a loving heart to watch over you.

Damn. Pat shook his head. He was getting maudlin. His eyes caught sight of the box he and Angel had hidden in the attic. Rather than wallow any longer in sentimentality, he flipped the box open. A framed photo of a six-year-old Angel lay on top. Pat picked it up.

"Why didn't you tell me you had kids?" he asked the smiling first grader. "Did you really hate me that much?"

The only answer was the buzzing from the microwave. His water was hot.

Pat tossed a tea bag into the water, then, taking the mug and still holding the photo, went upstairs. He put both on his dresser before he emptied his pockets. He needed some exercise, he thought, as he tossed his shirt on his bed. Considering the weather, a run was probably foolhardy, but he could work out with his weights in the basement. He tossed his pants next to his shirt and pulled some shorts from a drawer. There was nothing like a good sweat to get the craziness from your body.

Once dressed in his shorts and T-shirt, he reached for his tea, but the mug was hotter than he'd expected. He jerked his hand back. The cup wobbled, though, and hit Angel's picture, knocking it over so that it fell off the dresser toward the floor.

"Hell!" Pat cried and dived for the picture as if in saving it, he would be saving Angel.

He was too slow. The photo landed before he could catch it, shattering the glass in the frame. Pat landed on his knees on the broken glass as the picture bounced once, then landed faceup. Angel was smiling at him.

"Thanks a lot, bro," Pat muttered as he gingerly eased to one side, away from the broken glass. His knees hurt. And no wonder; they were covered with scratches, stinging little stripes of blood. Swell.

Moving slowly, he brushed the glass from his knees and was just starting to clean up the rest when the phone rang. "Now what?" he asked Angel. The kid just kept on grinning.

Pat limped over to the phone. It was Rulli.

"Pat, you gotta come over here," he said. No preliminaries.

"Where are you?" An icy fear took hold of Pat's heart. "What's wrong?"

"I'm at the club," Rulli said.

The boy's voice wasn't exactly panicky, but Pat's fears doubled. "Is it Trisha?" he asked. "Has something happened to her?"

"She sez she's leaving."

Pat's heart practically stopped. Trisha was going to quit? It wasn't what he had feared, but it was still not good news. "Why?"

"I don't know," Rulli said, then seemed to leave the phone a moment as there was muffled talking near him. "She's crying all the time and she's really sad."

"She's what?"

There was more muffled conversation at the other end before Rulli came back on. "You gotta come and stop her," the boy said.

"Me?" Pat said. "Why would she listen to me?"

"'Cause she won't listen to us. She don't listen to nobody anymore."

Pat thought of how lost the kids would be without her. How they'd miss all those little extra assurances of their worth that she gave each child there. How she'd be doing just what she said her father had done.

"I'll talk to her," Pat assured him and got off the phone. She couldn't leave. It might feel right now, but there'd come a day when she wouldn't be able to live with herself.

He grabbed his wallet and car keys, shoved his bare feet into some loafers and raced down the stairs. She should still be at the club, unless she'd already quit. No. Rulli would have known that.

Pat sped through the fading light of late afternoon to the club. It was all his fault. Once again, he'd stepped into somebody's life only to screw things up for them.

Trisha was zipping up her jacket as Angie came rushing over. "You aren't leaving yet, are you?" the girl asked. She sounded almost worried.

Trisha frowned at her. "I told you I was leaving about ten minutes ago. I'd be gone by now except that Douglas couldn't find his coat."

"Yeah, but I ain't hardly seen you all day," Angie said. "You know. We ain't had a chance to talk."

"About what?" Trisha asked.

Angie just shrugged. "I don't know. Girl stuff."

Trisha shook her head. Much as she cared for Angie, she wasn't up to a "girl talk" today. "Can we do it another time?" she asked. "I've got an awful cold and I just want to get home."

"I guess," Angie said as she walked along with Trisha. "Pat has a cold, too."

"Oh?" Trisha was concerned in spite of her best efforts not to be. "He's not too sick, is he?"

Angie made a face. "He didn't seem sick to me at all. Just kind of whiny. You know how guys are when they're even a little sick."

"'Whiny' doesn't sound like Pat," Trisha said.

Angie stopped walking, a strange look on her face. "Maybe you should drop over to see him," she said. "I could be wrong. I ain't a doctor, you know. He could be real sick."

Trisha allowed the idea to tempt her for only a moment. She doubted that Pat was sick, but there was no doubt that he was out of her life. And had to stay there. "I'm sure he's fine," she told Angie. "He's been taking care of himself for a long time now. He knows when he's sick and needs a doctor."

Angie slid in front of her as if to keep her from leaving. "But you never know. He's been acting real weird lately. He really needs somebody to look out for him."

"Well, that may be so, but it's not me." She stepped around Angie. "Now me and my cold are packing it in."

"Trisha!"

They both turned at the sound of Pat's voice. Her heart wanted to leap for joy, but it froze as she saw him. Though he had a jacket on, he was wearing shorts, no socks under his shoes and his knees were skinned. Plus, he was limping for the first few steps. Then he pulled off one shoe.

"I stepped in somebody's gum," he said, waving the shoe in the air.

"Oh, gross," Angie cried and grabbed the shoe. "Here, let me clean it for you."

Before either of them could speak, Angie had grabbed the shoe and run off. Since when had she become Little Miss Helpful?

"I have to talk to you," Pat said, grabbing Trisha's arm as if she might escape. "What's this about your leaving?"

His touch sent shivers of desire all through her and set her heart to racing. She wanted to throw herself into his arms. She wanted to make time go backward until it was before Halloween and her life still held laughter.

Trisha pulled back her arm. "I have a cold," she said stiffly. "I thought that an early evening was called for."

"That's not what I meant," he snapped.

But she didn't care what he meant. Tears were starting to burn in her eyes. His eyes looked so tired and his mouth looked tense and weary. She wanted to take him in her arms and bring back the smile to his lips. It was time she got out of there. She pushed past him and hurried to the door.

"Trisha!"

He was following her and suddenly it seemed terribly vital that she get away. She just couldn't talk to him again. She couldn't have him close enough to touch and not be able to. She couldn't have his arms close enough to hold her and know that they never would.

She fled out the door and into the wet snow. The ground wasn't frozen yet, but there was an inch or so of snow on the parking lot. Enough to make it slippery. She slowed a teeny bit, then stopped. Pat had parked his car behind hers, blocking her exit. Damn him.

"Trisha!"

The wet flakes were hitting her face and melting like tears to run down her cheeks. She headed toward the shops along Olive Street. Pat caught up with her in the playground.

"Trisha, for God's sake, slow down."

He had her arm, so she had to stop. She turned to discover he was running after her with his one foot bare.

"What do you want?" she asked wearily, sinking against the swing set. It was cold and miserable outside. She just wanted to go home.

"Is it true you're leaving here?"

It hurt so to be this close to him. She wanted nothing more than to be in his arms and know their protection. Yet that was one thing they didn't offer her. Maybe the cold was a good thing. Maybe it would make her numb.

"What are you talking about?"

"You can't leave," he said. "You won't be happy some-place else. You'll feel you're just like your father."

Oh, he was talking about *that* kind of leaving. But she wasn't. Where had he gotten the idea she was?

He shifted his feet and ducked his head into the neck of his jacket. "The thing I fear the most is becoming an alcoholic like my father. Letting the disappointments push me into drowning my sorrows and trying to forget. Deep down, you have to fear you could be like your father."

The snow wasn't melting here on the playground, but piling up so that her shoes were starting to get covered.

"You must be freezing," she said. "Let's go back inside."

"I'm not going anywhere until this is settled." He stomped his feet again, then stepped back, climbing onto the bottom bracket of the swing-set frame to keep his feet out of the snow.

She was starting to get annoyed with his officiousness. "Who are you to tell me what to do, anyway?"

He just stared at her for the longest time, then turned to gaze at the playground around them as he rubbed his knees. "I'm a male with skinned knees on a playground," he said.

If her heart had been cold before, it was frozen now. Frozen with horror. He couldn't be the one she'd been waiting for, not with his refusal to love. She wanted someone she could depend on, someone who would always be there.

But then she saw him—*really* saw him—standing there in the snow with his ridiculous skinned knees. With the snow dusting his hair and his one bare foot. Yet his eyes didn't show the cold or the wet or the miserableness of the night, just concern for her.

Her heart was ready to burst with love.

Love! She did love him. For his concern, for his pain and guilt, for himself. Oh, Lord, Lord. For all her careful tiptoeing around relationships, she had gone and done the very thing she'd been running from. She'd fallen in love with a fool who came running out in the snow barefoot—

A smile began to creep out onto her face and a tiny bit of warmth began to melt her fears. "You're barefoot in the snow. Does that mean I'm the woman you've been waiting for?"

It was his turn to go from fear to awakening. She saw the shock pass through his eyes, the realization take hold and then the struggle to overcome so many years of being alone. Love was before him if he only had the courage to take it.

She took a step forward and held a hand out to him. He took it. His clasp was strong, almost crushing.

"I love you," he said, his voice holding the wonder of sudden discovery. "Here I thought it was the flu."

"Couldn't sleep, couldn't eat and couldn't think straight?" she asked, and laughed when he nodded. The snow was magical now, the coming darkness their private shelter from prying eyes.

"This is scary," he said. "Half of our past conversations have come back to haunt us."

"Or push us together," she said.

But a cloud came to shadow his eyes. "It's not all a perfect ending though," he said. "There's still the kids. And what Angel said to me."

She just shook her head and clasped his hands ever tighter in hers. "We're standing in the snow, in the dark, next to a swing set, and a grand piano falls out of the sky on our heads and makes us see we love each other," she said. "If that kind of magic is around, anything is possible."

"Not going back to undo Angel's anger."

She glanced down at his knees. "How'd you do that?"

"Stupidity," he said. "I knocked over Angel's picture and then knelt—"

"Angel?"

He just sighed. "It doesn't mean anything. I was clumsy and the glass in the frame broke."

"I'm clumsy sometimes, but I don't skin my knees to fulfill a prophecy."

"Trisha." His voice was weary.

"He skinned your knees so we'd realize we love each other."

"And I suppose it was his gum I stepped in." His tone was skeptical. Resigned.

"It could have been," she said. She was fighting for everything now. She couldn't let him give in to realism. "If we can have love, we can have anything."

"You think so?"

"Miss Stewart!" They turned to find Angie and Rulli were running over. They stopped on the edge of the playground.

"Are you okay?" Rulli asked, but Trisha couldn't tell if he was asking her or Pat.

"I brought your shoe back," Angie said to Pat.

"Thanks." He took it with obvious gratitude and slipped it on.

"We're fine," Trisha told Rulli. "We're both fine."

"Then you'd better start making up," Angie said, her hands on her hips and a definite threat suddenly in her voice. "We're tired of all this goofing around."

"Yeah," Rulli agreed.

"You two are acting like a couple of jerky little kids who won't play with each other."

"Yeah," Rulli said.

"If we hafta get along, then so do you."

"Yeah."

Pat turned to smile at Trisha as he gave her hand a squeeze. "We are," he said softly, a slight question in his voice.

When she nodded, he let go of her hand and stooped down so that he was close to eye level with the kids.

"I've learned a lot from you guys," he said. "I thought my life was a success and my brother's was a failure. All because he never went to college, never had a job where he could wear a suit and buy a fancy watch. I was stupid."

By some miracle, Angie held her tongue and Pat went on "He had everything and I had nothing. He knew what was important all along. Love and trust and loyalty. I should have listened to him, instead of being so stubborn. Instead of being so afraid to love."

Something in Angie's face seemed to soften. She looked away for a quick moment, then back again. "I lied," she whispered. "When I said he didn't like you, I lied."

"Did he talk about me at all?"

Trisha heard the hope in Pat's voice and bit her lip to keep her own hopes from spilling out. *Remember, Angie,* she cried out. *Make up something, anything. Just give him Angel back.*

Angie shrugged. "I don't remember him hardly at all." Her voice was wobbly and tears glistened in the light from the security lamps by the building.

Trisha held her breath.

"I remember him carrying me on his shoulders when it was bedtime and how he'd tuck me in." Angie's voice died away. "That's all, though."

Trisha felt her eyes water and she turned away. *Damn you, Angel,* she cried out in her heart. *Damn you for dying and not ever forgiving him. He wanted you to have the world, and maybe it was the wrong world, but you had to know it was all because he loved you.*

"Well, it's time to stop fooling around, Patrick Michael Stuart," Pat said, his voice brisk as he stood up. "There's a time to honor wishes and a time to ignore—"

"I ain't foolin' around," Rulli snapped, suddenly glaring at them.

"Pat was just talking to himself," Trisha said. She came up next to the boy and slipped her arm around his shoulders. "Sometimes people do that, especially when they're serious about something."

"I thought he was talking to me," Rulli said. "That's my name, too."

"What?" Pat cried.

"Your name's Rulli," Trisha said, confused.

Rulli took a step closer to Angie, pulling away from Trisha, as if feeling under sudden assault. "Those are my middle names," he said.

"He's Rulli Patrick Michael Ingram," Angie said.

"You were named after me," Pat said. His voice was soft, almost a whisper. He knelt down in front of the kids, apparently oblivious to the snow. "You know what this means?"

"I get your car?" Rulli suggested.

Angie burst out laughing. "Good one, Rulli."

"Yeah, I know."

Pat just ignored the joke, pulling them both into his arms. "It means Angel isn't mad at me anymore."

"Huh?" Rulli was confused.

Pat only partially let them go as he stood up and pulled Trisha into the embrace. "I think it's time we went home. I got a house that wants its treasure back."

"Hey, great idea," Angie cried, backing away slightly. "But maybe you and Pat should go inside the club first. You know. Warm up a little."

Trisha frowned at the girl. "I'd rather warm up at Pat's."

"Yeah—us, too. Right, Rulli?" She nudged her brother sharply.

"Uh, yeah," he said.

"But we got some stuff to do before we leave and—" She was backing away faster now, dragging Rulli with her and getting farther ahead of them.

"Angie." Pat's voice stopped her dead in her tracks. "What's going on?"

The girl shuffled back slowly. "You sorta don't got any air in a couple of your tires."

"I what?"

"How do you know that?" Trisha asked.

"I'm not sure," Rulli said. "Maybe 'cause we let a little too much out."

"You what?"

"We had to," Rulli said. "We thought you were never gonna stop fighting and didn't want Pat to leave too fast."

"It was my idea," Angie said.

"Why am I not surprised?" Pat said dryly. "So how about if you call for a tow truck?"

"That's what I was gonna do," Angie cried and, pulling Rulli with her, raced for the club's front door.

Pat just sighed and slipped his arm around Trisha's shoulders. "Why do I see the ability to control my life disintegrating before my eyes?"

"Happy anticipation?" Trisha guessed. The snow was still lightly falling, but it seemed as warm as springtime here in his arms.

He tightened his hold. "You know I'll never survive on my own. I'm horribly outnumbered."

"Two against one," Trisha said.

"Angie counts as more than one. It's ten against one."

"Poor baby."

He turned so that both his arms surrounded her. "I was thinking we could form a partnership. An alliance of sorts," he said.

"An alliance?"

"Sure, it'll be us against the kids, but to fool them you'll go by the name Mom and I'll be known as Dad."

Her heart tingled as she snuggled deeper into his arms. "How's that going to fool them?"

"They'll never know that I consider myself the luckiest guy in the world." He paused. "So what do you say?"

"Do I have a choice?" she said with a laugh and laid her head against his chest. "If I don't agree, I could get stuck in gum and stay out here until I freeze. We've got a powerful angel watching over us."

His eyes were serious, though, when he gazed down at her. "We can fight him if we need to. We need to both want this."

She just laughed and tightened her own hold on him. "No problem. With or without an angel watching over us, it sounds like heaven to me."

Epilogue

"Congratulations, sweetie," a big old woman cooed just before she swooped down and caught Angie in a crushing hug. She gave her a big, sloppy wet kiss on the cheek before moving off.

"Yuck," Angie cried and tried to rub the kiss off of her.

"Angie!" a voice warned her.

Angie just glared. She and Rulli and Mom and Dad were standing outside this big room filled with people and four dorks playing dinky music. Mom said the four of them were a receiving line. And they were supposed to welcome people who came in and show them where they would be eating.

Jeez, how dumb. They were giving these people a free meal and then they had to show them where to go? Anybody walking in the front door could see the room with all the tables and chairs.

"Angie," Mom said. "Ladies don't wipe off kisses."

Boy, Angie thought. Falling in love sure changed a person. When Mom was Trisha, she used to be real cool. Now all she could talk about was this "how a lady behaves" junk. Angie knew that she sure as heck was never falling in love.

"I'm getting tired of this," Angie said.

"I told you everything about today," Mom said. "Including the fact that you'd have to wear a long dress. And you still agreed to be in the wedding party. Remember?"

"Yeah, yeah."

"She did, Angie," Rulli said. "She told us how it would all come out."

"Thank you, Rulli," Mom said.

Angie rolled her eyes. Rulli was really getting to be a mama's boy.

"I didn't know all these old women were going to hug me," Angie said. "You never told me about that."

"I'm sorry. Please accept my humble apologies."

Angie knew Mom wasn't sorry. Her cheeks were all rosy, her eyes all bright and she was as perky as some stupid little squirrel in a tree.

"That perfume they wear really stinks," Angie said. "It makes my mouth taste all bad."

"You know what perfume's made of?" Rulli said. "Whale poo."

"Do what I do, Angie," Dad said. "Take a deep breath just before they kiss. Then after the kiss, let it all out. You hardly smell any of it that way."

"Okay, Dad," Angie replied. "I'll try that."

Angie ignored Mom and her rolling eyeballs as she traded smiles with Dad. He was turning out to be okay.

"Whoowee." An old guy held the outside door open for a gray-haired woman. Then he came in, stomping his feet and rubbing his hands together. "It is bitter out there."

"Sure is, Ben," Dad said. "I heard we're setting a record today. Coldest day in the past fifty years."

"You could have waited until it got warmer," the old man said. "If not June, at least March or April."

"Oh, no, dear," the gray-haired woman said. "You never put off a wedding. Not if you got yourself a hot prospect. Right, Trisha?"

"What cold?" Mom asked, pretending to be really dumb. Angie was absolutely positive that she'd never fall in love. "I don't feel any cold."

Everyone laughed; then the woman looked down at her and Rulli. Angie took a deep breath and scrunched up her face.

"You look very nice in your beautiful dress," the woman said.

Angie wished the woman would kiss her quick because she was about to burst.

"Angie's got a slip on under it," Rulli said. "But Mom said she didn't have to wear a bra 'cause she's not big enough yet."

Angie's breath escaped in a burst as she gave Rulli her best triple-dagger, mean-dude look. He quieted down quick enough but the grown-ups all laughed as if he'd told a joke.

"Well, there's no need to rush anything, honey." The woman mussed Rulli's hair a little. "And you look very handsome in your suit."

Angie considered telling everybody that her brother was wearing long socks with his suit but no jockstrap, 'cause he wasn't big enough yet, but Mom was giving her one of those "cool it" looks. She was starting to see problems with having a mother who knew so much about kids.

"Well, I guess we should be going in," the man said.

"You're sitting at table seven," Angie said.

"Angie," Mom said, her voice carrying a firm warning.

The man and woman looked puzzled. "The caterer has decided that seven is our lucky number," Dad explained. "He put it on all the tables."

"Oh?" The woman laughed. "What does it stand for? Number of children, possibly?"

"It doesn't stand for anything," Dad said, looking all red and embarrassed. "Just go in and grab a drink. The dinner will start soon."

The older couple walked into the dining room, where everyone was talking at the same time like kids on the playground. Dad put his arm around Mom.

"We're not having seven," he said.

"That's a joint decision," she said.

They kissed so long, their spit musta got all mixed up, and Angie just had to look away, totally grossed out. Dad was looking all goggle-eyed, like when Mom gave him that old gold watch last night. They'd found it when she, Rulli and Mom were fixing up the attic for a playroom. Mom said it was Dad's grandfather's watch and really special. More proof Mom was losing it. The watch didn't tell the date, couldn't be a stop-watch and you couldn't put it in the water. That was special?

"All right," Dad said, trying to act as if he were in charge. "Let's eat."

"Can I have a hot dog?" Angie whined.

"Now don't start that," Mom said. "We're having the same meal you had when we were up here last week. And you said you really liked it."

"I know." Angie cranked up her whine. "But we've been eating all kinds of new stuff lately. Can't I just have a plain hot dog, please?"

Rulli started to open his mouth but Angie stepped on his foot. With the long dress covering her legs, Mom couldn't see what she did.

"Please," Angie whined.

Then Dad squatted down in front of her. "How about after the dinner we stop in at the Ice Cream Shoppe? You can have a banana split."

"Honey," Mom protested. "We have to change and go right to the airport."

"Grandma can take us," Angie said. They were staying with Mom's mother and the cats at her old apartment.

"Yeah, right," Dad said. "She won't mind."

Mom sighed kind of loud as Dad stood up and took her arm. "I'm really getting the hang of this father thing."

"You're doing wonderfully," Mom said.

"Hey, Angie," Rulli said. "I thought you really liked this food."

"Ix-nay, ulli-Ray. Ix-nay." Angie looked at her parents murmuring to each other and figured they hadn't heard what had spilled out of Rulli's big mouth.

"Oh," Rulli said. "I get it. You really wanted ice cream later."

"Shut up, Rulli."

"You're good, Angie."

"Somebody's got to be in charge around here. Might as well be me."

*   *   *   *   *

COMING NEXT MONTH

#985 D IS FOR DANI'S BABY—Lisa Jackson
That Special Woman!/Love Letters
Eleven years ago, Dani Stewart had no choice but to give up her
baby for adoption. Now she was determined to find her son—and
the last thing she expected was a reunion with Brandon Scarlotti,
the father of her child.

#986 MORGAN'S WIFE—Lindsay McKenna
Morgan's Mercenaries: Love and Danger
Everything was at stake when Jim Woodward accepted a dangerous
mission to rescue his closest friends. Pepper Sinclair was along for
the ride to ensure he got the job done—and to melt the ice around his
enclosed heart....

#987 FINALLY A BRIDE—Sherryl Woods
Always a Bridesmaid!
Katie Jones never expected a proposal of marriage from the man
who was once her best friend. She'd always loved Luke Cassidy,
but once they said their "I do's," Katie learned a few secrets about
her new husband....

#988 A MAN AND A MILLION—Jackie Merritt
A newly rich woman like Theo Hunter attracted her share of roguish
attention—and town bad boy Colt Murdoch made no secret of his
interest. Talk around town predicted Colt stealing Theo's land, but
the only thing she was sure of losing was her heart!

#989 THIS CHILD IS MINE—Trisha Alexander
Eve DelVecchio and Mitch Sinclair hadn't seen each other in years,
but the attraction between them still smoldered. Mitch was elated
to find his lost love, but would Eve's secret jeopardize their second
chance?

#990 AND FATHER MAKES THREE—Laurie Campbell
Premiere
Despite the wild attraction between them, Sarah Corcoran knew
Nate Ryan was not her type. After all, she was single-handedly
raising a teenager—but maybe footloose and fancy-free Ryan
could be convinced to settle down....

Take 4 bestselling love stories FREE

Plus get a FREE surprise gift!

Special Limited-time Offer

Mail to Silhouette Reader Service™

3010 Walden Avenue
P.O. Box 1867
Buffalo, N.Y. 14269-1867

YES! Please send me 4 free Silhouette Special Edition® novels and my free surprise gift. Then send me 6 brand-new novels every month, which I will receive months before they appear in bookstores. Bill me at the low price of $2.89 each plus 25¢ delivery and applicable sales tax, if any.* That's the complete price and a savings of over 10% off the cover prices—quite a bargain! I understand that accepting the books and gift places me under no obligation ever to buy any books. I can always return a shipment and cancel at any time. Even if I never buy another book from Silhouette, the 4 free books and the surprise gift are mine to keep forever.

235 BPA ANRQ

Name	(PLEASE PRINT)	
Address		Apt. No.
City	State	Zip

This offer is limited to one order per household and not valid to present Silhouette Special Edition® subscribers. *Terms and prices are subject to change without notice. Sales tax applicable in N.Y.

USPED-295   ©1990 Harlequin Enterprises Limited

It's our 1000th Special Edition and we're celebrating!

Join us these coming months for some wonderful stories in a special celebration of our 1000th book with some of your favorite authors!

Diana Palmer   **Nora Roberts**
Debbie Macomber   **Christine Flynn**
Phyllis Halldorson   **Lisa Jackson**

mini-series by:

Lindsay McKenna, Marie Ferrarella, Sherryl Woods, Gina Ferris Wilkins.

And many more books by special writers.

And as a special bonus, all Silhouette Special Edition titles published during Celebration 1000! Will have **double** Pages & Privileges proofs of purchase!

Silhouette Special Edition...heartwarming stories packed with emotion, just for you! You'll fall in love with our next 1000 special stories!

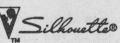

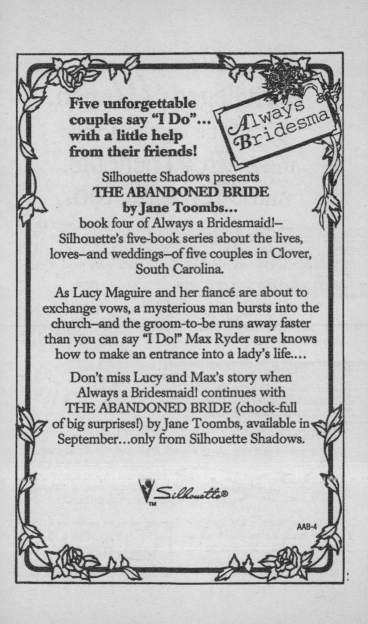

Five unforgettable couples say "I Do"... with a little help from their friends!

Always a Bridesma[...]

Silhouette Shadows presents
THE ABANDONED BRIDE
by Jane Toombs...
book four of Always a Bridesmaid!—
Silhouette's five-book series about the lives,
loves—and weddings—of five couples in Clover,
South Carolina.

As Lucy Maguire and her fiancé are about to
exchange vows, a mysterious man bursts into the
church—and the groom-to-be runs away faster
than you can say "I Do!" Max Ryder sure knows
how to make an entrance into a lady's life....

Don't miss Lucy and Max's story when
Always a Bridesmaid! continues with
THE ABANDONED BRIDE (chock-full
of big surprises!) by Jane Toombs, available in
September...only from Silhouette Shadows.

V Silhouette®
TM

AAB-4

Become a Privileged Woman, You'll be entitled to all these Free Benefits. And Free Gifts, too.

To thank you for buying our books, we've designed an exclusive FREE program called *PAGES & PRIVILEGES*™. You can enroll with just one Proof of Purchase, and get the kind of luxuries that, until now, you could only read about.

BIG HOTEL DISCOUNTS

A privileged woman stays in the finest hotels. And so can you—at up to 60% off! Imagine standing in a hotel check-in line and watching as the guest in front of you pays $150 for the same room that's only costing you $60. Your *Pages & Privileges* discounts are good at Sheraton, Marriott, Best Western, Hyatt and thousands of other fine hotels all over the U.S., Canada and Europe.

FREE DISCOUNT TRAVEL SERVICE

A privileged woman is always jetting to romantic places.

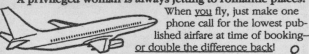

When <u>you</u> fly, just make one phone call for the lowest published airfare at time of booking—<u>or double the difference back!</u>

PLUS—you'll get a $25 voucher to use the first time you book a flight AND <u>5% cash back on every ticket you buy thereafter through the travel service!</u>